# The
# Wilt Inheritance

Tom Sharpe was born in 1928 and educated at Lancing College and Pembroke College, Cambridge. He did his national service in the Marines before going to South Africa in 1951, where he did social work before teaching in Natal. He had a photographic studio in Pietermaritzburg from 1957 until 1961, and from 1963 to 1972 he was a lecturer in History at the Cambridge College of Arts and Technology.

He is the author of fifteen previous best-selling novels, including *Porterhouse Blue* and *Blott on the Landscape,* which were serialised on television, and *Wilt,* which was made into a film. In 1986 he was awarded the XXIIIème Grand Prix de l'Humour Noir Xavier Forneret, and in 2010 he received the inaugural BBK La Risa de Bilbao Prize. He is married and divides his time between Cambridge, England, and northern Spain.

# TOM
# SHARPE

## The
## Wilt Inheritance

arrow books

Published by Arrow Books 2011

2 4 6 8 10 9 7 5 3 1

First published in Great Britain in 2010 by Hutchinson

Arrow Books
Random House, 20 Vauxhall Bridge Road,
London SW1V 2SA

www.randomhouse.co.uk

Addresses for companies within The Random House Group Limited can be found at:
www.randomhouse.co.uk/offices.htm

The Random House Group Limited Reg. No. 954009

A CIP catalogue record for this book
is available from the British Library

ISBN 9780099493136

The Random House Group Limited supports The Forest Stewardship
Council (FSC), the leading international forest certification organisation. All our
titles that are printed on Greenpeace approved FSC certified paper carry the FSC logo.
Our paper procurement policy can be found at www.randomhouse.co.uk/environment

**Mixed Sources**
Product group from well-managed
forests and other controlled sources
www.fsc.org Cert no. TT-COC-002139
© 1996 Forest Stewardship Council

Typeset by Palimpsest Book Production Limited,
Falkirk, Stirlingshire
Printed and bound in Great Britain by
CPI Bookmarque Ltd, Croydon CR0 4TD

To Nancy, my inspiration and my love.

# Chapter 1

Wilt drove down to Fenland University feeling in a thoroughly bad mood. He'd had a row with his wife, Eva, the previous night about the expense of sending their four daughters to boarding school when, in Wilt's opinion, they had been doing very well at their old school, the Convent. Eva, however, had been adamant that the quads must stay at the private school.

'They've got to learn good manners and they weren't doing that at the Convent. And in any case, you swear so often they've become quite foul-mouthed and I'm not having it. They're better off away from home.'

'If you had to fill in totally useless forms and supposedly teach Computer Studies to the illiterates I'm lumbered with – who actually know far more about

bally gadgets than I do – you would swear
ilt had said, choosing not to point out that
they'd become teenagers the quads' repertoire of
obscenities put his own to shame.

'I can't afford to carry on paying for another God
knows how many years just so that you can boast to
the damn' neighbours about where your damn' daughters go to school. Even the Convent was already costing
a small fortune, as you well know.'

Altogether it had been a most acrimonious evening.
To make matters worse, Wilt had not been exagger-
ating. His salary really was so small he couldn't see
how he was going to go on paying the boarding-school
fees and still maintain the modest standard of living
his family presently enjoyed. As merely Head of the
so-called Communications Department he was paid
less than the heads of academic departments, all re-
titled Professors when Fenland College of Arts and
Technology had been designated a university and, as
a result, earning a great deal more than he was. Eva
had, of course, made that point several times over
during their row.

'If you'd had the gumption to leave years ago, like
Patrick Mottram, you could have got a really decent
job with a much better salary in a proper university.
But, oh, no, you had to stay on at that stupid technical college because "I've got too many good friends
there". Utter rubbish! You've No Get Up And Go in
you, that's what you've got.'

At that Wilt got up and went. By the time he got back from the pub, resolving to have it out with Eva once and for all, she had given up on him and gone to bed.

But as he drove into the 'University' car park the next day, Wilt had to admit to himself that she was right. He ought to have left years ago. He hated the wretched Communications Department and actually could probably number his friends still working there on one finger. He should probably have left Eva too. Come to think of it, he should never have married such an infernally bossy woman in the first place. She never did things by halves: the quads were proof of that.

Wilt's spirits sank even lower when he thought of his daughters, all four of them exact replicas of his ghastly wife and just as loud and overbearing as she was. No, more loud and overbearing than she was, given the combined effect of their quadruple efforts. All four girls were inexhaustible in their petty squabbling and inter-sororial battles, and he was pretty sure that the demise of his get up and go had pretty much coincided with their arrival.

There had been a moment in their early infancy when, in between the nappies and bottles and the disgusting pap-like baby food Eva insisted on shovelling into them, he had briefly entertained great hopes for his offspring, imagining shining futures ahead of them. But the older they grew the worse their behaviour became, from torturing the cat to tormenting the neighbours – though pinning anything on any one of them was impossible since they all looked exactly the same. He supposed that at least now they were boarders they were someone else's problem, although it was a bloody steep price to pay for it.

Wilt cheered up on his arrival when he found a note inside a sealed envelope on his desk. It was from the Chief Administrator, Mr Vark, telling him that his presence was not required at the meeting of the recently created Academic Apportionment Committee. Wilt thanked God he didn't have to attend. He wasn't sure he had the patience to sit through another interminable session of paper-shuffling and self-important pronouncements about nothing.

Feeling in a better mood, he went off to check the classrooms but found them largely empty except for a few stray students who were playing on the computers. It was the end of the summer term in a week's time and with no exams in the offing most of the staff and students saw no point in sticking around. Not that the lazy sods stuck around much in the first place. Wilt was back at his desk, making yet another attempt to sort out the following term's timetable, when Peter Braintree, the Professor of English, poked his face round the door.

'Are you coming to Vark's latest nonsensical gathering, Henry?' he asked.

'No, I'm bloody well not. Vark has sent me a note

saying I'm to stay away and for once I'm going to do what he wants.'

'I don't blame you. Rotten waste of time. Wish I could get out of it as well, I've got stacks of exam papers to mark.' Braintree paused. 'I suppose you wouldn't think of . . .'

'No, I wouldn't,' Wilt said firmly. 'Mark your own papers. Can't you see I'm occupied?' He waved airily at the timetable in front of him. 'I'm working out how to fit the Digital Future into Thursday afternoon.'

Braintree had long since given up trying to make sense of any of Wilt's more obscure remarks. He simply shrugged his shoulders and let the door bang loudly behind him.

Wilt gave up the timetable as a bad job, and for the rest of the morning sat filling in the forms the Administration Department concocted practically every day to justify employing more staff than the 'University' had lecturers.

'Suppose it keeps the sods off the street,' he muttered to himself, 'just like having so many so-called students makes the employment figures look far better than they really are.' He could feel his bad temper returning,

After lunch he sat for an hour in the Staff Room, reading the newspapers piled up there. As usual they were filled with horror stories. A pregnant woman had been stabbed in the back for no apparent reason by a twelve-year-old boy; four louts had kicked an old man to death in his own garage; and fifteen insane murderers had been released from Broadmoor after five years – presumably because they hadn't been allowed to kill anyone in that time. And that was in the Daily Times. Wilt tried the Graphic and found it just as sickening. In the end he skipped the political pages, which were full of lies, and decided to go for some air. He went out to the park and was walking round it when he spotted a familiar figure sitting on a bench.

To his surprise Wilt realised it was his old adversary Inspector Flint. He crossed over and sat down beside him.

'What on earth are you doing here?' he asked.

'As a matter of fact, I was sitting here wondering what you were getting up to.'

'Not a very interesting topic. I should have thought you'd have been concentrating on something more in your line,' said Wilt.

'Like what?'

'Oh, arresting innocent people perhaps. You're good at that. Trying to convince yourself that they're criminals. I know you were certain I was one when I was idiotic enough to dump that beastly inflatable doll down a pile hole, but I was drunk at the time and anyway it was years ago.'

Flint nodded. 'Quite. Then there was the drug stunt and the terrorist business in Willington Road. You were involved in all those rotten affairs. Not intentionally, I agree, but it's interesting how you repeatedly seem to find yourself in the middle of particularly curious situations. There must be something criminal about you for you to get caught up in quite so many nefarious activities, don't you think?'

'No, I don't think. And nor, quite often, do you. Though you've got a really fantastic imagination, I'll grant you that, Inspector.'

'Not me, Henry. Oh, definitely not me. I'm just quoting your old friend, and my old colleague, Mr Hodge. Superintendent Hodge to you, of course, Wilt. And I can tell you, Mr Hodge still hasn't forgotten the quagmire you led him into over that drug business . . . nor has he ever got over it. Speaking frankly, I myself don't think you could commit a real crime if it was handed you on a plate. You're a talker, not a doer.'

Wilt sighed. The Inspector was only too damned right. But did everyone have to keep reminding him of how impotent he was?

'Well, apart from thinking about me, what on earth are you doing sitting out here?' he asked. 'Have you retired or something?'

'Been thinking seriously about that too,' said Flint. 'I think I may do. I'm never given anything interesting to do, thanks to that bastard Hodge. He goes and marries the Chief Constable's daughter, and gets promoted to Superintendent as a result, while I'm desk-bound, filling in forms and doing nothing but paperwork. It's as boring as hell.'

7

'Join the club,' said Wilt in spite of himself. He hated the expression. 'I'm doing the same. Forms, agendas, bumf of all sorts . . . and all I get in return is hell from Eva when I go home because I earn a miserable salary and she insists on our paying a small fortune to send the quads to an expensive boarding school. God alone knows how we're going to continue doing it.'

They chatted on, grumbling about the economy and politicians in general, and it was some considerable time before Wilt glanced at his watch and realised it was later than he'd thought. He wondered if the Academic Apportionment Committee meeting had ended yet.

He said goodbye to Flint and went back to his office. It was past four o'clock before Braintree stuck his head round the door again, this time with the news that he'd only nipped out for a pee and the committee was still at it hammer and tongs.

'You were bloody sensible deciding not to go even if Vark would have let you. They're all having a hell of a row. Mostly the usual topics,' he said. 'Anyway I'll definitely be finished by six. Do you want to hang on for me?'

'Suppose so – I've nothing better to do with myself. Thank God I kept away,' Wilt muttered as Braintree hurried back out. For the remainder of the afternoon Wilt sat in the Staff Room, occasionally wondering about Inspector Flint's assessment of his ability to attract crime. 'I am a talker, not a doer,' he said to himself. He'd have given anything to have had the old Fenland Tech back. He'd had a sense of doing something useful in those years, even if that only amounted to having arguments with apprentice technicians and making them think.

By the time Braintree returned, Wilt was thoroughly depressed.

'You look as if you've seen a ghost,' Braintree said.

'I have. The ghost of things past and opportunities lost. As for the future . . .'

'What you need is a stiff drink, old chap.'

'You're damned right I do and it won't be a pint of beer this time. Whisky is what I need.'

'So do I after that verbal punch-up.'

'Was the meeting as bad as all that?'

'Let's just say that in the end it couldn't have been much worse . . . Which pub do you want to go to?'

'In my present mood I suggest the Hangman's Arms. It will be quiet and I'll be able to walk, or at least stumble, home from there,' said Wilt.

'I'll say! By the time I've had a few, I'm not going to risk driving either. Nowadays those buggers will breathalyse you as soon as look at you if you're within a bloody mile of a pub.'

There was no one in the bar when they entered. The place was as grim as its name, and the barman looked as though he'd been a hangman himself once and, given the opportunity, would be happy to demonstrate his skills on either of them.

'Well, what's it to be?' he asked gruffly.

'Two double Scotches and go easy with the soda,' Braintree told him.

Wilt noted the order and sat down in a dark and grubby corner. The situation must be genuinely dire for Peter Braintree to order doubles and go easy on the soda.

'Well,' Wilt grunted when his friend brought the drinks over to the round table, 'spit it out. Was it that bad? Yes, clearly it was. Out with it then.'

'I'd say "Cheers", but in the circumstances . . . Well, mud in your eye!'

'All I want to know is, have I been given the boot?'

Braintree shook his head and sighed.

'No, but you're not out of the wood yet,' he said. 'You were saved by the Vice-Chancellor. Correction: the Vice-Principal. Sorry, I know how you feel about these pompous new titles. As you're bound to know also, Mayfield was in the Chair and doesn't exactly like you.'

Wilt bridled.

'That's the understatement of the decade.'

'Agreed. But he loathes Dr Board even more, and since Board is Head of Modern Languages, and languages are vital if they're going to go on calling the place a university, there's damn all Mayfield can do to get rid of him. So, because you're a friend of Board, and because Mayfield doesn't like you in the first place, it was starting to look bad for Computer Studies . . .'

'Meaning my job is at stake?'

'Well, yes, but wait for it: the Vice-Principal came to your rescue by pointing out that the Communications Faculty . . . sorry, the Communications Department . . . has many more students than any other, and now that History has gone and Maths is down to around forty which is even lower than Science, the Univers— the College can't afford to dispense with Communications. And that includes you.'

'Why? They could find someone else to take my place.'

'The V-P doesn't think so. He put the boot into Mayfield by asking him if he'd care to volunteer to take your job on, and Mayfield said he wouldn't dream of dealing with the hooligans in your department. Oh, yes, the V-P had him by the short and curlies there! Mayfield had gone quite white by then but the Vice-Principal still hadn't finished. He said you handled the brutes very deftly and . . .'

'That's very decent of him. Did he actually say "deftly"?'

'His exact word, and he was backed up by Board who said you had a real gift plus years of experience in dealing with blighters he wouldn't go near with an AK47 or something even more lethal. At one point he called you "something of a genius".'

Wilt gulped at his whisky.

'I must say, Board's always been a good friend,' he murmured. 'But he's gone above and beyond this time. No wonder Vark didn't want me there.' He looked down at his glass gloomily. 'They may be hooligans but some of my lads are good-hearted enough. The main thing is to let them get on with what they really like to do.'

'You mean, muck around playing games and surfing the internet for porn?'

Wilt shook his head.

'They can't get on to the pornography sites. I got a couple of technicians over from Electronics to block that area off, and in any case it costs money to download the really hard filth and none of my lot have credit cards. Or only ones they've stolen from someone, of course, which don't usually work on the internet.'

'Oh, well, that puts paid to Mayfield's argument that they should never have forced all those computers on to you,' Braintree said.

Wilt finished his whisky.

'Shouldn't have closed the old Tech down,' he declared. 'Still, I've got something to celebrate. At least my job's safe for the time being and the Vice-Principal isn't going to resign any time soon. He earns such a whacking great salary, lucky bugger, and so long as he's around it sounds as though dear Professor Mayfield's scuppered. I'm going to have another Scotch. No, don't move. I'll get them.'

This time he ordered triples.

'I'd love to have seen Mayfield go white. He's no more a professor than I am. Let's drink to the V-P . . . and to Dr Board.'

# Chapter 2

Despite the row with Henry the previous night Eva
had had one of her better days. In fact, it had been
her best day for a long time. For some months now
she had been cultivating a very upper-class woman who
regularly visited the Harmony Care and Community
Centre where Eva helped out. Lady Clarissa came
down once a week from North Fenland to see her uncle,
a retired colonel who had lost a leg in the Second
World War.

'I've found a perfect home for Uncle Harold,' she
told Eva when she arrived. 'It's called the Last Post.
It's quite near here in Clarton Road, and a doctor
lives just two doors down the street. But, best of all,
it's especially for retired officers and the woman who

runs it has a son who was in the army. Obviously he wasn't in the army during Uncle's war because he was far too young if he was even born at the time . . . but he was definitely some sort of officer in a war somewhere. He works in the Black Bear Hotel now. In fact, he's the manager according to Matron, but he still puts his old uniform on from time to time and she's awfully proud of him.'

The old man sitting in the wheelchair beside her, a tartan rug draped over his knees, looked up at her with a livid expression and swore that he wasn't going anywhere called the Last Post because that was what the buglers played when they buried the dead, and he'd seen too much of that in his time.

'Well, it's a lot better than some of the other places I've visited and the Matron there was only too pleased to take you in. She's got a son who was an officer in some county regiment or other so you'll have special treatment.'

Lady Clarissa turned to Eva to explain, 'Uncle lost his leg at Arnhem.'

'At the crossing of the Rhine, damn it,' grumbled the old man. 'Can't you get anything right?'

'Oh, well, somewhere in Europe.'

Uncle Harold raised his voice.

'In Germany, confound you!' He scowled. 'What about women? I suppose that place is crawling with old hags. I see enough of them here already.'

16

Lady Clarissa sighed and shook her head.

'There are no female residents. Well, except for Matron, of course.'

But the old man still wasn't satisfied.

'Trust you to choose a nursing home in Clarton Road. There's a graveyard there, you know.'

'Well, it was a choice between that or one called Journey's End which, come to think of it, is conveniently close to the Crematorium. Perhaps you'd prefer that,' Lady Clarissa suggested sweetly.

'The Crematorium, damnation!' squawked Uncle Harold. 'I wonder why you don't call it the Incinerator. I don't want what remains of my body crisped up, thank you very much. Bad enough that the ruddy Hun barbecued my leg when they blew it up.'

'Oh, all right, I'll see to it that you aren't cremated then. And since we're on the subject, where exactly do you want to be buried? Not that I hope it is any time soon, Uncle dear.'

'Hmm, you must think I was born yesterday. I know you have a very good reason for coming to visit me . . . damned if I can work out what it is, though. God knows, I haven't got two pennies to rub together. But I've been thinking about this and I want to be buried in Kenya, where I was born and brought up.'

'But that's in Africa! It would cost a fortune to get you there . . . and anyway it's too far for the family to visit.'

'As though I care! Not one of them has visited me for years and years while I'm still alive. What could it possibly matter once I'm dead?'

'Well, I must say, that's not a very nice thing to say and anyway it's not even true,' protested Lady Clarissa. 'I come all the way down here, week after week, and where would that leave me if you were buried in Kenya? I'd have nothing local to visit. You're being very ungrateful, if you don't mind my saying so, and after I've found you a really good nursing home too.'

'Possibly,' said the old man. 'Though you could have found one with a more cheerful name.'

'Well, if you don't like it there I'll try to find somewhere else,' she sighed. After kissing her uncle on his forehead she left him there, still muttering bitterly.

'I'm more than ready to go back to the hotel,' Lady Clarissa told Eva as they went out to the car park together. 'Uncle isn't the easiest person to deal with. And I'm so delighted you can join me there for lunch, my dear. Why not come in my car?'

They got into her Jaguar and drove to the Black Bear in silence.

'I think I'll have a nice sherry,' Eva said when Lady Clarissa asked her what she'd like as an aperitif. Instead of her usual sweet sherry, though, she was given a Tio Pepe while Lady Clarissa had a very large dry martini.

'That's better,' she sighed as she took a great gulp of her drink and settled back in a chair. 'Now then, last week Miss Clancy at the day centre mentioned that your husband lectures at Fenland University so I suppose he must be a very good teacher. Do you know which university he went to himself?'

'Cambridge,' said Eva, who actually had no idea.

'Mmmm. You wouldn't happen to know which college, would you?'

'I didn't know him then but he's spoken about one called Porterhouse.'

'But that's marvellous! My husband was there too so he'll be delighted to have a fellow Old Porterthusian up at the Hall. Someone for him to talk to. I'm afraid he gets terribly lonely.

'Now, Eva my dear, what I want to know is whether you think your husband might be prepared to tutor my son Edward in history to A-level standard? You see, I'm determined to get him into Cambridge, and preferably Porterhouse.'

'I'm sure he would,' Eva said with a demure smile. 'In fact, I know it.'

'Oh, that's wonderful. Of course Edward should have been taught much better at his laughably named public school – I can't think of anything less public given that it costs an absolute fortune and schools like that are usually miles and miles from anywhere! The one we sent him to near Lidlow was useless. He has yet to pass history despite sitting it three times. The place cost us a fortune, my dear,' she repeated, signalling to the wine waiter. 'Another dry martini – and this time use Tanqueray fifty per cent and less Noilly Prat. I could hardly taste the gin in the last one, it was all vermouth. And another fino for my guest.'

'Oh, I don't think I'd better,' said Eva, who'd never had a dry sherry before and hadn't liked it either. 'You see, I've got to drive this afternoon and I don't want to lose my driving licence.'

'My dear, two finos aren't going to put you over the limit,' Lady Clarissa told her.

Under the influence of the previous sherry and an obviously rich woman who called her 'my dear' and treated her as an equal, Eva relented.

'I do wish you'd let me pay for this round,' she said but, fortunately, Lady Clarissa waved the offer away.

'It goes on my room bill. I always stay down here and do some shopping when I visit Uncle.' She lit a cigarette. 'In any case, my husband pays for everything. Such a sweet man.'

'But what happens when you drive home? I mean, if the police breathalyse you.'

'You don't seriously think I'm going to drive? I have a chauffeur. Actually he's the local garage man but he doubles as a chauffeur. I gave him the morning off but he'll be lurking somewhere, ready to take me back. Of course, I never drive over the limit at home either, but then the police there never stop me. That's one of the advantages of being married to George. You see, he's a JP,' said Lady Clarissa, and, realising that Eva still didn't understand, continued, 'Well, actually, if he'd been more ambitious he would almost certainly have been a QC by now but he's too lazy. We live virtually separate lives.' She finished her gin and modicum of Noilly Prat and got to her feet. 'Let's go through and have lunch.'

Eva, whose knowledge of acronyms was virtually non-existent, especially those beginning with a 'J', and who had even less of an idea what a 'QC' might be, was only too glad to move on. She left her sherry and followed Lady Clarissa into the dining room. By the time they'd finished lunch, with which Eva had been persuaded to have a glass of white wine, she was in a decidedly good mood. With coffee Lady Clarissa, who had finished the bottle of white burgundy they'd had with the meal, ordered two Armagnacs and insisted Eva try one. She sipped at it but Clarissa ordered her to drink it all.

'Down the hatch,' she said, and drained her own glass. 'You'll find it a perfect digestif.'

Eva did as she was told and wished she hadn't. Only then did the subject of Wilt's salary for tutoring Lady Clarissa's son come up.

'We're prepared to pay your husband fifteen hundred pounds a week and all found. If he can get Edward into Porterhouse there'll be a bonus of five thousand pounds. I mean, the summer holidays last two months so there's plenty of time. I realise this is frightfully short notice and you might already have a holiday planned . . .'

'The Lake District,' said Eva, with some difficulty, 'we go every year.' The spirit had gone to her head. And the thought of a £5,000 bonus made it reel even more.

'Well, you can cancel and come to us instead. There's a furnished cottage in the grounds you are welcome to use, rent-free. And we're not far from a delight-fully sandy beach. I'm sure you'll love the Estate too.' She paused for a moment. 'I suppose you'll have to discuss the idea with your husband, and I must meet him too.'

Eva hurriedly stopped any suggestion of that. The notion horrified her. Wilt wouldn't make the right impression at all.

'I'm afraid he's gone down to see his mother this weekend. She's not been at all well lately.'

'Oh, I am sorry. Still, I'm coming down again next weekend to get my wretched uncle into the nursing home. He really is a curmudgeonly old man! I do everything for him and nothing seems to please him. Perhaps I'll be able to meet your husband then?'

Eva gave a small nod which could have been inter-preted either way. She would have to rehearse Wilt endlessly if he weren't to go and spoil everything.

Lady Clarissa stood up. 'Time for a catnap before I head off. It's been a great pleasure talking to you, my dear. And I am so glad that you're a fairly normal size.'

She left a puzzled Eva still sitting at the table wondering what on earth her size had to do with anything. Perhaps the boy was a dwarf or height-impaired or whatever you had to call it nowadays. But then Lady Clarissa would surely have asked about Wilt's size and not hers? How very strange the whole lunch had been . . . and, come to think of it, how very strange she herself felt after all that alcohol. She went out and took a taxi, abandoning her car at the day centre. Once back home she took an unplanned catnap of her own, waking up several hours later on the floor of the sitting room with no clear memory of how she'd got there. Thank God Henry hadn't come back and found her! she thought as she groggily came to.

She needn't have worried. Several hours later the supper she had hastily prepared for him was still uneaten. Thinking of the difference Lady Clarissa's money would make, she hummed happily to herself as she took Wilt's steak and broccoli out of the warming oven and put it in the fridge. After that she sat in front of the TV for a little longer, watching a movie, but finally gave up waiting. She turned out the light and went to bed, hoping Henry had a front-door key. She was sure now he'd been in a pub all evening and would be drunk when he came home.

Wilt was. He'd switched from double whiskies to pints of strong bitter. Even more ominously, when he and Braintree had left the Hangman's Arms they'd found themselves unable to see a thing as the street lights in that part of Ipford were out. As a result he'd stumbled down several wrong turnings before retracing his steps and, eventually locating the one that led to the bridge across the river, finally finding his way home. Here at least the street lights were on though the house was in darkness. It took him some time to find his front-door key and, after several attempts, to manage to insert it into what he supposed was the lock. It was the wrong one. Eva had become so terrified of burglars she had installed a second lock, much stronger than the first, the previous month. The useless key dropped to the ground.

'Shit!' Wilt slurred, and groped around for it, but before he could find it the pressing need of his bladder had to be answered. He stepped on to the small front lawn and was in the process of peeing when a light came on in a house on the other side of the road, revealing Mrs Fox peering out of her window. Wilt promptly swung round – or would have done if he hadn't been so drunk. Instead he tripped over his own feet and fell face down on a most unpleasantly wet patch of grass. He lay there with the consoling thought that at least Mrs Fox couldn't see him now for the low hedge bordering the front garden.

He might almost have drifted off to sleep were it not for the sound of the phone ringing inside the house, followed by the bedroom light coming on above him and Eva clumping down the stairs. Wilt tried to think. Even in his drunken stupor he realised what had happened: Mrs Fox had phoned Eva to say that someone was trying to break into their house. He struggled to get to his feet and failed, so crawled over to the front door and pleaded through the letter box to be let in.

'It's only me,' he squawked. But Eva wasn't listening. She was too interested in discussing whether or not to call the police. Wilt tried to hear what she was saying. The only words he caught were, 'No, not the police. I'll double bolt the door.' And: 'Thanks for calling. Yes, I'll definitely tell my husband.'

She put down the receiver and waited. Like Eva herself, Mrs Fox had a phobia about burglars. She took her time over going back to bed and turning off the light. Eva wasn't about to admit it to a neighbour but, having heard the cursing at the front door, she was certain she knew the identity of the 'intruder'.

Wilt resumed his pleas.

'It's only me. For goodness' sake, let me in. I'm soaking wet and if I'm out here much longer . . .' He was about to say he'd go down with pneumonia but Eva had had a flash of inspiration and interrupted him there. She was going to get her own back for his rudeness the night before.

'Who is "me" exactly?' she asked, to prolong Wilt's agony.

'Oh, for God's sake, you know who I am! Your bloody husband, Henry.'

'You don't sound like him. And whoever you are, you're obviously drunk.'

'I don't give a tuppenny damn what I sound like, I'm soaking wet! And, all right, I'm sloshed.'

'If you're who you say you are, you must have a key on you,' said Eva, determined to prolong his misery. 'Why don't you use it?'

'Because I've dropped the bloody thing!' Wilt shouted through the letter box. 'Why did you turn off the outside light? I can't see a bleeding thing out here. It's pitch dark.'

Eva considered turning the light back on and decided on another tactic.

'I'll call the police . . .' she began, noisily putting the door chain on.

'Are you off your rocker? That's the last thing we need.'

Even Eva had to agree with that. The notion of having police cars arriving, with sirens almost certainly blaring, and giving the whole street something to gossip about, did not appeal. All the same, she wanted to extend Wilt's misery just a little longer. She turned the overhead light on and, keeping the chain in place, opened the door a few inches and peered out. Wilt had mud all over his face and looked awful.

'You're not my husband,' she insisted. 'You look nothing like him.'

'I've had enough of this, Eva. I'll break the bloody door down!' shouted Wilt. 'If you don't open it this minute, I'm going to go straight across the fucking street and pee through Mrs fucking Fox's letter box. Then see what the damned neighbours have to say.'

'Well, I suppose I'll have to let you in,' Eva hastily decided, and shut the door slightly before undoing the chain. By the time she'd opened it again Wilt had slid to the ground and was being sick into a flower bed.

'All right, you can come in,' she went on when he'd finished vomiting.

Wilt tried to get to his feet and failed. Instead he crawled across the doormat while Eva, with a smile of satisfaction, went outside in her dressing gown and found his key. Back inside, she locked the door and regarded her husband with disgust. She'd never seen him quite so drunk before and was looking forward to his hangover next morning. He'd be in no condition to oppose her plan for him then.

'You go upstairs straightaway and have a shower.

Then you can sleep in the spare room. You're definitely not sleeping next to me.'

And she went back to bed, leaving Wilt to drag himself upstairs

Half an hour later, after he'd tried to take a shower only to fall in the bath twice, a bruised and bitter Wilt crawled into the spare room feeling like death warmed over and fell asleep.

Next morning he phoned the 'University' to say he was in bed with some bug and wouldn't be coming in. No one answered the phone.

'It's Saturday,' said Eva. 'Of course you aren't going in. No one does at weekends.'

Wilt thanked God and went back to bed. Presently he was woken by Eva who had learned more from her treatment at the hands of her Auntie Joan the previous summer than she had realised. She'd been turned out of the Starfighter Mansion in Wilma, Tennessee by Auntie Joan – kicked out would be the more strictly accurate expression – and as a result her own attitude had hardened. She had endured years of Henry's drunkenness and obscenity. Auntie Joan's style of retaliation was an example she intended to follow. It was about time she stood up for herself.

'Now, you listen to me,' she snapped when she'd shaken Wilt awake and dragged the bedclothes off him. 'You're going to do exactly what I say.'

She looked down at his naked body with disgust.

'Oh, for goodness' sake,' Wilt moaned. 'Do you want me to freeze to death?'

'It's a hot day. If you're cold, it's your own fault. You came home last night drunker than I've ever seen you.'

'All right, so I did. I'd been celebrating with Peter.'

'Celebrating what?'

'It's a long damned story. Can't it wait?'

'No, it can't.'

'Well, if you really want to know, I haven't been made redundant. That's what we were celebrating.'

'Thank goodness for that,' said Eva. She was about to leave then but changed her mind. She knew her Henry and he lied whenever it suited him. She wasn't going to be hoodwinked this time.

'Who said you were going to be made redundant? And I don't care if it is a long story, I want the truth.'

Wilt stared up at her with blood-shot eyes and wished to God she'd never been to America to visit her aunt. Previously she always used to leave him alone with his hangovers, and he wasn't sure he could cope with a newly assertive Eva, particularly not in this state.

'Give me back the bedclothes and I'll tell you,' he whimpered.

Eva threw the sheet and blanket over him.

'Go on. Tell me.'

'First, I was supposed to attend the ACC,' he began.

She hated it when he used those damn' acron . . . anachron . . . abbreviations.

'What's that mean?'

'The Academic Apportionment Committee. It's where they decide which courses to get rid of and, of course, who the next head of department to get the chop will be. Communications isn't considered sufficiently academic, though, so I wasn't required to attend. Peter told me what happened. May-bloody-field wanted to have me replaced.'

'What's he got to do with it?'

Wilt sighed.

'He just happens to be the Chairman of the ACC, if you must know.'

'And?'

'Fortunately the Vice-Principal was there too. He pointed out that they couldn't get rid of me because no one else could deal with the blokes in Communications as well as I can, and no other department has so many blasted students. You've got that?'

Eva nodded.

'Right. Then, to put the boot in, he asked Mayfield if he would like to take over from me himself – and the bastard shut up like a shot. Peter said the ass practically fainted at the thought and there was no more talk of my being replaced.'

'Thank goodness for that,' said Eva, who was almost convinced. She could always check with Peter Braintree.

'May I please go back to sleep now?'

'No, you may not. I want you up and dressed and

downstairs in fifteen minutes. I've got some exciting news to tell you.'

Wilt groaned. He knew from long experience that Eva's idea of exciting and his own were two very different things.

# Chapter 3

Wilt stumbled downstairs with two minutes to go, having hastily pulled on his underpants from the previous night – all he could find in his hurry. Eva sat at the kitchen table, a glass of water and some Aspirin in front of her but just out of his reach.

'Now, Henry,' she began in a loud voice, 'I've found you a job for the summer. Fifteen hundred pounds a week and all found. Isn't that wonderful? She wants her son to go to Cambridge.'

Wilt slumped down on to a chair and held his head in his hands. It was still hurting desperately.

'Who is "she", and what do you mean, a job? And fifteen hundred pounds a week?' For that sort of salary it couldn't be that wonderful . . . and what on earth was the meaning of 'all found'?

'She is Lady Clarissa Gadsley, and she's offered you a temporary job.'

'Doing what?'

'Tutoring her son Edward Gadsley, up at Sandystones Hall. Lady Clarissa wants you to see that he gets his A-level history, and I said you'd be delighted.'

'Charming!' said Wilt. 'So I've got to spend the Summer Vac cramming some horribly snobbish young oaf to get him into Cambridge? I don't suppose it occurred to you that I haven't taught history for thirty years, and that when I did it was to Plasterers Two and louts who couldn't even remember where Austria was.'

'It can't be that difficult, and in any case you've two months to do it. We'll be getting enough money to keep the girls at St Barnaby's and having a free holiday at the same time.'

'You may be . . . Hang on, what do you mean, free holiday? I won't be getting any holiday at all.'

Eva smiled and tried not to look at his stained Y-fronts.

'Lady Clarissa's offered us a furnished cottage in the grounds rent-free,' she said. 'And there's a delightful beach not far away.'

'There would be. And fat chance I'll ever see it. Instead I'll be closeted with a moron, trying to make him understand the causes of the French Revolution or even which century it happened in. Come to think of it, I'm not sure I remember myself.'

'Then you'd better find out,' Eva told him. 'Fast.'

'All right, let's drop the subject for now My head hurts too much even to think about it. I'm starving, I had no supper last night, and I suppose I've missed breakfast as well.'

'Well, whose fault is that?' Eva eyed his pitiful state and finally relented. 'If you go and have a shower, and put those disgusting pants in the washing machine, I'll make you some sandwiches.'

Wilt sighed and went upstairs.

'Some bloody shitty holiday,' he muttered halfway up.

'I heard that,' Eva called out. 'Swearing again! You've got to learn not to use that filthy language. We're going to be in very select company after all.'

Wilt kept his thoughts about that to himself and went into the bathroom

When he came downstairs half an hour later, dressed in a pair of grey trousers and a shirt, he found Eva on the phone spreading the ghastly news to Mavis Mottram, to make her jealous. He took his brown bread and sardine sandwiches through to the front room and stared at a cricket match on telly without taking any real interest in it.

Instead he was mulling over the change that had come over his wife ever since she had returned from

America last year. Wilt didn't know why, and Eva refused to tell him. In fact, she wasn't prepared to say anything at all about what had happened to her in Wilma, Tennessee the previous summer. Occasionally she murmured 'Bitch' when she didn't know he was listening. It was either that or 'Stupid cow'. All in all, it was as clear as daylight that the trip to visit her Uncle Wally and Auntie Joan, with the quads in tow, had been as disastrous as his own quest in search of Old England which had been made at the same time.

He had ended up in a mental hospital after landing on his head in the back of a pick-up truck, and then been falsely implicated in the disappearance of a Shadow Minister. Eva's stated reason for returning early had been that Uncle Wally had suffered two heart attacks. Secretly, Wilt suspected the hand, or rather hands, of his daughters in Wally Immelmann's misfortune, but given that he loathed the ghastly man he didn't much care. The only thing he did find disturbing was Eva's new-found determination to dominate him, a trait she'd evidently picked up in Imperial America. 'Dominate' was too mild a word, in fact. So was control. Ever since last summer she'd been insisting he do whatever she wanted, whenever she wanted.

Well, Wilt most certainly didn't want to spend the summer kowtowing to some damned snobs who would undoubtedly patronise him. And what sort of moron was this son he would have to tutor? He was just considering where on earth he could find the relevant A-level history syllabus when Eva came marching in.

'Oh, there you are,' she said. 'For your information, I told Lady Clarissa you'd been at Porterhouse and it turns out that you have that in common with her husband, Sir George. He was a student there, too, so you'll have something to talk about together.'

Wilt gaped at her.

'For Christ's sake, I never went anywhere near the place! I went to Fitzherbert. And you expect me to chat the bastard up about the good old days at bloody Porterhouse and who the present Master is? He probably comes down every year for the Annual Feast and regularly uses his Dining Rights. He'll spot me as an imposter straightaway.'

'Well, surely you can find out that sort of thing and just let him do the talking?'

'Bugger!' groaned Wilt.

'And that's another word you can cut out,' snapped Eva, leaving the room again. With another groan, Wilt followed her out and headed for the front door. Having made sure that he had the right keys, he stepped out into the afternoon sunshine. He needed to get out of this house and to talk to someone sane.

Wilt headed for the allotments and his old friend Robert Coverdale. For some years now Robert had lived in a shack there in preference to his own house which was, as he put it, 'Infested with shrews. Namely my wife and her two maiden – that's a joke too – sisters.'

Wilt found him on all fours, weeding his asparagus bed. The old man prised himself to his feet.

'You look like something the cat dragged in,' he said, fetching another chair from the shack.

'I feel like it,' said Wilt, sitting down. 'My wife . . .'

'Don't tell me,' said Robert, and lit his blackened pipe. 'I know all about them, don't I just? You're damned lucky yours hasn't any sisters. Look at me, stuck with a pair of them. Unmarried hell-cats is what they are. What's Eva been up . . . beg your pardon . . . been down to this time?'

Wilt told him, pointing out for good measure that despite his lack of sisters-in-law, he was lumbered with four diabolical daughters.

'The wages of sex,' Robert told him. 'I reckon the amoeba has the right idea. Lives on its own, completely single, and when it feels like having some offspring, it simply discards part of itself and lets the other half get on with its own life. The perfect solution. No responsibility, no hassle, no nagging – and, best of all, no sex. Certainly no jobs in the holidays tutoring some young oaf whose father is an earl – or whatever this blighter is up to in North Fenland.'

'Added to which the old fellow went to Porterhouse and Eva's told his wife I was there too.'

'What's porterhouse? Sounds like a steak to me.'

'A Cambridge college, and about the worst example you can find. Full of hearties with big bank accounts and no brains. I don't even see why this moron thinks he needs A-level history to get in. Sounds like he more than meets the entrance requirements already.'

'Thank God I never went to university,' said Robert. 'I went straight into carpentry as an apprentice, and made what money my wife hasn't spent yet creating "antique" furniture and flogging it. Did kitchens too, and parquet floors when things got tight.'

By the time Wilt went home an hour or so later he was feeling decidedly better. Old Robert had his priorities right. He did his own cooking on a Primus stove, heated the shack in winter with a paraffin burner, used an oil lamp to see by, and generally kept himself to himself. Nobody disturbed him because few people knew he was there, and the neighbouring allotment holders were grateful to him for keeping an eye on their vegetables and ensuring no one nicked them. No nagging wife, no awful daughters, and no bloody job to worry about either.

Wilt wondered what the waiting list for allotments was like.

# Chapter 4

In North Fenland Lady Clarissa dropped off the young man she'd spent the night with at the Black Bear, popped his chauffeur's uniform into the boot of the Jaguar and then drove the two miles to the Hall to announce her good news to Sir George.

'You've done what?' he demanded, annoyed at being woken from his afternoon nap.

'I've arranged for Edward to pass his A-level,' she said. 'And I've also found a really good old people's home for Uncle Harold. It's called the Last Post.'

'Very suitable. And damned expensive, I expect. Well don't forget I'm the one coughing up for the old devil's keep, though Christ knows why. He's your confounded uncle, not mine.'

'There's absolutely no need for you to pay,' she said icily. 'I will.'

Sir George almost smiled.

'Fat chance of that. But anyway, that's all right. For half a moment I thought you were going to say you were bringing him here. That was what you implied when you left.'

'Oh, you're always so pessimistic, and you think I'm just a fool.'

'In some respects . . .' He gave a sigh. 'Well, never mind. What's this about getting your blasted son educated?'

It was Clarissa's turn to sigh.

'He's your son too. In name, at any rate. You may not like it much but the fact remains that Edward is your step-son'

'I know. Just as I know your first husband died on an ungated level crossing . . . and I for one don't blame him for it.'

'And what precisely do you mean by that? Is it another of your beastly cracks about Edward?'

'Not about dear little Eddie, as you like to call him.'

'I don't call him Eddie, and he's not in the least bit little as you know . . . but what exactly were you not blaming my late husband for? At least he wasn't mean about money.'

'Quite. Though I do blame him for being over-generous and indulging you in your ridiculously expensive tastes. I actually meant I didn't blame him for taking his own life. I've had some dark thoughts on the same subject myself, but on the whole I'm against leaving you a wealthy widow like he did, the idiot. And I'm damned if I want your awful boy Eddie to inherit my estate.'

'What on earth are you talking about?' snapped Lady Clarissa. 'My first husband met with a terrible accident under the five-fifteen from Fakenham.'

'Tommyrot, and you know it! That story was put about purely because of his insurance policy, my dear. If he were known to have committed suicide, you wouldn't have smelt hide nor hair of a pay-out. I thought you realised that.'

'Typical of you to assume the worst!' she cried, marching out of the room only to return a few minutes later. 'Where's Cook? I want some tea.'

Sir George stood up and adjusted the portrait of his mother which was hanging over the fireplace.

'I have no idea. Probably hawking her pearly in Norwich. I'm sure lots of blokes there like thin women. In short, I sacked her.'

'Sacked her?'

'Do you have to repeat everything I say? Yes, I sacked her. I'm afraid you'll have to make the tea yourself. Oh, and make it strong. I can't bear weak tea.'

Lady Clarissa sat down on a chaise-longue by the window and stared venomously at her husband's back.

She had hoped he'd be in a good mood when she

returned. Instead he was in one of his most difficult ones. If only she'd married a more amiable man.

'May I ask why you sacked her? Was it perhaps because she was thin and remained so, despite all your attempts at fattening her up? Well, I will make myself a pot of tea but I'm damned if I'll make you one! And speaking of weight, you can lose a bit tonight because I'm certainly not making supper. You can starve.'

'Oh, I'm going out to dinner tonight,' he replied, turning to face her with a smile. 'In fact, I think I'll go and have a bath and change now.'

And with that he strolled out of the room.

In the kitchen, Clarissa refused to let her husband's behaviour rattle her composure. God knows who he was going out with tonight. He would come home and sleep in his own room as usual. And with any luck, plus the help of his usual excessive after-dinner intake of brandy, he would sleep well and be more amenable to her plans in the morning. She wasn't worried.

Nor was Wilt. Talking to old Coverdale had cheered him up. And in any case, the more he thought about it, the more interested he became in seeing how the landed gentry lived. And North Fenland was a part of the country he'd always liked. Cold in winter, of course, with the east wind blowing straight in from the Urals, unimpeded by the flat expanses of the

Steppes and the North German Plain. But in summer it should be mild enough and certainly peaceful, with only the few resorts beside the sea over-run by ghastly holiday-makers.

If Eva were right about Sandystones Hall and it had both parkland and lake it could be very pleasant there. He'd be cut off from the outside world and could wander at will through the woods when he wasn't having to cram the boy . . . may even have something of a holiday after all. Eva and the quads could spend their days on the beach, and he'd be earning his fifteen hundred quid a week which might stop his wife from grumbling at him all the time.

By the time Wilt had had supper and taken himself off to bed in his own room he was almost looking forward to the summer holiday. And so the weekend passed relatively peacefully and on Monday he went back to Fenland University and his office there, feeling almost light-hearted.

# Chapter 5

At Sandystones Hall Clarissa was still mulling things over as she wandered around the garden and stared down into the water of the moat. It was as green and murky as usual, if less so than the soup the under-gardener's wife had served them at lunch. Given the choice, Clarissa wasn't sure she wouldn't have chosen heated moatwater in place of that soup. Sir George had tried a spoonful and promptly left the table to pour the filth out of the window.

'Where the hell did you get that woman?' he demanded. 'From a sewage plant?'

'She's Herb's wife.'

'Good God, I wonder he's still alive. Must have a cast-iron stomach to survive her ghastly cooking.'

'She was the only so-called cook I could find in the village. If you will make a habit of sacking decent ones, simply because they're too thin for your particular preference, you can't expect me to whistle up an haute-cuisine replacement overnight. Anyway, I'll tell her we'll do without soup in future as we're both on diets.'

Sir George had moved over to the sideboard and the decanter of cognac set upon it.

'What are you doing now?' asked his wife as he poured himself a glassful. 'You don't usually drink cognac during lunch.'

'Washing the taste away,' he replied, after spitting a mouthful into the moat. 'Probably kill the damned fish!'

Although the rest of the meal hadn't been quite so bad, one could hardly say that it was to their liking either. Sir George had compared the blancmange pudding to an extremely obese jellyfish, and unfortunately Herb's wife had overheard and taken umbrage. Clarissa had intervened, blaming her husband's remark on his lunchtime drinking, but privately was amazed that Sir George had escaped having it tipped over his head.

Afterwards he'd taken himself off to watch a cricket match, saying that he couldn't be at all sure when he'd get back. Clarissa couldn't have cared less as she most certainly wasn't in any hurry to see him. All in all, they'd had a relatively peaceful time of it for what was left of the weekend. Somewhat predictably he had exploded about the blasted fifteen hundred pounds she'd promised to pay the blasted tutor and the blasted free cottage for his blasted wife – but she had been expecting that and had assured him he didn't need to worry.

'If this man can get him into Porterhouse, Edward will soon be off your hands. And, besides, you'll both have something to talk about. You can reminisce about your good old days at Cambridge.'

'What? This fellow must be a genius if he can get your son into any dashed university. Now what did you say his name is?'

'Wilt . . . Henry Wilt.'

'Wilt? Sounds an appropriate name, at any rate. By the time he's done his damnedest to get that son of yours through any exam, he'll have wilted all right. That is if he's as intelligent as you say he is.'

'He must be. After all, he's a lecturer at Fenland University.'

'All the same, I'd keep your eye on Eddie. I mean, for all you know, the bloody fellow could be a paedophile, and next thing he'll be messing about with your son. Yes, better watch him.'

'Oh, don't be so ridiculous, George! Even if Eddie wasn't more than big enough to look after himself, which he is, having met his wife, I'm absolutely certain that Wilt is nothing of the kind. Or she'd have killed him long ago. With her bare hands.'

And on this ominous note she'd left her husband to stew.

Now, as Lady Clarissa wandered through the garden, she planned her future tactics. She'd managed to calm down Herb's wife for the time being, and ought to be able to keep things ticking along if she forbade her to serve any more soup, just sticking to sausages or roasts with potatoes and a variety of veg. For afters it might not be a bad idea to have rice pudding or tapioca, both of which she knew Sir George loathed, with just occasionally a fruit salad thrown in, to make him realise it was time they got a proper cook.

In fact, the more she thought about it, the more convenient it seemed to have yet another reason to make frequent trips back to Ipford. She would tell George that there was a first-rate agency there where one could hire a really good cook. She rather thought that he'd been becoming a little suspicious of her Ipford jaunts of late and couldn't afford to have him find out what she really got up to there. Clarissa smiled to herself at the thought of her usual suite at the Black Bull.

In fact, she decided, she ought to make another trip there very soon, in order to check Uncle Harold into the Last Post and to make absolutely sure Mrs Wilt's husband was prepared to tutor Edward. It would actually be doubly beneficial if the presence of an educated man about the house made George less irritable. She'd have to warn Mr Wilt – what was his first name? Henry? – to keep off the subjects of taxation and politics at any cost, though. Forewarned was fore-armed, after all.

On this cheerful note she went back into the Hall to get the key of the vacant cottage in which she intended to house Wilt and Eva. She would walk down there, to check that it was relatively clean and not harbouring any bats or other unwelcome intruders. To be on the safe side she took a notebook with her, so as to write down anything she may need to buy. But the place was in good shape and only required a spring clean. She presumed the children could all share one bedroom. Eva had spoken of their having teenage girls. Clarissa only hoped they wouldn't prove to be too much of a distraction for Edward. Not that he had showed much sign of being interested in girls so far.

The truth was he hadn't actually showed much sign of being interested in anything on his brief visits home from school. Apart from a rather alarming tendency to throw stones at anything that moved, that was. Nothing, be it small animal or small child, was entirely safe when Edward was around. There had been a couple of unfortunate run ins with some of the towns-folk, who seemed not to accept the argument that if their children would trespass on the Estate then they only had themselves to blame. A lot of silly fuss about nothing really. After all, what were a few stitches here and there? And it wasn't as if the child was good-looking in the first place.

Lady Clarissa sighed as she walked back to the house, reflecting that if only George would take more of an interest in Edward – include him in a bit of hunting or fishing – all of this inconvenience might have been avoided. After wandering into the drawing room, she helped herself to two large dry martinis and decided to spend the rest of the day in bed, knowing her husband would be back late as usual. Thank goodness he slept in a separate room and was too old to take any interest in her sexually.

At 35 Oakhurst Avenue lived someone who shared her views on the desirability of separate bedrooms: Henry Wilt. For one thing it put a stop to Eva's spasmodic and thoroughly undesirable attempts to arouse him for sex by what she termed 'manual stimulation'. Wilt had frequently feigned sleep in the face of that, though without much success. Eva had once consulted Mavis Mottram, who had advised that the use of scrotal pressure was a sure way of waking him.

'I always use it when I want Patrick,' she'd said. 'I've never found it to fail.'

Wilt had. He called it the 'nutcracker method' and, on the few occasions when Eva used both hands, had leapt out of bed with a yell, demanding to know if she was trying to castrate him.

'If you want to prove you're bloody strong, try using two blasted walnuts!' he'd squawked one night, hobbling downstairs to fetch a bowl of the things.

His reaction had had the desired effect from his point of view, if not from Eva's.

His screams inevitably woke the quads when they were at home from boarding school, and all too often they'd surge out of their two bedrooms to ask what had happened.

'Nothing,' whimpered Wilt on that occasion as he crawled upstairs, holding the bowl with one hand and his scrotum with the other. 'It's just that Mummy is hungry.'

'For walnuts?'

'Yes, for walnuts. You know she says they're good for you.'

'Then why are you all doubled up?' Penelope had asked on that memorably agonising night.

'Because she mistook me for a damned tree,' groaned Wilt, and shut the bedroom door.

The quads were not deceived. Emmeline's penetrating voice could be heard quite clearly. 'Mummy's got the hot pants again,' she told the others on the landing. 'I think she's into S&M.'

An observation that put all thought of sex from Eva's mind. She got out of bed, poked her head round the door and gave the quads hell. Then she got back into bed and gave Wilt hell, too, though in a way which thankfully didn't involve anything physically disabling.

Tonight he went to sleep with the consoling thought that having the quads at home for the holidays would have its advantages after all.

# Chapter 6

Meanwhile at the police station Inspector Flint had time on his hands. He spent it staring out of the window and mulling over that perennial puzzle, Mr Henry Wilt. Ever since the sense of liberation he'd felt when Wilt had been mugged the previous summer, he'd come to the conclusion that the man was some sort of born victim, with a genius for getting himself into catastrophic situations and then wriggling out of them like a greased eel. On the other hand, he had a truly God-given and at times diabolical capacity for equivocation and, while being interrogated, for giving answers of such dizzying inconsequentiality that they had on a number of occasions driven Flint almost to the point of lunacy himself. The Inspector had looked

55

up both 'equivocation 'and 'inconsequentiality' in the dictionary at the public library and had concluded both words definitely applied to Henry Wilt. In fact, the fellow was almost admirable in his own diabolical sort of way.

Flint's feelings about Superintendent Hodge were, however, quite the opposite. There was absolutely nothing to admire about Hodge. In short, Flint loathed him, and would have termed him a 'bloody nincompoop' to his face if Hodge hadn't wielded influence higher up the chain of command.

Instead he expressed his opinion in private to Sergeant Yates, who demonstrated that he shared Flint's feelings for the Superintendent by referring to Hodge as 'that stupid bugger'. Outside the sun shone down. Staring across the park from his window, the Inspector idly wondered what Wilt was up to now.

Wilt was definitely not looking forward to being inspected by Lady Clarissa.

'Now you've got to be on your best behaviour,' Eva had told him rather more often than he liked. 'And don't forget to say you went to Porterhouse College in Cambridge.'

'In other words, lie through my teeth? I told you, I never went near the place.'

'That isn't a nice thing to say to me, and it's only a small fib anyway. You've got to impress her.'

'Oh, sure. And all she's got to do is phone the

college, ask if I went there, and then she'll be hellishly impressed, won't she just! And her bloody husband's bound to ask me if I was in the First Boat and what I think about the new Master who's probably a woman in any case.'

Eva was looking puzzled.

'I don't see what boats have to do with it. We've all been in boats at some point or other. Even I've been on a boat . . . it was on the Norfolk Broads, and rather jolly now I come to think of it.'

'They have to do with rowing, dear, and Porterhouse is a rowing college. It has frequently been Head of the River and is renowned for being filled with hearties. Do you know the difference between a hearty and an arty, by the way?'

'No,' said Eva, 'I don't. And if you're talking about gays, I don't want to hear any more.'

'Nothing could be further from my mind,' said Wilt. 'What I'm trying to din into your head is that when I was at Fitzherbert, a hearty was an undergraduate – all right, a student – who was good at sport. An arty was lousy at sport. If I was anything, I was an arty. Is that clear?'

'As mud,' said his wife. 'I shouldn't have thought you were good at anything.'

'Agreed,' said Wilt. 'On the other hand, this Gadsley bloke must have been a rowing or rugger sort, and thanks to your telling his wife I went to Porterhouse, the bloody man will undoubtedly talk sport – if he bothers to take the slightest notice of me at all, that is. I'll just have to try and keep out of his way.'

'You'll be too busy tutoring his step-son to have to go anywhere near Sir George. Besides he's probably too busy being a landowner, and playing golf, and hunting, shooting and fishing . . . or whatever it is that landowners do.'

'There is that, though I'm not going to spend all day, every day, teaching the boy if I can help it.'

'Of course not. It will be a lovely peaceful holiday for all of us,' Eva said, then went back upstairs to carry on packing the suitcases, satisfied that Henry fully understood the importance of his coming interview.

'Peaceful?' muttered Wilt. 'Fat chance of that.' And with the accompanying thought that the quads would almost certainly create chaos wherever they were, went back to reading about the First World War since it seemed Edward's examining board had based their syllabus around modern European history.

Meanwhile at St Barnaby's School, Sussex, the Head-mistress was in consultation with two teachers there, Miss Sanger and Ms Young, about the quads.

'I simply can't cope with them any longer,' Ms Young was saying. 'They create havoc in their house practically every day. Take last night, for example, when the fire alarm went off at two in the morning and we had to evacuate the dormitories. Who do you think was responsible? One of those horrid Wilt girls, that's who.'

'Are you absolutely certain?' asked the Headmistress.

'I can't prove it but I'm pretty certain. In the first place there was no fire, and secondly, Sandra Clalley told me that one of them – Emmeline, I think – had left the dormitory not long beforehand, ostensibly to go to the lavatory. By the time she came back to her bed, the glass had been smashed on the alarm.'

'It could have been broken before or by someone else.'

'Hmmm, I would agree with you there were it not for the fact that she was wearing gloves, and leather ones too, Sandra told me she was.'

'Did you ask Emmeline about it? What did she say?'

'She looked at me blankly and had the cheek to say she didn't know anything about leather gloves or fire alarms. For all I know, it might have been another one of them . . . I still can't tell those girls apart. In any case, she accused Sandra Clalley of lying and trying to get her into trouble because she was jealous of her and her sisters.'

'But that might well have been the case. After all, Sandra has come up with absurd stories about other girls,' said Miss Sanger. 'In my experience, she is not to be trusted in the slightest. Anna Mayle was nearly expelled because Sandra accused her of stealing her knickers, all of them, from the laundry while she was in the Sanatorium with glandular fever. That turned out to be a downright lie. We eventually found them behind one of the washing machines.'

The Headmistress nodded.

'Mrs Bluwell admitted she'd left a pile of wet underwear on top of the machine and so Sandra's could have fallen down behind it. There was absolutely no proof Anna was involved. Besides her father is a bishop and she's always been very well behaved. I don't see how we can ask Mr and Mrs Wilt to remove their girls just because Sandra Clalley accuses them of setting off the fire alarm last night.'

'But the fire alarm is the very least of it!' cried Ms Young, who went on to produce a catalogue of other misdemeanours – putting it mildly – that the Wilt girls had committed, and was in nearly all cases backed up by Miss Sanger. By the time the little meeting was over the Headmistress was forced to admit it was very difficult to know how best to deal with the four girls. In the end she agreed she would write to Mr and Mrs Wilt, telling them that she would have to consider asking them to remove their daughters the following year unless their behaviour improved

'It's probably a waste of time,' sighed Ms Young as she and Miss Sanger walked down the corridor. 'Have you ever seen their mother?' Miss Sanger hadn't. 'A dreadfully vulgar woman – and I do mean vulgar. I don't know why the Headmistress agreed to let them come here in the first place.'

'Possibly because their father is the head of some sort of university faculty,' Miss Sanger suggested.

'I think it more likely it's because we've never had

quadruplets in the school before. And because enrolment figures have shrunk so. I suppose having quads in the school makes us appear interesting. The little bitches are certainly unique, but in a truly dreadful sort of way. I'm just hoping they do something really appalling and get themselves expelled. I can't take much more.'

They parted and Ms Young marched back to her house with a very nasty expression on her face.

Outside the Headmistress's study, Samantha waited until she'd heard her leave the room before emerging cautiously from the shrubbery next to the window. She raced off to report back to the other three.

'The old cow is going to write to Mum and Dad to warn them we'll have to leave if we don't behave really well next term.'

'Ms Young said Emmy's setting off the fire alarm was the last straw. She thinks we're a pack of savages.'

'I like that! They're all snobs. Especially the Young bitch. I vote we do something to her car,' said Emmeline. 'That'll teach her.'

'Like what? Stuff a potato up the exhaust pipe like we did to that beastly old man at home, Mr Floren? He had to have the engine taken to bits before they found it.'

Emmeline shook her head.

'Something much better. Something that will wreck the motor and stop her driving for a long time.'

'Sugar in the petrol tank would do that,' said Penelope, thoughtfully. 'It takes some time though. Coats the pistons and valves gradually and then the engine seizes up.'

'Wait, I know,' interrupted Josephine. 'I heard the mechanic who services our car telling a man that carborundum powder ruins an engine for good.'

'And where do we get carborundum powder? Sugar's easier.'

'What if she locks the petrol-tank cap?' asked Samantha.

'She didn't when she took Martha and me to the dentist last week,' Emmeline told them. 'She needed more petrol and just got out and unscrewed the cap with the keys still in the car.'

'You mean, she left the engine running?'

'Of course not. She's not a complete idiot. She turned off the engine and left the keys in the car, which means it must be the sort which doesn't lock. Should be easy to pour a bag of sugar down it.'

'And have it stick to the side of the inlet where she can see it? Don't be so lame,' Samantha dismissed this suggestion.

'Oh, brilliant,' retorted Emmeline. 'Have you ever seen anyone peering down into their petrol tank? Even at the garage they're only looking at the pump to see if it's working properly and how much they're putting in.'

'All the same, we ought to test if sugar dissolves in

alcohol,' was Penelope's comment. 'I've got some eau de cologne we could use, and we can buy a bag of sugar from the shop in the village.'

'We don't need to. I've got some in my locker. I pinched it during Cookery when Mrs Drayton wasn't looking. We can use that,' said Emmeline.

An hour later they'd tried dissolving sugar in eau de cologne, which didn't work, and then in hot water, which did.

'Great! We'll just have to dissolve a lot of sugar in hot water and keep it in a bottle. That way Ms Young won't see any traces of it even if she looks.'

'She's going up to Scotland for the summer holidays. If this works, she'll end up having to go by train, which will serve her right. I know! I know! We ought to put it in right at the very end of term then she might break down on her way up there, miles and miles from a garage with any luck.'

And on this happy note the quads came out from behind the hockey pavilion and split up.

# Chapter 7

At home Wilt was swotting up his notes on Edward's A-level history course. He was planning to run through a few points with Braintree over a beer at the Dog and Duck, after having first had his hair cut on Eva's instructions.

'We can't have you looking like some of these footballers you see on telly,' she had told him, determined to remain optimistic in spite of the recent warning letter from St Barnaby's. 'So don't let whoever cuts it leave it too long. I've had your suit dry-cleaned too. You've got to look really smart and be very polite.'

'I'll look smart enough in my best sports jacket, which does at least fit me. More than I can say for that ridiculous outfit you bought me. Anyway that's the sort of thing university lecturers wear. They don't dress up in pink chalk-stripe suits.'

'Oh, all right, wear the sports jacket if you insist. I still say the suit looks better.'

'It may to you, but I know damned well it wouldn't impress a wealthy landowner,' Wilt said before returning to his notes. Thank goodness history A-level was a lot more interesting than he'd remembered. And also sufficiently violent to interest even the dimmest – and doubtless most conceited – teenage boy.

'You'll just have to get to the hairdresser early and . . .' Eva carried on, but Wilt intervened.

'Barber,' he said. 'I know it's an old-fashioned word, and refers to a more elegant age when men wore proper beards and one could get a shave too, but the correct word is barber, Eva.'

'I don't care. All I want is that you don't look like some long-haired hippy. A nice short back and sides, please.'

'All right, I heard you the first time,' said Wilt. 'Rest assured, I've no desire for you to blast the hell out of me when I get home.'

'Well, I have had a particularly disturbing day,' said his wife, and handed him the Headmistress's latest letter before storming into the kitchen.

Wilt read it through and followed her.

'I sort of expected something like that,' he said

cheerfully. 'If you will send our darling daughters to a very select and expensive school, you shouldn't be surprised when they inevitably create havoc and are threatened with expulsion. They're lucky not to have been expelled long ago. You should have sent them to a reformatory – it would have saved time and been a lot cheaper.'

'They're not being expelled. Mrs Collinson only says their behaviour has to improve or they may be asked to leave.'

'Where there's life there's hope,' said Wilt. 'And there's no hope of that. Well, at least in future years I won't have to subsidise their awful activities by taking tutoring jobs in my summer holidays.'

And before Eva could find words to express her annoyance, he had retreated to the front room and was watching the news.

The subdued friction that was part and parcel of the Wilts' marriage, and which occasionally broke out into open warfare, had a full-scale eruption later that day when Wilt came back from having his hair cut.

'You call that a haircut?' Eva demanded. 'It's far too long.'

'Well, I only asked for a trim. Did you want me to have my hair shaved off and come back looking like a skinhead?'

'Of course not. But mark my words, you're going to have it cut properly. So go back right now and see

67

the man does a thorough job. It's got to be a short back and sides. And another thing . . . your sports jacket has holes in the elbows so I want you to wear that lovely suit I bought for you instead.'

'If you really think a light grey suit with a pink chalk-stripe is going to impress Sir Bloodhound and Lady Claptrap . . .'

'Sir George and Lady Clarissa Gadsley, for goodness' sake . . .'

'Sir George, eh? He probably has his suits tailor-made in Savile Row.'

'What's so special about this Civil Row or whatever you said?'

'Savile Row, Eva, Savile Row. It's just about the most expensive place to buy a suit in London. Lady Claptrap and Sir Gadsley wouldn't give me house room if I turned up in a bright chalk pink stripe. I mean, a pink chalk stripe bright.'

'Have you been drinking, Henry?' Eva asked suspiciously. 'I thought that haircut took an awfully long time. Come over here and breathe on me.'

'Breathe on you? Good God, woman, do you never stop? First you sign me up for some fucking silly job teaching an upper-class cretin things he should have learned years ago, and then you decide how long my fucking hair should be! Well, I've had enough. I'll wear my hair however I like, do you hear me?'

On this note Wilt left the house and cycled back to the men's hairdresser to give him Eva's instructions.

'She says you've left it too long and it's to be shorter at the back and sides.'

'Your missus?' asked the barber sympathetically.

Wilt nodded.

'I wonder she didn't ask for a crew cut,' the barber went on.

Wilt shuddered.

'She said I wasn't to look like a footballer. And all this because I've got to meet Lady something or other. Anyone would think I was going to see the Queen.'

'Well, you're certainly not going to be mistaken for Bob Geldof.'

'That's a mercy,' said Wilt.

The barber grinned.

'I don't think I'd be in business still if I only had customers like him.'

Using an electric razor, he thinned the hair on the sides of Wilt's head.

'Reckon that ought to do or is she going to want more?'

'Oh, she's bound to want more off than that, but I most certainly don't,' said Wilt, getting out of the chair. The barber shook the loose hair off the sheet and removed it. Wilt studied his head critically.

Just then Eva arrived. Wilt got back into the chair

and the barber draped the sheet around him again before starting to trim the back of his head, studiously avoiding catching the eye of either his customer or his customer's dragon of a wife.

Not until Wilt bore a close resemblance to a sheep that had been made ready for the spring did his wife relent and proclaim herself satisfied. Wilt sullenly pushed his bike back to the house, trailing a clearly delighted Eva, and went to bed before she could inflict any more damage on him.

The following morning Eva brought him breakfast in bed, in an attempt both to make amends and to put him in a better mood before his interview with Lady Clarissa. Her plan might well have succeeded had she not also hidden all of his clothing save for the offending suit. By the time he came downstairs Wilt was in a foul temper.

'That's much better!'

'It will serve you right if she takes one look at me and runs off screaming, you stupid bloody woman,' Wilt muttered. 'So when are we going to meet her ladyship?'

Eva made a tactical decision to ignore his swearing for the moment. Looking at the clock, she said, 'We may as well go and have a cup of tea first. Lady Clarissa isn't expecting us until twelve-thirty.' At Eva's insistence they took their bikes rather than the car, calling in first at a café near the Black Bear. Half an hour later they walked into the hotel lobby, Wilt continuing to feel like a prize idiot in his outlandish suit.

'Lady Clarissa is in the lounge,' the receptionist told them.

Eva turned to her husband and brushed some imaginary fluff from his lapel.

'Now if she asks you if you want a drink, you're to say a sherry.'

But Wilt had had enough.

'I don't like bloody sherry. What does she drink?'

'What she calls dry martinis, whatever they are.'

'Then that's what I'll ask for. A dry martini will make me feel more confident. And God knows I need some confidence, dressed like a spiv and practically bald up top.'

'All right, have a martini then, but you mustn't have a second. She drinks very strong ones with a lot of gin in them. The last thing we need is for you to get drunk. And will you stop using that horrible language?'

Wilt grumpily followed her into the lounge where he was surprised to find that Lady Clarissa was not the starchy middle-aged woman he had expected. She was in fact very good-looking and extremely well dressed. Best of all, he would have said she was at least half seas over – as indeed she was, although she held her liquor well.

'Ah, my dear Mrs Wilt,' she greeted Eva. 'And this must be your clever husband Henry. My goodness, what a very lively suit you have on, my dear.'

She smiled invitingly at Wilt who, somewhat to his own astonishment, heard himself say he was honoured to meet her.

'Mrs Wilt drinks sherry, I know,' she continued. 'May I offer you a . . . ?' Lady Clarissa left the question open.

Wilt barely hesitated. 'I think I'll join you. I take that to be a dry martini,' he said, almost purring as he indicated her glass.

Lady Clarissa signalled to the waiter who came over at a rate of knots. Her Ladyship was evidently a respected drinker here.

'Mrs Wilt would like a sweet sherry, an oloroso . . . I think you'd prefer that, my dear . . . and Henry and I will have dry martinis – and go light on the Noilly Prat.'

Eva wasn't looking too pleased. She disliked being called Mrs Wilt while her husband was addressed as Henry. She also found the expression on Wilt's face oddly disturbing. He was looking like a cat that had swallowed half a dozen canaries.

'Now, Henry, about my son . . . Edward's not stupid but he's simply not academic,' confided Lady Clarissa. 'He calls history "old-fashioned". I've told him it's bound to be because it's in the past, but he remains unconvinced. And my husband's attitude doesn't help. Edward's not his own son, you see, and George will insist on calling him Eddie . . .'

Eva interrupted here.

'When you say he's not Sir George's son . . .' she began than stopped hurriedly, much to Wilt's regret. For a moment he'd thought she was going to ask if the boy was illegitimate.

'My first husband died in a car accident.'

'How dreadful. I am sorry.'

'I don't think I am,' said Lady Clarissa. 'I know one ought to be but he was a frightful bore. Still, I haven't dragged you out here to talk about him.'

'You were saying that Edward doesn't like history,' Wilt reminded her. 'Is it his only weak subject?'

'Well, he failed English the year before last. Probably because he said that was old-fashioned too. But, you know, I don't think that's the real reason. Failing his A-levels is Edward's way of getting his own back on my husband. You see, George considers the past to be so much more important than the present. And besides, he's an elderly man himself – though younger than my Uncle Harold. As bad-tempered as him, though.'

Wilt considered all this and found it to be thoroughly illogical. Lady Clarissa was perhaps further into her cups than he'd first thought. He managed to catch Eva's eye and she hastily broke in on the conversation.

'Did you get your uncle into the old people's home all right?'

'Oh, yes, after the usual struggle. First of all he claimed it was noisy, which it wasn't, and then when he found out there was a black woman in the kitchen he kicked up an awful fuss about Aids in Africa. I had to point out she had been born in Manchester and spoke with a Moss Side accent. It's all been very difficult and he still says he's not going to stay.'

Listening to all this, Wilt wondered what sort of people he was going to have to mix with at Sandystones Hall. He decided he'd prefer to break the news that he hadn't been to Porterhouse now, rather than wait and be caught out by Sir George.

'By the way, I think I ought to tell you straight-away that I went to Fitzherbert and not Porterhouse.' Wilt ignored Eva's furious glare and added, 'Long before I came up to Cambridge, Fitzherbert was known as the townies' college, but I expect that was before your husband's time too.'

'What an odd name . . . the townies' college. I think Fitzherbert is much nicer. Smarter, if you know what I mean,' observed Lady Clarissa.

'I absolutely agree,' said Eva, with huge relief, and with that they went into lunch. Wilt was fairly glad too. That dry martini was the most lethal he'd ever drunk. The glass had been unusually large and the gin the strongest he'd ever tasted. He hated to think what two of them would have done to him. Total befuddlement was the term that suggested itself when he'd racked his brains for longer than usual. One thing was certain: Lady Clarissa was definitely a most accomplished drinker.

'And when does your university term end?' she asked Wilt once they had ordered and she had had a minor wrangle with the wine waiter. After a lengthy look at the wine list she had chosen a bottle of Château Latour, only to find that they were out of it. The wine waiter had suggested instead a claret which was infinitely cheaper. Lady Clarissa agreed only reluctantly but, upon tasting it, declared herself won over.

'Goodness, who would have believed it? Do you know, I think I actually prefer this after two Tanqueray martinis,' she said when the waiter had filled their glasses and departed. Wilt concentrated on her previous question.

'I'm free from the end of the week', he told her.

'But the qua—' Eva began before he could intervene.

'Our daughters come home from St Barnaby's in twelve days' time,' he said to forestall a diatribe from Eva on the subject of the quads. The Gadsleys were in for a nasty surprise there. They may not be so keen on his tutoring their son when they'd endured a few weeks of the quads making merry in their grounds. Merry hell was more like it.

'Do you have to wait for them? I want Edward to get into Porterhouse straightaway when he retakes the exam this autumn.'

Wilt kept his thoughts to himself. Even if the lad retook A-level history and passed it in the autumn, it was almost certain that he wouldn't get in to Cambridge for another year. At least, Wilt didn't think he would. With Porterhouse one never quite knew. The college was one of the poorest and least academic in Cambridge. But unless he'd lost touch completely, it was also the least likely to stand on convention. Anything was possible when dealing with Porterhouse, he concluded.

'So I'd be grateful if you could start as soon as you can,' Lady Clarissa was saying. 'You could stay in the Hall if you'd rather not go straight into the cottage. See how you get on with my husband . . .'

'I'm sure I can make it,' said Wilt, glancing at Eva. 'Aren't you, love?'

'Of course you can. After all, it's only a few days until we all arrive,' said Eva with false enthusiasm. To be called 'love' by Wilt was an unusual experience for her and in recent years had almost always signalled trouble. And she was puzzled by his amenable attitude too. He was usually the last person to do what someone else wanted. She was even more alarmed by the way Lady Clarissa, now with two-thirds of a bottle of wine inside her, was openly gawping at him. It had begun to dawn on her that Wilt was attracting more of her ladyship's attention than Eva found entirely desirable. She'd have to keep a close watch on the situation. Fifteen hundred pounds a week plus board and lodging was surely a lot to pay a mere tutor. 'Hanky-panky' was the expression that suggested itself to her next, and the one she used as they cycled home after lunch.

'If you think you're going to get up to any hanky-panky with that woman, you can think again,' she shouted at Wilt when they came to a Stop sign.

He grinned at her.

'You're the one who set this job up,' he yelled as they started off again. 'Anyway I don't understand why you're saying that now. I was only trying to fit in with your plans. And in any case, Lady Clarissa was as pissed as a newt.'

'I daresay, but you didn't have to fawn all over her.'

'I thought that was what you wanted, love,' said Wilt, giving the word a rather different intonation than he'd used in the restaurant. At least all her warnings to him about looking respectable and not getting drunk had worked.

They cycled on in silence to Oakhurst Avenue, but once they were in the house Eva became newly aggrieved.

'She kept calling you Henry while I was merely Mrs Wilt. I thought that was rather unnecessary. She could have called me Eva.'

'She called you "dear Mrs Wilt" several times. After all, she's employing me, not you, and in her circle they probably always use Christian names with the servants. I can't see why you're making such a fuss about nothing.'

'It's going to stay nothing, too, if I have anything

to do with it,' warned Eva before remembering another suspicious circumstance. 'And when she said she'd drive you up, you jumped at the offer. I didn't like that much either.'

'I only did that because you'll need the car to fetch the quads. Anyway I didn't jump at the opportunity, and I'm damned if I fawned on the ruddy woman. I was just doing what you told me to do: being very polite to her. Dressed up and made to have a short back and sides . . . What did you expect me to do? Insult her?'

Eva had to admit that he was right. All the same, she hadn't liked the way Lady Clarissa had gazed at Henry with such obvious interest. True, the woman certainly had been drinking before they arrived, but how could Eva be sure she wouldn't drink like that again while Henry was living in the same house as her? In fact, it was almost certain that she would.

Eva went upstairs to make the bed – Henry, who was still sleeping in a separate room, could make his own – wondering what she ought to do about the potential threat. The quads were more important to her than anything else in her life; she couldn't stand in the way of them receiving the education they deserved. And anyway, Henry was so sexless that Lady Clarissa could make as many eyes at him as she liked but was it really likely he would respond? All the same, Eva definitely needed to get up there herself just as soon as the quads finished school, and once safely installed she would keep her eyes pinned on him, to make quite sure he behaved himself.

# Chapter 8

Uncle Harold – or the Colonel, as he'd insisted on being addressed – wasn't having a pleasant time at all in the Last Post. On his second night there he'd no sooner got to sleep in his room on the ground floor than he was woken by a crash above him – the sound of what he supposed was someone falling out of bed – followed by Matron's scurrying footsteps. He couldn't hear what the ambulance men were chattering about as they headed upstairs in what were surely hob-nailed boots, but they were fast followed by several other people, including the doctor who was loudly summoned from across the road. They all stayed in the room above for an age, seemingly in constant motion, and when they finally came out the doctor's tactlessly loud voice reached him from the landing, saying: 'They may be able to do something for the poor old sod at the Hospital, though I very much doubt it. What on earth was he doing getting out of bed like that?'

'Probably forgot he'd a catheter in and wanted to urinate. Very forgetful, the Brigadier is. And obstinate too.'

'Was by the look of things,' announced the doctor. 'Must have hit his head on the locker when he fell.'

Five minutes later the Colonel heard the siren of a police car arriving and more heavy footsteps on the stairs. Why couldn't they use the lift? Five more minutes passed and they did – or at any rate tried to.

'He's too bloody tall! He's never going to fit in here . . . should have been on the ground floor.'

'What? And have him where visitors could hear him using such foul language all the time?' Matron replied. 'Anyway, we always put the most difficult old bastards down there, so they can't make things too awkward for the staff who have to get them up and dressed and so forth.'

From his room, the Colonel decided to make his feelings known.

'I am not a difficult old bastard!' he yelled, and heard someone say he could see what Matron meant.

Presently she opened the door and poked her head inside.

'Now don't you worry,' she cooed into the darkness. 'You just go back to sleep like a good boy.'

'I am neither an old bastard nor a boy,' shouted the Colonel. 'And you're the ones who've woken me up, pounding up and down the stairs without a thought for anyone else. I won't have it, and I won't have your rotten rudeness either, do you hear me? In fact, in future you'll call me "sir" when you address me. Now bugger off!'

'Naughty, naughty,' answered Matron. 'There's a catheter going spare for nasty old men who won't behave themselves.' And shut the door with a loud bang.

The Colonel roundly cursed all women and then lay grimly contemplating his future. It would be an unpleasant one and probably short. His thoughts drifted back to the days when he'd still wielded some authority. It all seemed a very long time ago.

Before he got back to sleep he had worked out the rudiments of a plan to get himself out of this hell-hole, preferably before that old bag could do anything involving catheters. He had remembered hearing that Matron had a son who had been an officer in a county regiment. A man of that calibre would have more respect for anyone connected to the army than for his old bat of a mother. No point in throwing himself on Clarissa's mercy: she'd made it quite plain when she'd come down to settle him into the Last Post that it was this or the even more Godawful-sounding Journey's End where, according to her, you could practically smell the Crematorium on a busy day.

No, he'd had it with Clarissa. He was pretty damn' sure he knew why she visited so regularly and it was nothing to do with love. Or, rather, nothing to do with any kind of love for him.

Now if he could only get a message to this army chap, he might just be able to get out of here.

# Chapter 9

Next morning Wilt was awake surprisingly early and over his standard breakfast of muesli – which Eva insisted was good for him – continued mugging up on the First World War. Eva was still in bed, much to his delight. He probably wouldn't have been so relaxed if he'd known she was thinking dark thoughts about him and Lady Clarissa. Eva eventually came downstairs in her mauve and yellow dressing gown and was relieved to find him sitting at the kitchen table, obviously engrossed in his book.

'What's that you're reading?'

'Just an account of the decisive battles of the First World War,' he answered. 'I thought I'd better go through it again myself before trying to make it even faintly comprehensible to what's-his-name? You know, the Gadsleys' puppy . . . Edward. I must say, the prospect doesn't exactly enthral me. It's very bloody reading – but I daresay that'll make it more interesting to the young brute.'

Eva didn't want to know. Instead she made a pot of tea for herself and some coffee for Wilt.

'I hope you had a nice time last night,' she said sarcastically as she put the cup on the table just out of his reach. 'Out drinking again, I suppose.'

In fact, Wilt had been driven to seek refuge in the pub after spending an unpleasant afternoon being badgered by his wife about behaving properly at Sandystones Hall: not getting drunk or using bad language or having sex with Lady Clarissa. Or letting Lady Clarissa have sex with him. In desperation he'd gone down to the Braintrees' and dragged Peter out to the Duck and Dragon where they had sat outside and drunk beer, watching the boats pass by on the river.

'What's this Lady Clarissa like?' Peter had asked him.

'Drinks huge dry martinis as if they're water. She has to be an alcoholic . . . or at least that's the impression I got at lunch. I'd be very surprised if she hasn't a lover on the side, too, the eyes she made at me. One thing that is certain is I'm going to stay well clear of that sort of thing. Not that I'm planning to put Eva out of her misery. any time soon. The truth of the matter is she's only really concerned about the fifteen hundred quid a week I'm going to be paid for tutoring the dimwit son.'

Wilt had only stayed out for as long as it took to ensure Eva had gone up to bed ahead of him, and was actually pretty much sober when he made his way home.

Eva finished her tea and went back upstairs, leaving him concentrating on his book. To Wilt's surprise and disgust she came back down moments later, this time wearing a sheer dressing gown through which he could see her vivid scarlet panties. That meant only one thing and Eva put it into words.

'I've been thinking about it, Henry, and I've come to the conclusion that it's about time we had some gender,' she said, using the word Wilt had come to detest.

'If by that you mean sex . . .' he began.

'I do,' interrupted Eva. 'We haven't had any for ages, and at Sandystones Hall I don't suppose we'll get the chance. Besides the girls will be there too and . . .'

Wilt interrupted her.

'. . . you make such a din they're bound to know what we're up to. Not that it matters. They know more about sex than I do. Haven't you heard Emmeline going on about it? Anyway I had a sleepless night and I'm whacked out. I couldn't get it up even if I wanted to. Which I don't.'

'Hmm, yes, and I wonder what you've been up to that you're so "whacked out", and whether it's got something to do with the fact that you've taken to sleeping in a separate bedroom from me? Mavis Mottram thinks that if you're a man of normal appetites, you must be satisfying yourself if you aren't satisfying me. Not that "normal" is a word I would usually apply to any of your activities. In any case, you'll be glad to know she has given me some Viagra just so you can get an erection. I know it went wrong for us before but she says the dose was . . .'

'Take bloody Viagra? And possibly go blind into the bargain,' said Wilt, almost wishing he was. Those blasted panties were a practically inflammable red.

'What on earth are you talking about . . . going blind?'

'Oh, didn't you know? It's been in the papers. A number of men in the States have gone blind after taking Viagra.'

'I don't believe it. They'd probably just been masturbating, like you do.'

'Oh, for heaven's sake! If you believe that . . .'

'Of course I do. Definitely.'

Wilt raised his eyes to the ceiling in despair.

'So why haven't I gone blind? Either I masturbate and don't go blind or I'm not blind because I don't masturbate. Which is it?'

'Some men don't, I suppose,' said Eva, now thoroughly confused as to what it was she was accusing Wilt of doing.

'But on the whole they do? So most of the blind men you meet in the street – you know, the ones with sticks and guide dogs – are wankers?'

'Of course they're not! And how many times do I have to tell you to stop using such foul language?'

'And do you also check for hair on the palms of their hands?'

'No. Why should I?'

'Because that's another hoary old story stupid women like you and Mavis Mottram put about. You can try it out on the Gadsley boy. When I was at school we used to tell younger ones that if they did it they'd grow hair on their palms, and they always looked to check.'

'You must have gone to a very peculiar school.'

'All schools are peculiar. They have to be, considering the number of morons they turn out.'

And before Eva could think of a retort to this, Henry had gone out of the kitchen and down the hall to the front door.

'I'm off to the Tech to get some peace and quiet. Come to think of it, you can give yourself some DIY sex while I'm gone. Those flaming pants are dying for some.'

He left Eva to work out that last remark. Ten minutes later he was sitting in the sun outside old Coverdale's shack, with a cup of tea in his hands.

'Do you ever miss sex?' he asked his friend.

'Gave it up years ago,' said the old man. 'I reckon

it's an overrated pastime. Besides you should see my missus. She's an anti-aphrodisiac if ever there was one. Only a sex maniac would want her – and then he'd regret it.'

'Don't go on,' Wilt pleaded. 'My wife's walking about the house in a pair of pants that would put a sex-starved rapist off for life. She wears the beastly things whenever she wants what she mis-calls "gender".'

'That's a grammatical term surely.'

'Not in our house it isn't,' Wilt said bitterly. 'Let's talk about something else. Like how I'm going to get this young idiot to pass his exam when every time I sit down to swot up, my blasted wife sticks her oar in.'

'It's not her oar you need worry about, from the sound of it! You want to watch she doesn't sneak some of that Viagra stuff into your food, you do.'

Wilt nodded gloomily. He still remembered only too well the débâcle that had ensued last time Eva had fed him an aphrodisiac. He'd be lucky if he even made it to the Hall at this rate.

# Chapter 10

Lady Clarissa arrived back at Sandystones Hall feeling in a good mood. She'd had an energetic night in Ipford with her young man, and now that she had met him she was also greatly looking forward to the arrival of Wilt the following weekend.

He was obviously a well-educated man and she was sure he'd be just the right tutor for Edward, who was due back from school next Monday.

Even Sir George was more amiable than usual, having heard that a neighbour he had always detested had been sentenced to three months for dangerous driving, and to the loss of his driving licence for two years on the additional charge of being drunk at the time.

'That'll teach him to trespass on my land,' he added inconsequentially. 'I've warned him to keep off it time and time again, as you know. Anyway, you're back at last. How's your uncle doing at that new nursing home? Enjoying himself?'

'Far from it, I'm sorry to say. No, he kept on telephoning me at the hotel, complaining about the traffic noise and the fact that the Brigadier upstairs had fallen out of bed just when Uncle Harold had got to sleep and they couldn't get him into the lift because he was too tall. And how Matron told him not to be a naughty boy when he asked her to tell them not to make such a din. He doesn't like the place being called the Last Post either. Says it's morbid. Oh, yes, and he also dislikes having to sleep in what he calls "a premature shroud".'

'A premature shroud? What the devil's that?'

'A long nightshirt. It's because he's only got one leg and they think it's more manageable than pyjamas. Apparently they've also told him he'd be better off with a catheter, but he objects to that too. I can't think why.'

Sir George could but he wasn't going to argue about it. He'd had one after an operation and wouldn't wish the experience of the procedure on anyone, even Uncle Harold, miserable old bugger that he was. He decided to move the conversation on to a more pleasant subject.

'By the way, I've found an excellent cook,' he said. 'She's been here since Friday, and by God she's pretty special! Her name is Philomena Jones but she doesn't mind being called Philly. What she can do with a goose is quite remarkable . . .'

Lady Clarissa tried to think what one could do with a goose other than roast it. She couldn't see it being fried or boiled.

'First she smears it with bacon fat and butter. She calls that "schmatzing it". Then she stuffs it with pâté de foie gras and blood pudding and . . . oh, yes, I forgot. She cuts the head and neck off first then puts them back just before she serves it up. She's extremely artistic. For pudding last night there was a choice of zabaglione or plum duff, followed by Limburger cheese the like of which I've never tasted before.'

'I can well imagine. I had some once and found it absolutely revolting. Just the smell was enough to put me off the stuff for life,' said Lady Clarissa with a shudder.

'I suppose it's an acquired taste, but I can tell you that I've never dined and lunched so well in my life as I have over the course of this weekend. Goose, duck, partridge, pheasant . . . you name it, Philly can cook the lot. Of course, she varies the stuffing. She's been mixing fried snails with garlic and . . .'

'Hold it there. Just tell me where she gets the snails from. I hope they come in a tin?'

'Great heavens, no. She goes into the kitchen garden and collects them. Eating off the land and all that. Philly's a forager, Clarissa. And damned good at it she is, too. Yesterday we had stuffed breast of hedgehog for an hors d'oeuvre. She'd baked it in clay to remove the prickles, of course. Utterly delicious.'

'And doubtless extremely healthy,' said Clarissa sarcastically. 'In other words, I've only to leave you here alone for a couple of days and you completely ignore the cardiologist's strict instructions not to eat vast quantities of fat and to stick to chicken and fish as much as possible. Instead I come home and find you indulging yourself in a positively lethal diet of goose stuffed with foie gras and black pudding, not to mention the other disgusting ingredients. And where on earth did you find this Myra Hindley of a cook?'

Sir George smiled.

'As a matter of fact, in court. She was sentenced to a month's community service for poaching. So to save money I took her on here to do her community service, which means she's extraordinarily cheap. Actually she costs nothing except for what she eats herself. I mean, I give her bed and board. That way I get to eat magnificently and we save money into the bargain.'

'Perfect,' said Clarissa. 'Just tell me one other thing before you drop dead. Is this woman Philomena Jones a gypsy?'

Sir George hesitated for a moment.

'Do you know, I hadn't thought of that,' he said finally. 'She certainly lives nearby and the man she usually lives with has been sentenced to six months for something or other. I think it was causing bodily harm to a gamekeeper. Had I known his wife, if that's what she is, was such an excellent cook, I'd have used my influence to see the court gave him a much longer sentence.'

'Brilliant! Utterly brilliant. No wonder she wants you dead,' said Clarissa, staring out of the window while considering what to do about this. She did not want to become a widow again. Not just yet. On the other hand, she had no intention of sharing her husband's notion of gourmet cuisine. Garden snails and hedgehogs were . . . she tried to think of an adequate description and failed. Instead she tried another tack.

'Am I wrong in thinking this creature is fat?'

'As a butterball,' said Sir George. 'Whatever a butter-ball is.'

'In other words, extremely fat.'

'Oh, I wouldn't say that. Overweight, perhaps, but not really obese.'

'You and I have a different definition of obese. I can't say that I have ever understood this predilection of yours for enormous women – God knows why you ever married me.' She glared at Sir George, daring him to respond to this last point, and he at least had the good grace not to reply.

'Oh, well, I'd better go and see what this paragon of cordon bleu cookery looks like.'

'Well, you can always ring for her. She rather likes me sending for her.'

'I'm sure she does, but I rather want to see for myself what denizens of the wild she is preparing for us tonight. Toads' legs from the dry moat, perhaps? Hare's testicles on toast? I despair of you, George, I really do.'

And on this cheerless note Clarissa marched down the long corridor to the kitchen, to be confronted by a woman who did not look in the least like a gypsy given her fair hair and pasty complexion. She had rather a snub nose, and rosy cheeks that bulged out below deep-set eyes. In fact, she bulged grotesquely just about everywhere.

'You must be Philomena,' Lady Clarissa said. 'Philomena Jones.'

'You can call me Philly. Most everyone does.'

'And is that your real name? Not that it matters.'

'Yes, mum, except the last bit. I made that up for the court.'

'Well, I am Lady Gadsley and you will address me as "my lady".'

'Yes, mum. I call himself Mr Gadsley.'

'You can call him whatever you like, though I'd prefer it if you dealt mainly with me from now on. And what are you proposing to poison us with tonight?'

'Poison, mum? Was there anything in particular you were thinking of?'

'I told you not to call me "mum".'

Philly grinned.

'Know you did, but if I called you "my lady" I'd have to curtsey, wouldn't I? And then I'd probably fall over and have trouble getting up. I have to get out of bed real careful. I fell over in front of a steamroller one time and only managed to crawl out of its way at the last moment . . .'

'What a dreadful pity,' said Clarissa ambiguously. 'Anyway I haven't come here to discuss the world's misfortunes. I want to discuss the menus.'

'Men yous? I don't know about men yous. Not here, that is, though I know Mr Gadsley fancies a bit of crackling at night, if you take my meaning?'

Lady Clarissa shuddered.

'Are you talking about pigs cooked or pigs uncooked?'

But the implication behind this question escaped the cook.

'Oh, never mind,' said Clarissa as Philly struggled to answer or at any rate appeared to. 'I just want to make it absolutely clear that I do not share my husband's taste for snails, hedgehogs, blood pudding and foie gras stuffing, to say nothing of all the lower forms of wildlife you seem to serve up. From what Sir George has said, I wouldn't be at all surprised if you were offering up fricassees of slugs and the like. It's simply absurd.'

'Oh, no, mum. I never heard of anyone wanting slugs for breakfast. Or dinner either, come to that.'

'Well, that's a mercy,' said Clarissa. 'So what are you preparing for dinner tonight?'

'I thought, 'cos Mr Gadsley keeps asking for a savoury, that for starters we'd have toadstools . . .'

'Toadstools?' squawked Lady Clarissa. 'Don't you mean, mushrooms? Toadstools are frequently poisonous.'

'Perhaps some are. Depends what you pick,' said Philomena. 'My old man says the ones what are white on top and sort of white underneath, too, are all right. The red ones on their hats aren't.'

'You can take all of them off the menu for a start! I'm not having my husband killed off just yet. And for the main dish?'

'Suckling pig roasted to a crisp. Like I said, he does enjoy his bit of crackling.'

'No, absolutely not. We'll have a light supper tonight. Some tinned asparagus, followed by sardines with a lettuce salad and some tinned beans. And afterwards plain Cheddar cheese,' Clarissa ordered, then stormed out of the kitchen again in search of Sir George.

'You may wish to die a premature death from food poisoning but I most certainly do not,' she snapped at him. 'And that ghastly creature in the kitchen knows as much about healthy cooking as I do about the structure of the atom. I've just ordered her to serve a salad for supper tonight.'

'Oh, God, no. Just when I was looking forward to some delicious hors d'oeuvre followed by suckling pig.'

'I doubt you'd still have been around for the suckling pig. She was going to give you toadstools for starters. Yes, toadstools, dear. Assorted toadstools. You know, the ones that are white underneath . . . like death-caps. Yes, I thought that would make you sit up and take notice.'

'I'm not sitting down or up, as a matter of fact,' said Sir George. 'And I'm quite sure Philly knows what she's doing. After all, she's a child of Nature. Been living off the land since she was born.'

'Suckled by Nature, too, I suppose.'

'You know what I mean. Gypsies have a gift for survival. That is, if she is a real gypsy.'

'Whatever the creature is, you'd better get it into your head that I mean to see we survive her lethal cooking. I'm not having you dying in agony or, even worse, being paralysed by a cerebral haemorrhage. In other words, a stroke.'

'I am fully aware what a cerebral haemorrhage is, thank you very much.'

Lady Clarissa took perverse comfort from the anger in his tone and decided to press home her point. 'I had an old friend once who had a stroke and turned into a human cabbage overnight. I remember the occasion well. He insisted that all this fuss, as he put it, about fat clogging the arteries was a lot of nonsense. He was smoking a cigar at the time, as I recall, and had just eaten two extra helpings of crackling at dinner. He was standing in front of the fireplace holding forth

99

when he suddenly keeled over and never spoke again. Or even moved his hands. He made pitiful noises, which his wife tried and failed to interpret. She sat by his bed for three years although the stroke specialist she called in did tell her he would never recover his speech or ability to move. But she hung on out of devotion. It was only when she met a top man in the Foreign Office and fell in love with him that she finally agreed her husband could be taken into a nursing home. I can give you his name too. It was . . .'

'I don't want to know!' shouted Sir George.

'All right, I won't tell you then. Anyway he lingered on like a living corpse for another seven years before he popped his clogs. I went to his cremation, too, and I do remember hoping he was really dead when the coffin began to slide through the curtain towards the furnace. I mean, he might not have been. Oh, and another thing . . .'

But Sir George had heard quite enough.

'For God's sake, shut up, will you?' he screamed, and hurled his Montecristo No. 2 cigar into the empty fireplace.

But Lady Clarissa had yet to deliver the coup de grâce.

'His name was Henry Hogg, which seemed appropriate considering how much he loved roast pork. A fitting end, I suppose some people would call it.'

'I don't believe it. You made the whole disgusting story up,' her husband said in a whimper.

'You don't have to. You can look up his name in Who's Who: he died in 1986. Actually, come to think of it, you'll need to look in Who Was Who.'

Sir George almost smiled.

'There's no such bloody thing, you stupid woman.'

'All right, try the latest Who's Who and see who Leonard Nocking married. I can tell you now to save you the trouble. It was the widow of Henry Hogg, the year after his decease. Nocking was knighted shortly afterwards for services to medicine. He was a great man, and for all I know still is.'

Later that evening, after a light supper of asparagus and sardine salad, Sir George sneaked off to his study and took down Who's Who. He found the entry for Nocking. The bitch had been telling the truth after all.

In the kitchen Philomena was tenderly stroking the uncooked piglet. If it had been alive she might well have offered it a nipple. She felt sorry for it, enduring rejection even after death.

# Chapter 11

Had Ms Young's car had any feelings, it would have felt the same way. The quads' efforts to make the trip to Inverness a difficult one had succeeded. The pound and a half of sugar dissolved in hot water and added to the petrol tank had been augmented by a potato shoved up the exhaust pipe with the help of a broom handle.

That the potato had first been coated with super-glue made it impossible to remove without dismantling the exhaust. And, in fact, it was the potato which caused the first problem. The car, a brand new Honda of which she was particularly proud, had had to be taken down to the local garage to be repaired. Ms Young, who had been given permission to leave school six days before the end of term so as to attend her cousin's wedding, was to put it mildly not amused and nursed her suspicions about just who had delayed the start of her journey. After two days the car had been returned with a new exhaust and she had set off again – but then the sugar water had kicked in.

She had just reached the Dartford Tunnel when the car ground to a halt. Unfortunately it was rush hour and the traffic was in its usual appalling state, so a broken-down car in the tunnel was the last straw for other drivers whose vehicles stacked up for miles behind hers.

Horns were blown, drivers cursed – those closest to her in crude language she had never heard before and most certainly didn't wish to hear again – and it was over an hour before a recovery vehicle managed to reach her. And even then the process was made even more difficult because the Honda had stopped so close to the lorry in front of it the number plate was caught on its bumper, and the car behind couldn't be moved at all easily. The driver of the car behind Ms Young tried to cross into the second lane in his desperation to escape, only to be hit and badly damaged by an enormous French lorry which shouldn't have been in that lane in the first place. Altogether it took two hours to disentangle the Honda and get it out of the tunnel, by which time Ms Young was not the sane person who had left St Barnaby's School so many hours before. In fact, she could best have been described as demented and, while the car was towed away, was herself taken in hysterics to the nearest hospital where she was heavily sedated.

'I'll kill the little shits!' she screamed when she'd just been informed that it would take at least a week to get the Honda back on the road again and before the massive dose of tranquillisers took effect. 'I'm supposed to be attending my cousin Sarah's wedding in three days' time.'

The paramedics doubted that. So did the Ghanaian doctor who had been called in to deal with such a difficult case. But by then Ms Young had fallen asleep.

When she woke late the following afternoon she immediately insisted on leaving the hospital.

'I'll catch a train,' she screamed, struggling out of bed, and, when an attempt was made to stop her, went on to use the most foul language which she'd never used before but had picked up from the drivers trapped in the tunnel.

'But you're still in shock, dear,' the Sister told her. 'You're not fit to go anywhere. You need to rest.'

'And you need to be bloody well fired,' Ms Young yelled as she staggered to the door. The Sister sighed. If the stupid bitch insisted on leaving there was nothing she was prepared to do to stand in her way. Life was difficult enough without hysterical and evidently well-educated young-ish women telling her she ought to be fired.

'She insulted me in the foulest language,' she later

explained to the Ghanaian doctor who wholly sympathised. He was used to being insulted by racially prejudiced patients.

'Well, it will serve her right if she goes to the wrong station,' the Sister said with satisfaction. 'In her condition I wouldn't be at all surprised if she does.'

Ms Young did. Two hours later she was on her way to Cardiff and, still suffering the after-effects of the sedative, asleep again. The Ward Sister had been right. She had chosen the wrong station and completely ignored the insistent denials of the ticket-seller that he had any tickets for Inverness.

'Well, give me one that will let me get there by taxi then.'

'Listen, madam, this is a railway station not a taxi office.'

'Of course it is. I know that. Just give me a ticket, you oaf! I'm in a hurry,' she snarled at him.

Convinced he was dealing with a lunatic – and a rude one at that – the railway clerk eventually sold her a ticket to a small Welsh town whose name was unpronounceable, in the hope that it had a good mental hospital or at least a rehab unit, and where the Welsh would know better than to speak to a deranged Englishwoman.

Having slept nearly all the way, Ms Young awoke with a start when the train stopped at Cardiff. By now she was sufficiently de-tranquillised to understand the ticket-seller's reluctance to provide her with a ticket to Inverness, and the peculiar expression on his face when she'd said she'd catch a taxi there.

Still determined to attend the wedding, she tried to hire a car only to find that somewhere along the way since she'd left the damned school she'd lost her driving licence. Ranting at the unfortunate Avis man who refused to accommodate her without it was satisfying but to little avail. In fact, it was only when he threatened to call the police that she gave up and walked into the centre of town. Fortunately for her, she still had her credit card and could book into a hotel. She was feeling desperately hungry as well as murderous towards those infernal Wilt girls, absolutely certain they had been responsible for her awful experiences of the last two days.

Finally accepting defeat, Ms Young sent an urgent message to her cousin explaining that she was sorry to miss the wedding but her car had broken down and she was stuck in Cardiff, thanks to the idiocy of a taxi driver. Then she went to her room and ordered sandwiches from Room Service. She was asleep again when they arrived.

# Chapter 12

At St Barnaby's School the quads were planning a final act of revenge on Mrs Collinson, the Headmistress, who had ordered them to stay away from the other girls until they left for the summer holidays.

'The silly old bag!' said Penelope. 'Anyone would think we had some infectious illness. I vote we put something horrid in her study when she's not there.'

'Like what?' asked Samantha.

'What about a snake? If we got hold of a grass snake and painted it black, the old bitch would have a fit.'

'And where are we going to get a grass snake? Anyway all snakes give me the horrors,' said Josephine.

'All right, snakes are out. Surely we can think of something she'll hate and won't be able to pin on us.'

'What about breaking into her office and getting lots of porn from the internet on to her computer and then reporting her to the police?'

'And how are we going to find out her password, stupid? It was only because you guessed that Mum's password was Disappointed that we managed to do it last time. And anyway she caught us before we even had the chance to show Dad, let alone ring 999.'

'Well, what if we did the sugar in the petrol tank again?'

'Boring. And besides we may get caught,' Penelope said. 'That might have worked with Ms Young but you don't do the same thing twice if you want to get away with it. It's got to be different and subtle, like . . .'

'Well, go on. Like what?'

'I can't think. We've got to come up with something before the end of term, though, if we really do want to get rid of her.'

They sat behind the hockey pavilion and applied their diabolical minds to the problem but none of the ideas they discussed seemed adequate. They were all agreed that it had to be something so horrible and nasty, something so absolutely unthinkable but also very public, that the Headmistress's position would become untenable. She'd be leaving then instead of the quads.

Emmeline still favoured ruining Mrs Collinson's reputation by implying she suffered from some sexual perversion. I was reading about a man called Driberg the other day. He liked tramps' socks – and really dirty ones. They turned him on. I think he sucked them.'

'Oh, do shut up,' Penelope told her. 'You make me sick.'

'You're just too innocent to be true. I bet you have really filthy fantasies.'

'If anyone's a pervert, you are, you weirdo!'

'Tart!'

'Cow!'

'Bitch!'

After swapping insults in language which grew fouler by the moment, and could even have taught the drivers in the Dartford Tunnel a word or two, all four of them ended up on the ground, fighting and pulling one another's hair.

Much to their chagrin, the school groundkeeper reported them to a prefect who had them confined to their dormitory for the rest of the week.

At Sandystones Hall Sir George was feeling less cheerful too. Lady Clarissa had imposed a frightful series of healthy meals on him and had been so rude to Philomena Jones that the new cook had refused to stay.

'I don't care if you send me to prison,' she'd announced one evening as he munched his way through a salad of cos lettuce, lentils and raw carrots, all of which he detested. 'You get treated better by warders than you do by her.' And Philly had marched out of the dining room before Clarissa could even say, 'Good riddance to bad rubbish.'

Sir George stared at his wife venomously and was about to point out that he owned the Hall and had every right to employ whomever he liked when Clarissa announced that she was becoming increasingly worried about her uncle and would be driving down to Ipford the following day, to find out how he was getting on. She added that she would also take it upon herself to see if she could engage a proper cook there, to replace that awful creature who would undoubtedly have poisoned them if she'd stayed.

At this Sir George finally exercised his right as master of Sandystones Hall and exploded.

'To hell with your bloody uncle!' he shouted, so loudly that Philly was bound to hear him in the kitchen. 'You've just seen off the most interesting cook I've ever had, and you think you can just march away to fawn on your relatives and leave me to starve? You can go to hell. Philomena's staying, come hell or high water. Get that into your fornicating skull but fast! It's either that or I'll have Philly hurl you out on your ear. She's twice the woman you are.'

For a few seconds Lady Clarissa stayed silent. Then she spat back, 'She may be sizewise, but if you let that gypsy slut loose on me, I'll tell everyone your sexual fantasies about fat women and have you known all over the world as the Butterball lover! I can't imagine your living that down. I'll see to it personally that every news-paper in the country sends reporters to besiege this house and publicise your disgusting peccadillos. I can just see the headlines in the News of the World and the Sun. "Knight of the Girth" or "Gorging George's Orgy" some-thing like that. And you can be sure I'll get our excellent previous cook to give evidence that you harassed and then sacked her because she wasn't fat enough for your filthy tastes. That'll really make the divorce court sit up and take notice. Oh, yes, I'll file for divorce too. I've every reason to and will, you'd better believe me, if you carry on in this revolting fashion.'

Faced with this counter-threat, Sir George could only wish he was living in a previous age when women knew their place and, if they answered back too often, were strapped to a ducking stool and given a taste of pondwater. He'd happily have had Clarissa held under-water in the moat at that moment. Better still would have been a metal scold's bridle, which would have prevented her from talking at all. After one final murderous look at her, he took himself off to his study with a bottle of brandy for consolation. The only way out he could think of was that he'd find Philly a cottage somewhere on the estate and have a proper dinner down there every night, instead of munching his way through some awful mixture of raw vegetables with his wife. He could always say he'd been down to the golf club for a drink.

# Chapter 13

Mrs Collinson wasn't having a pleasant night either. She'd been up to London to see her dentist and have a new set of dentures fitted. Her old ones had begun to drop whenever she smiled, which wasn't often but had happened several times while she had been giving the sixth form a Latin lesson. Since then she had overheard some of the senior girls referring to her as Toothless Annie. She was feeling quite confident with her new false teeth firmly in place when she drove into the school grounds and parked. By the end of the evening that confidence had completely evaporated. The quads had struck.

They'd been down by the river that afternoon and had watched a young man having a swim in the nude.

More to the point, they'd found his clothes on the bank and appropriated them on the spur of the moment.

Samantha suddenly had a bright idea.

'It's Mr Collinson's evening out. He comes back from Horsham and has his dinner at the pub in the village then stays on and drinks,' she said as they examined the abandoned trousers and emptied the pockets. 'And when he comes home he's usually pissed.'

'I don't blame him,' said Emmeline. 'Being married to that old gumboil can't be any fun at all.'

'Why don't we put this man's trousers in her bedroom so that Mr Collinson thinks she's been up to something?'

They were interrupted by Penelope who had been poking around in the bushes with a long stick.

'See what I've found,' she cried excitedly, and held up a condom. It was unrolled and appeared to have been used. The quads stared at it and then at one another. Josephine then held up the young man's underpants, which were not particularly clean.

'Yuk! You're so disgusting . . .' the other three chorused together '. . . but . . .'

This was just what they needed to complete the scene when the Headmistress's husband came home.

'He'll think she's been into rough trade,' said Samantha, who had picked up the term from Wilt talking on the phone. 'Oh, how wonderful, she's gone to London. The house will be empty!'

The Collinsons' house stood some distance from the main school buildings. Best of all, it was surrounded by a neatly trimmed yew hedge which would give them some cover. The quads went in by the back gate. 'Suppose there's someone inside, like the cleaner?' said Josephine. 'I mean, we ought to make sure.'

'All right. You can go up to the front door and ring the bell and find out,' the others told her.

'Oh, well then, I jolly well will, you scaredy cats!' Josephine came back in five minutes to say that no one had answered. 'I tried the door and it was locked.'

'Then we'll have to get in by going up a drainpipe or using a ladder,' Penelope said.

But Samantha had spotted a way up to an open window on the first floor.

'Look at that climbing hydrangea. It's really strong, I'll show you.' And she climbed up the thick stem and slithered over the sill into the house. The rest of the quads were about to climb up too when she peered out. 'I think I'm in the bedroom,' she called down. 'There's a big double bed and all their clothes are in a long cupboard and there's a bathroom attached with his razors in it and the old cow's dressing gown on a hook beside the door.'

Emmeline climbed halfway up the climbing hydrangea after her and handed up the pair of pants.

'The condom's wrapped up inside them.'

Five minutes later the quads had left the garden

unseen and were back in the school buildings, trying not to laugh.

It was 8 p.m. when the Headmistress returned from London happily wearing her new dentures. She had a bath and then, after going round the school, returned and had dinner before she went to bed. She was asleep when her husband got in from the pub and, knowing how she would react if he woke her, he got into his pyjamas and slid into the bed as far away from her as possible.

As his feet encountered the underpants he paused for thought. These didn't feel like women's underwear. And certainly not like Mrs Collinson's underwear, which was – and this would have hugely surprised the quads had they known it – quite frilly and lacey. Very quietly he reached down for them and encountered something that no woman could possibly wear. The next moment he had dragged the blankets off his side of the bed and was staring incredulously at the unwashed pants and, with even more disgust, the condom. The sight of it had an extraordinary effect on him. From being a drunk but considerate husband, he became a sober and furious one. The pants themselves didn't improve matters either.

He turned on the light and became further infuriated. That his wife should be having an affair with anyone was bad enough, but that she had been having it off with some man whose underpants needed washing . . . He couldn't find words for his fury.

Instead he acted. He shook her so violently that she fell out of bed and landed with a thump on the floor, dislodging her new teeth in the process. As she stared glumly up at him he loomed over her.

'You filthy whore!' he yelled. 'I go out to work and come back to find you've been getting yourself shafted by some revolting animal in my absence. Well, this is the end of our marriage, that's for certain. Tomorrow I'm going to see the most experienced divorce lawyer in London. I'll get him to start proceedings immediately.'

Mrs Collinson got to her knees. To be woken from a deep sleep by a demented husband, who stank of booze and hurled her out of bed while accusing her of having sex with someone, was worse than any possible nightmare. As for the threat to divorce her, she could only suppose he was drunker, far drunker, than she'd ever known him to be. Her head was aching and, while normally an assertive woman, she felt surprisingly vulnerable without any teeth in. Worse: when she got to her feet she was confronted by the condom and the pair of underpants he was brandishing.

'There you are, the proof,' he snarled. 'I found them in our bed. I suppose you thought I was staying in Horsham tonight and didn't bother getting rid of them? Well, I'm not staying here, and I don't think I'll have any problem getting a divorce either.'

Mrs Collinson slumped down into a chair and tried desperately to think.

'This scandal is going to ruin you,' he continued. 'You'll have to give up this house, and the school, and I can't see you ever getting a teaching job after these have been produced in court'. He was smiling at her cruelly now. 'Not that I ever liked the wretched place . . . all those snobby little tarts. Well, you've brought it on yourself.'

But Mrs Collinson was thinking very hard indeed. She hadn't slept with anyone, and even if a man had been with her, why on earth would he have left these filthy things in their bed? And where was he now? It didn't make any sort of sense. Someone must have put them there deliberately to ruin her. But who?

Mr Collinson stormed out of the room, carrying the pants and the condom at arm's length, telling her that he was going to sleep elsewhere for the night and would be leaving at first light.

Mrs Collinson got up from her chair and retrieved her teeth, and with them something of her dignity. She was putting on her dressing gown to go after her husband when she spotted the open window and, on the floor beneath it, a bloom of climbing hydrangea. A closer look out of the window, this time with the aid of a torch she kept on her bedside table, showed her a branch hanging away from the stem. It had obviously been broken by someone making their way up the main stem which was unusually thick. Mrs Collinson rushed into the spare room.

'What do you want, damn you?' her husband

demanded. 'Don't imagine for one moment I'll change my mind. I'm going to get that divorce and . . .'

'I want you to come out into the garden and look at something.'

'In the garden? At this time of night?'

'That's what I said. I've found something that will stop you making any more of a fool of yourself.'

'Oh, all right, but it isn't going to help you,' he grumbled.

They went downstairs and round the side of the house to the climbing hydrangea where she shone the torch on the broken branch.

'How did that break, do you think? And another question. How did this get into our bedroom?' She showed him the bloom. 'Tell me that.' Oh, yes, she wasn't a headmistress for nothing!

Her husband shook his head.

'God only knows. Perhaps your lover boy . . .'

'Are you saying he climbed up? If you are, let's see if you can,' she said. 'Go on. Don't just stand there.'

But Mr Collinson was feeling the main stem and knew there was no way a full-grown man could climb up it without ripping the hydrangea off the wall. He turned back to face her.

'Are you suggesting one of your girls did it? I mean, where on earth could they have got those pants, not to mention that filthy condom? And why on earth would they?'

'I have no idea, and frankly I hate to think. But

I hope you're satisfied now that I haven't been having an affair. Can't you see that I'd have been mad to have left the evidence in our bed?'

They went back into the house where Mr Collinson made a shame-faced apology and then helped himself to a whisky and soda.

More practically, Mrs Collinson went to the boot cupboard and took out a pair of gym shoes.

'I'm going down to the dormitories to see if anyone's giggling,' she told him as she went out of the front door. 'I've my own suspicions as to who did this. And, by God, if I'm right those disgusting girls won't know what's hit them.'

Five miles away, a naked young man who had wasted several hours in the darkness, searching for his clothes, was cycling home, painfully and without any lights, when he was stopped by a police car. He'd already been spotted by several drivers, three of them middle-aged women who'd used their mobiles to phone the police and inform them that there was a naked flasher on a bike in the vicinity. Unfortunately two of them had driven past as he'd been relieving himself into a hedge.

Rounding a sharp corner, he found his way blocked by a police car. Twenty minutes later, strategically covered by a blanket, he was being questioned by a thoroughly bad-tempered Inspector who'd had his car windows smashed the night before by hooligans and regarded all young men as swine. Naked ones riding bikes without lights at ten o'clock at night, and pissing with complete abandon into hedges, came into an even worse category.

'So you'd been having sex with some slut and couldn't remember where you had left your clothes, is that what you're saying?' he asked belligerently.

'No, I've told you, I went for a swim . . .'

'In the nude. Right?'

'All right, naked, in the river. I'd left my clothes on the bank. There's no law against that, and there was no one about that I could see.'

'So they just disappeared of their own accord, I suppose?'

The young man sighed.

'Of course they didn't. Someone pinched them,' he said.

'That someone being the girl you'd been having it off with.'

'I've told you, I was alone.'

'Oh, sure.'

All in all it was a most unpleasant interview. Finally they sent him home in a police car for another distressing hour of furious questioning by his father, the local Vicar, who had searched the young man's room when he hadn't come home and found a packet of condoms in a drawer.

The implied threat to his own reputation was too much for the Vicar, and his consequent ferocious reaction was definitely too much for the young man. He went to bed naked, badly bruised, and without any supper. After today he was of the opinion that sex was not all it was made out to be, and seriously considering joining the priesthood of the Catholic Church, to spite his father.

# Chapter 14

Lady Clarissa had spent a very difficult day in Ipford trying to persuade her Uncle Harold to stay in the Last Post. He had flatly refused.

'It's not just the Last Post: it's the last place on earth I'd want to be. I'd rather be in prison for the rest of my life. At least if anyone shouts or screams in the middle of the night there you can be pretty sure someone will stop them, and even prisoners don't have to wear a ridiculous premature shroud. That sadistic Matron keeps trying to shove a catheter up my penis and she won't let me have a chamber pot. If you don't get me into a really decent guest house, I'll make things extremely awkward for you with that husband of yours.'

Clarissa couldn't imagine how.

'Well, I'll try, but I can't guarantee anything . . .'

'You'd better put your mind to it then. I know what you get up to every time you come down here, supposedly to see me. Do you think Gadsley knows you sleep with the man who drives you down?'

'What are you talking about?'

'Adultery. Or fornication, if you prefer. You see, the manager of the Black Bear is ex-army. Long after my war, of course, but I've got to know him quite well when he calls in to visit his mother, that horrible old bag of a Matron. He's been most helpful to me. Old soldiers stick together, don't you know? You always stay in the same suite, apparently, and at my request he had it bugged with miniature cameras. The pictures are most interesting.

'Now, my dear, off you go and find me somewhere pleasant to live. I'll need to inspect it first, of course. And in the meantime, you'll pay for me to stay at the Black Bear instead. I think you'll find that they're expecting me.'

'But . . .'

'No buts. Just go.'

Lady Clarissa went. She knew when she was beaten. That evening the Colonel sat in the bar of the hotel, toasting his victory with a number of very large malt whiskies. He had fooled his wretched niece: there'd been no cameras, although Matron's son had been most obliging in confirming his shrewd suspicions

126

about the cheating bitch. He sent for the menu and decided to push the boat out by ordering lobster for dinner.

Wilt had spent most of the week sitting in his office, reading a life of Kaiser Wilhelm II. He seriously doubted that the young Gadsley blighter knew anything at all about the causes of the First World War despite his three previous attempts at the exam. From the sound of it this was only going to work if Wilt cut out all the difficult parts and stuck to basics. He'd decided that the best course was to make Edward learn all the easy stuff by heart, so that he was able to regurgitate it at will: if the moron had at least half a brain that ought to do it.

He was periodically interrupted by so-called students asking inane questions about the autumn-term timetable. And then there were the so-called students asking broadly sensible questions about inane subjects. Earlier in the year he and Braintree had invented the most ludicrous seminar topic they could think of and inserted it into the brochure for the autumn term just as it was going to press. So far 'Cultural Obesity: the study and appreciation of the contribution made by the overweight to Western Civilisation since the Fall of the Roman Empire' appeared to be heavily over-subscribed – so much so that there was an eager queue of idiots anxious to join the waiting list.

On Thursday he got home to find that Lady Clarissa had phoned to say she wasn't coming down to Ipford this weekend after all and suggesting that Wilt should instead catch the train to Utterborough where she'd send a taxi to pick him up.

'That's fine by me. The less time I'm closeted with that woman the better pleased I'll be,' he told Eva, and went back to twentieth-century German history. Half an hour later the phone rang again. Wilt left his wife to answer it.

'That was Lady Clarissa,' she said. 'She wants you to catch the 10.20 train on the thirteenth. That's tomorrow.'

'Why the change?'

'She said something about Edward getting on Sir George's nerves.'

'And she wants him to get on mine instead, I suppose? Did she say how much she was paying me for half a week?'

'I didn't like to ask. She seemed to be in a bit of a state. In fact, I wondered whether she'd been drinking. She started saying something about the cook being an old cow and her uncle being a fat bastard . . . or perhaps it was the other way round. I really didn't like to interrupt her.'

'Bloody hell! What on earth have you let me in for? Oh, well, I suppose I'd better go up and pack.'

'I've done that already,' Eva told him.

Wilt went upstairs and checked his suitcase to make

sure Eva hadn't put the pink chalk-stripe suit in. She had. He removed it and hid it underneath a jacket in the wardrobe. Then he sat on the edge of the bed and cursed his wife for having got him into this infernal situation. One thing he definitely wasn't going to do was take a dinner jacket; the Gadsleys probably dressed for dinner but he intended to maintain an independent stance.

The next morning Eva drove him down to the railway station and by twelve o'clock he was in the taxi at Utterborough, on the road to Sandystones Hall.

Built in the nineteenth century, the Hall had a mile-long drive which culminated in an amazing moat. The architect who designed it had been instructed by his client, General Gadsley, that Hunstanton Hall in Norfolk had one and so Sandystones must too. The building itself was such an extraordinary conglomeration of conflicting styles that it was commonly conjectured that General Gadsley – who had been in India at the time – must have changed what there was of his mind every month, removing any last shred of architectural coherence from the original design. More charitable critics would have it that the General's horrific experiences in the Indian Mutiny had turned him into an opium addict, and this accounted for the series of bizarre instructions he sent back. Whatever the truth of this, the architect was known to have become so confused by them that he became a semi-deranged alcoholic himself. His client died of dengue fever after being bitten by a mosquito and never came back to England to see the indescribable monstrosity which was the result of his many and varied instructions.

Fortunately the discriminating passers-by were spared any accidental glimpse of it by the high wall surrounding the grounds. This was augmented by the unnecessarily long and tortuous drive, and by the half-mile-wide belt of beech woods planted by subsequent generations of Gadsleys, to hide what some of the more sensitive of the General's descendants considered the family 'shame'.

As the taxi wove its way up the drive through the encroaching forest, frequently swerving round deliberately sharp and narrow corners to avoid crashing into tree trunks and overhanging branches, Wilt decided to insist that Eva and the quads should be met at the gates and driven down to the Hall by someone more accustomed to this death trap of a road. By the time they reached open parkland he was black and blue from tumbling about in the back of the taxi and determined that he would never drive this way himself. And then he saw Sandystones Hall half a mile ahead.

'Whoever called it Sandystones must have been blind,' muttered Wilt, surprised to find that the extraordinary house was not as enormous as he had expected. 'More like Greypebbles.'

'You can say that again,' the driver agreed.

'Is there any sand round here?'

'Look to your left. See the nine-hole golf course? Bunkers have to have sand. Of course, they could have brought it up from the beach . . . I don't believe that, though. It's too expensive. Mind you, they're as rich as hell. I mean, they have their own private cemetery and chapel.'

They stopped beside the drawbridge across the moat. Beyond it loomed a massively ornamented front door, though both door and moat looked ridiculously overblown against the relatively small scale of the Hall itself. Wilt got out and reached for his wallet but the taxi driver shook his head.

'They've got an account,' he said, and carried the suitcase across the bridge to the front door where he pulled the bell rope. Presently an extremely plump grey-haired woman dressed in black opened it.

'Mr Wilt? Do come in. I'll show you up to your room. I'm afraid the cottage you were promised isn't quite ready yet but I do assure you it will be by the time your family arrives. Lady Clarissa apologises for her absence but she has been suddenly called away. I'm Mrs Bale, Sir George's secretary. I come over and act as housekeeper when either of them is away.'

'I must say I've never stayed in a house with a draw-bridge before,' said Wilt, gazing around him at the furniture which, like the house itself, was extraordinary. Everything had clearly come from India. Even the portraits of what he presumed were family ancestors on the ornately panelled staircase wall were of people dressed in the uniforms of the Indian Army during the heyday of the Empire.

'And this is your room,' Mrs Bale told him, opening a door at the top of the stairs. 'The bathroom's through the door over there. If there's anything you need just let me know. There's a bell on the desk.'

But Wilt hardly heard her. He was gaping at an enormous bed which looked as though it had been designed for six overweight adults.

'All the beds in the house are that size,' said Mrs Bale, evidently reading his mind. 'Very difficult for the maid to make in the morning. You have to run round them to tuck in the other side. I personally find them quite comfortable.'

She went to the door.

'If you're hungry, the kitchen's downstairs along the passage to your right by the back door. That's where I eat and have my tea.'

Wilt thought to himself that from the size of her it must be quite some tea, but refrained from commenting and thanked her as she pulled the door to.

Left to himself he wondered what sort of household he'd come to, and for the umpteenth time what on earth he'd let himself in for. Then, having unpacked, he went out on to the landing and down the stairs, wandering from room to room exploring the house. Everything inside the Hall was as peculiar as the exterior had promised. Through the windows overlooking the draw-bridge he could see what looked like a lake with a chapel on its far side, and to his right a walled kitchen garden with a cottage standing beside it. That presumably was where he would be staying with Eva and the quads when they arrived. In the end he wandered outside and followed the moat round to the back of the house where he was surprised to find a wide and solid metal gate set in a wall, with beyond it a cobbled yard in front of a garage big enough for several cars.

'That's the family's way in. You have to press the bell beside you on the right three times for the gate to open,' called a woman's voice. Wilt looked up and saw Mrs Bale standing at the top of a flight of steps at the back of the house.

'Come in and have a cup of tea,' she invited him. He went up the steps and followed her into what seemed to be the kitchen, judging from the stove and racks of cooking equipment. But the room's sheer size was astonishing: it was enormous in relation to the rest of the house.

'Sit yourself down,' Mrs Bale instructed him. 'The corners are the best places for conversation in here otherwise one has to shout. I doubt if you've ever been in a stranger place – this whole house, I mean.'

Wilt agreed. He hadn't.

'I think you ought to be warned that Sir George is a weird old devil too,' she went on as she handed Wilt his tea. 'He used to be called Smith or something equally ordinary. From what my late husband told me, he wasn't a real Gadsley at all, let alone a Sir. Apparently the line died out when old Sir Gadsley, the real Sir Gadsley that is caught a bad case of mumps, so that was that. His sister had married a Mr Smith and their eldest boy inherited Sandystones and the Estate. They do say he has no right to the title at all, though I wouldn't like to comment. In fact, if I'm honest, there are some who say that old Sir Aubrey – the last real Gadsley – didn't even get mumps.' She paused to draw breath. 'Now I don't hold with gossip, but I have heard it said that he was a bit . . . you know . . . funny.'

'Funny?' asked Wilt, who didn't have a clue what the woman was rabbiting on about.

'Yes. Funny. You know, batted for the other side. In any case, I don't hold with gossip but the upshot of it all is that Lady Clarissa is no lady, if you see what I mean.'

'I found her to be completely respectable when I met her,' said Wilt hastily, just in case either of the Gadsleys was within earshot of this embarrassing series of revelations.

'No, no. I mean she isn't a Lady with a capital L. Even if Sir George were a baronet, she wouldn't be called Lady Clarissa, she'd be Lady Gadsley. But she's not. She thinks she is but it's about as real as one of those titles you can buy on the internet. Or so I'm told. I never have, of course . . . although my late husband did once get a plot of land on the moon as a birthday present. Fat lot of use that was!'

Wilt felt as though he had landed on Mars, never mind the moon. This was becoming increasingly surreal. It looked and sounded as though everyone at the Hall was completely batty.

'You were talking about Sir George,' he said, trying to steer the conversation back on course.

'Oh, him. Well, he's been a magistrate for years now, though the way he carries on you wouldn't know it sometimes. In fact, I find it's best not to disagree with him else he stomps around, shouting the odds.'

Wilt made a mental note of this advice.

'Thanks for telling me. What's Lady Clarissa like?'

'Drinks. Come to that, they both do. And . . . Well, you'll soon find out for yourself. As I understand it you've come to get her son Edward through some exam. I can't say I envy you. Strange boy, that one. Skulks around the place, throwing stones and the like . . . In the old days he'd probably have been put in one of those homes, you know, for children who had a bit missing. Two bob short of a shilling, if you get my meaning . . . Anyway he went out first thing this morning and none of us have seen hide nor hair of him since.'

On this dour note she got up and trekked to a very large stove where she poured some more water into a catering-size teapot.

'Another cup?' she asked.

Wilt nodded and thanked her. A bit missing? Good God, the boy really was an idiot.

'You don't think he's – well, bright enough?'

'I don't know what he is. What I do know is that Sir George loathes him. In any case, the boy's not his real son, only his step-son, so maybe that's why they don't hit it off.'

'Oh, well, it certainly doesn't sound like a very happy household,' said Wilt with a sigh. 'I'm surprised you stay on here.'

'Have to because my husband was killed in a car accident . . . just like Lady Clarissa's first one was, although it was a different level crossing, of course . . . and Sir George needed a secretary so I applied. I need to work and the pay is good so I stay on and just keep myself to myself. As I said, I don't hold with gossip.'

'Absolutely not. Of course not,' said Wilt hurriedly. 'Well, all I can say is that you've been remarkably helpful, giving me all this information. I really appreciate what you've done. Thank you very much.'

'Not at all. It's just that I have seen so many people walk innocently into this rat trap . . . actually, no, I think madhouse is a better description . . . that I thought you ought know what you are up against. They're not a normal couple – she married him for his money – and as for her ladyship's son, if you manage to teach him anything at all . . .' Here she stopped abruptly. Edward was evidently not a topic she cared to dwell on. Wilt tactfully changed the subject.

'I suppose no one would mind if I phoned my wife, to tell her I've arrived and that she's not to use the main gate when she comes? That route through the woods is horribly dangerous. What I saw of the back lane struck me as far safer.'

'The old road is meant to deter unwanted visitors. And of course you can use the phone. I'll show you where it is.'

She led the way along a corridor. Halfway down she looked over her shoulder to check that no one was observing them before stopping beside a half-concealed door. 'This is his private lavatory,' she said with a grin. Sir George has had a telephone installed in there. He can be inside for hours sometimes – he claims it's constipation but I'm certain he uses it for illegal purposes. To make the sliding door open you have to shine an infra-red torch at it . . .'

'And what's inside?'

'Exactly what you'd expect in a lavatory . . . with the addition of a telephone, fax machine and computer. Oh, and it's sound-proofed too.'

'This is the strangest house I've ever been in,' Wilt muttered to himself, then looked at her suspiciously. 'How do you know what's in there?'

Mrs Bale laughed quietly.

'He went to London one day and forgot to hide the torch . . . so I used it.'

'But how did you know what the torch was for in the first place?'

'Because I happened to be on my knees at the top of the stairs one day, fixing the carpet, and he didn't see me above him.'

'Blimey! You don't half take chances,' Wilt said, privately wondering how on earth she'd managed to get down on her knees in the first place, given the size of her.

'Have to in this loony bin,' she said with a snigger.

'I guess so. Well, where's the phone I can use?'

'Outside his study. He likes to be able to hear what people are saying.'

'Thanks. I just want to tell my wife to be sure to get a taxi. I don't want her driving through that awful wood.'

Mrs Bale nodded. 'Tell her to use the second gate instead of the main one. It's painted black and will put her on to the road to the back of the house.'

Wilt relayed all this to Eva when he got through to her mobile. 'It's the one the family use and far less dangerous,' he told her. 'The alternative is for you all to come by train and I'll ask them to provide a taxi.'

As usual Eva objected.

'Anyone would think I couldn't drive very well,' she grumbled.

Wilt sighed. Eva always objected to taking his advice. Not that she did drive that well come to think of it.

'I'm not saying that. But I wouldn't come down that awful track through the woods myself, and with the girls in the car it would be very unwise, to put it mildly.'

In the end she agreed and, to Wilt's relief, changed the subject.

'Have you met Edward yet?'

'No. Apparently he's gone off somewhere on his own. I have to say, Eva, he does sound very strange. Might even be an actual idiot. I'm beginning to wonder whether I'll be able to do anything with him.'

'You've got to do something with him.' Eva had neglected to tell her husband about the bonus payable if Edward got through the exam, thinking it would leave her with something of a trump card to play should Wilt show any signs of not wanting to see the job through. 'I'm sure you'll feel differently once you've met him.'

'God knows when that will be if he spends all day out in the woods playing silly buggers. And it does seem as though Sir George – who might not be Sir George after all, but that's too long a story for now – really does hate him. Anyway must go as I'm not paying for this call.'

Wilt rang off and turned round – to find himself face to face with a grossly overweight man in his sixties who looked as though he was surprised to find a stranger using the telephone.

'Am I to assume you are my step-son's tutor?' he

enquired in a tone of voice Wilt associated with the one occasion he had been fined for exceeding the speed limit.

'Yes,' he mumbled. 'I was just telling my wife that I had arrived safely. Mrs Bale said you wouldn't mind. I take it you are Sir George?'

'I am indeed. What's your name?'

'Wilt. Henry Wilt.'

'Well, that's all right. I had been led to believe you were arriving later in the week. My wife tends to be so infernally scatterbrained that half the time she doesn't know what day of the week it is.'

He led the way into his study and indicated a chair for Wilt to sit in while he busied himself with a decanter and glasses arranged on a silver tray.

'I always have a brandy after a morning in court,' he said. 'I wonder if you'd care to join me?'

'I think I'd prefer something less strong,' said Wilt. 'Perhaps a beer.'

'Just as you like, though I fancy you'll change your mind when you meet my step-son.'

'Not the easiest of boys?' Wilt enquired as Sir George half-filled a balloon glass from the decanter and then produced a bottle of beer, an opener plus glass for Wilt before lowering himself heavily into a large leather armchair.

'One of the most damnably difficult youths I've ever met. I'm not surprised my wife's first husband chose to commit suicide. Had I known Clarissa had a ghastly son like Eddie, I would never have married her. And that's no overstatement. Worse still, the woman bosses me about far too much for my liking.'

Wilt said nothing. If the Hall was a disconcerting place, the people living in it were just as peculiar.

'If you can get Eddie-Gawd-Help-Us into any college in Cambridge you'll be a miracle worker. We had difficulty getting him into a minor public school, and keeping him there required what I can only call bribery.'

'Your wife said something about Porterhouse. I gather you went there?' said Wilt.

Sir George turned up his nose in horror.

'I told you she was a complete scatterbrain – I was at Peterhouse. The last thing I'd want to do is inflict the mindless creature on my old college. Not that there's the slightest chance of getting the brute into any college. More likely to get a place in Pentonville.'

'You mean, the prison?' said Wilt, beginning to regret he hadn't accepted the brandy after all.

'I should imagine he'll end up there in any case. Best place for him, in fact. The public would be a lot safer by far.'

'Someone mentioned that he likes to throw things.'

'Throw things? He's a bloody maniac, that boy. The times I've had to bail him out when he's half killed some poor bugger or other . . . No, I'm afraid you've rather got your hands full with Eddie, old chap.'

By the time Sir George had finished his second

brandy, while continuing his diatribe against his step-son, Wilt's feelings had undergone a radical change. From initially appreciating the man's problem, he had begun to feel slightly shocked by his appalling attitude towards his step-son. Although, from experience, he did know just how difficult boys could be. He was half tempted to share with Sir George his own experience with apprentices in the Liberal Studies classes at the now defunct Fenland College of Arts and Technology.

In his early years there Wilt had been faced every day with rooms full of blank-faced youths who saw no point in reading Candide or The Lord of the Flies, as part of their cultural hinterland and it had been Wilt's task to try to show them how literature could equip them with life skills. Nowadays they were all called Communications students and weren't asked to think or discuss anything, merely to sit in front of computers and, as far as he could see, practise manipulating the machines at greater and greater speed. Most of the time they played violent virtual games on them or pored over their Facebook pages, uploading vile and ridiculous photographs of one another. The quads had told him that Social Networking sites were 'cool', to which Wilt had retorted that he preferred it when social networking meant looking at someone's face and not a bloody screen.

In fact, when he thought about it, Wilt felt extremely bitter about the way things had changed. Although, as annoying and badly behaved as the quads were, he hoped he wasn't ever as vile about them as Sir George Gadsley was being about his step-son. For whatever reason, he obviously loathed the boy.

In other circumstances Wilt would have asked more questions, but he was living in the arrogant old fellow's house and had to earn enough money from him to keep the quads at that damned school or else get hell from Eva.

All the same, he felt a bit guilty.

After a third brandy Sir George said he was going out to lunch and told Wilt that Mrs Bale would give him something to eat in the kitchen. Wilt duly noted the implication. He didn't care. The kitchen would be fine by him. He was glad to be out of the way.

# Chapter 15

Lady Clarissa had had another extremely trying day. She had cancelled her plan to drive down to Ipford at the weekend when, despite her begging and pleading, Uncle Harold had adamantly refused to leave the Black Bear and move into less expensive accommodation. It meant she couldn't possibly stay there too, not least because he'd taken over the suite she usually stayed in. Besides which the bill he was running up was astronomical and she'd rather not draw it to George's attention right now. The wretched Colonel had been doing himself exceedingly well at the hotel. His consumption of malt whisky before lunch and during the afternoon, often followed by a second bottle in the evening, was costing a small fortune.

She had spent the previous night trying to think of some way of making her uncle's stay so uncomfortable he'd be only too pleased to take leave of the place. She'd tried phoning his room in the middle of the night and had listened to him curse the bastard who'd woken him. She repeated this at 3 a.m. but by the third time she tried it it was clear that he'd disconnected the telephone.

Having spent such a broken night herself, she wasn't best pleased to be woken by a phone call from the hotel manager at 6 a.m. reporting that her uncle appeared to have locked himself in his suite. The maid who brought him his breakfast early each morning had knocked repeatedly, without success, and his phone appeared to have been pulled out of the wall whenever Reception tried ringing it.

'Can't you just let yourself in?' demanded Lady Clarissa, feeling a trifle guilty at the thought of Uncle Harold tugging the phone out of the wall in the early hours.

'He must have put the bolt across because the master key doesn't work,' explained the manager.

'Well, can't you go in through the window or the fire escape?'

'There's no fire escape to that room, and the window is locked with the curtains drawn. No, there's only one thing for it and that's to break down the door. I wanted to make sure first that you knew you would have to pay for a replacement.'

'Of course I do, you stupid man!' cried Lady Clarissa,

and slammed the phone down, starting to feel a little alarmed at the thought of what her night-time phone calls might have done to her uncle.

After what seemed a very long time but was actually only a matter of minutes the phone rang again. Clarissa eagerly answered it.

'I'm extremely sorry to have to tell you that the Colonel is no longer with us, Lady Clarissa,' the manager informed her.

'He isn't? You mean, he's left? Where's he gone?' she asked with some relief.

'I'm sorry to say . . .' The manager hesitated. Telling the niece of a guest that her uncle had probably died of alcohol poisoning wasn't a pleasant task, but Clarissa spoke again before he could think of a tactful way of breaking the news.

'I imagine you are. I can't say that I am. He was costing me a fortune! And where is he now?'

'By "left us" I meant that . . . Well, actually he . . . er . . . died. In his sleep.'

'Died?'

'Yes. Quite peacefully, of course,' the manager lied. In fact the Colonel had been found face down on the rug, purple-faced and with one fist still raised as if in anger. He assumed the poor chap had been hopping over to the en-suite bathroom since neither his stick nor his false leg was anywhere near, although it was odd that he'd somehow pulled the phone out of the wall as he fell.

As if that were not a bad enough start to Lady Clarissa's morning, to make matters worse she had had to drive herself down to Ipford because the man who ran the garage had caught summer 'flu.

By the time she arrived at the hotel she felt very out of sorts but had at least resigned herself to the old man's demise. She wouldn't have a convenient reason to come to Ipford any more but neither would Uncle Harold be able to carry on fleecing her. She went to the hotel manager's office and found his lounge suit augmented by a black armband.

He saluted as Lady Clarissa walked in and she quickly took out a handkerchief to hide her delight and feign tears.

'Oh, poor Uncle,' she sobbed. 'I had so hoped that getting him out of that awful nursing home and into this delightful hotel would raise his spirits.'

For a moment the manager almost reversed the expression, to say that in his opinion it was precisely because the old man had raised so many spirits, in the form of large and exceedingly strong whiskies, that he'd died.

Instead he merely offered her his condolences but Clarissa wasn't really listening, too busy considering what she was going to do now. Of one thing she was certain: Uncle Harold wasn't going to waste any more of her money by being buried in Kenya. But nor could she bring herself to think of him being cremated or, as he had so aptly put it, 'incinerated', after all that he had said about it. He might have been a nasty old man at the end but he was still family and she ought to do right by him.

'Is my late uncle still in his room?' she asked. 'I'd like to have a last look at him.'

The manager said he quite understood and took her up in the lift, discreetly tucking the final bill, to which he had already added the cost of a new door, into her bag.

'I'll leave you to spend a few private moments with him,' he told her, and hurried away down the stairs.

Lady Clarissa stopped sniffing and went into the room. From the strong smell of whisky it was clear that, although her phone calls had no doubt been a little unsettling, there were other reasons too for Uncle Harold's abrupt demise. He was lying on the bed with a sheet over him but, strangely, seemed to have one fist raised. She tried pushing it back down but unfortunately rigor had set in and the more she pushed the harder it sprang back. Clarissa gave up for fear of snapping it off and leaving him with only one arm to match his one leg.

She turned her attention away from her uncle's corpse and started looking around the suite for the 'bugs' he'd told her the hotel manager had installed, to film her having sex with the man from the garage. She knew they must be exceedingly small and were almost certainly hidden in obscure places, but there really was nothing to be seen of them. She went round the sitting room several times and even climbed on to the dressing table in the bedroom to get a closer look at the ceiling rose and coving. In the end she was convinced that there weren't any to be found and realised that the old devil had been bluffing her. With a silent curse, she went down in the lift and bearded the manager.

'The Colonel told me you had installed hidden video cameras in that suite. I want to know if there's any truth in his story?'

The manager gasped. 'He told you that? What utter nonsense. It's against the law and more than my . . . I mean, I'd have been insane to do anything like that. I'd have lost my job if such a story got out. And what on earth for?'

'Oh, I'm just telling you that's what he said. Not that I believed him, of course.'

'I should hope not. He must have been exceedingly drunk at the time. I hadn't wanted to say it before now but I think that your uncle probably killed himself with the amount he drank every day.'

Lady Clarissa was still dubious but there was nothing to be gained from starting an argument.

'I suppose he was suffering from some sort of persecution complex. I just thought you ought to know what he told me. I do apologise for mentioning it.'

And leaving the flabbergasted manager still muttering angrily to himself, she went back to the car and rang directory enquiries for the number of an undertaker.

Finding a firm nearby, she went round to make arrangements for the Colonel's funeral.

'You can send the body to me at Sandystones Hall, Fenfield,' she told the undertaker. 'We will be conducting a private committal in the Estate cemetery. I'll pay you for the coffin and transportation costs now. No, there'll be no flowers required nor any sort of ceremony. The Colonel was not a popular man.' And having written out a cheque, she gave it to the owner.

'Blimey, we get some extraordinary customers,' he told his assistant after she had left. 'Fancy having a burial ground on your own estate. No flowers, no ceremony, and from the way she spoke it sounds as though there will be no mourners either. Still, she must be rolling in money. Paid up without a murmur.'

In the street Clarissa changed her mind about not bothering further with her uncle's alleged bugging of her room. The hotel manager had seemed wholly convincing in his denials that it had taken place, but to make sure she decided she ought to see her uncle's solicitor. The Colonel had once or twice mentioned the man's name. It would be as well to check the old devil's will while she was here.

She went back to the hotel and asked for the number of the solicitor's firm. She then rang and asked the receptionist for an appointment with Mr Ramsdyke.

'Are you a present client of Mr Ramsdyke's?'

'How can I be present if I'm here?'

'Here where?'

'Here, not there, you stupid girl. Tell Mr Ramsdyke that I am Lady Clarissa Gadsley, wife of Sir George, the magistrate, and that if you do not fix me an appointment to see him immediately, you will both have cause to regret it.'

Twenty minutes later she was shown into Mr Ramsdyke's office and offered a seat.

'I'll come straight to the point,' she told the man with a grey moustache sitting behind the desk. 'My uncle, Colonel Harold Rumble, has died. I presume he left his will with you.'

'Colonel Harold Rumble? How do you spell the name?'

'Like "grumble" without the "g".'

'Nobody of that name . . .' Mr Ramsdyke began, and then hesitated. 'Now that I come to think of it, someone called Grumble did consult us a year or two ago. I think it was about suing a motorist . . . or was it a boarding house? I remember he didn't seem at all well and I advised him then to make a will. Did your uncle have a wooden leg?'

'Yes, that's right. And what I came to see you about was his will. He's just died.'

Mr Ramsdyke's face fell as he realised he wasn't about to acquire two wealthy new clients. 'In that case, he must have died intestate because he rejected my suggestion. Unless, of course, he went to another firm of solicitors. Although he claimed to have nothing to leave.'

'Nothing stored in boxes?' Lady Clarissa persisted. 'For you to keep in your strongroom?'

'Good gracious, no,' said Mr Ramsdyke. 'As a matter of fact, we don't have a strongroom as such. Safes, yes, but actual room, no. Though we do have lots of room for new clients . . .' he added in a last pitch for Lady Clarissa's business.

'Frankly, I'm surprised you have any clients at all,' she said, rising to her feet and banging the door loudly behind her.

Lady Clarissa left the solicitor's office with mixed feelings. On the one hand, her uncle had evidently made something of a fool out of her. But on the other, he'd very conveniently drunk himself to death, very rapidly. Wonderfully consoled by this thought, she collected her car and began to drive back to Sandystones Hall.

# Chapter 16

Down at St Barnaby's School, the Headmistress still had no idea who had clambered up to her bedroom to plant the condom and pants in her double bed. When she'd crept round the dormitories to check on them, the Wilt quads weren't giggling but were apparently fast asleep. They had been her first suspects but she still had no evidence. She had questioned the prefects, though for obvious reasons hadn't gone into too much detail, merely stating that a prank had taken place in her house. The prefects were as puzzled as she was.

'Something's up,' one of them said. 'It's probably to do with her husband. He's always drunk when he comes back from wherever he's been away to.'

'But she asked about the girls in the dormitories,' said another.

'Could be he's tried to sleep with one of them.'

'He'd be mad to do that!'

'Anything's possible. He always gets so drunk when he goes to Horsham on business.'

In the end they concluded that they really had no idea what the Headmistress had been so agitated about, although they rather suspected the ghastly Wilt girls were involved in it somewhere.

A furious phone call from Ms Young, who had finally made it to Inverness, only added to Mrs Collinson's bewilderment. Ms Young told her she was staying in Scotland and resigning from her teaching post forthwith. The Headmistress knew her to be an excellent teacher, almost certainly the best in the school. She couldn't afford to lose her.

'But why? If it's a matter of your salary, I'd be happy to increase it substantially.'

'My decision has nothing to do with what I earn and everything to do with those four fiendish girls! I can't prove it, but I swear they tampered with my car to such an extent that I missed my cousin's wedding. I could well have been killed in an awful accident in the Dartford Tunnel.'

'Good gracious me, how dreadful! And you're certain they were responsible?'

'I told you, I haven't any direct evidence but, yes, I am certain they were responsible. Ever since they came to the school, they've created havoc time and time again. Surely you must realise that? They ought to be expelled.'

The Headmistress hesitated. What Ms Young had just said was perfectly true. Until the Wilt quads had come to St Barnaby's there had been no serious trouble in the school, only a few minor quarrels and the occasional fight: matters she could deal with easily and certainly nothing that warranted expulsion.

'You may well be right,' she admitted. 'But unless we have definite proof, I don't see how we can expel them. If we can find that proof and they go, will you return? Naturally with the increase in salary I've already mentioned.'

Ms Young said she'd consider it and put the phone down. Left to herself, the Headmistress tried to think what to do next. She could not expel the quads without good reason, and in spite of her growing suspicion that they had been responsible for putting those revolting objects in her bed, couldn't for the life of her imagine where they had obtained the things. At the same time she was determined to retain the services of Ms Young. She would have to find a way of getting the wretched girls out of the school without officially expelling them. But how on earth could she do it? She'd already written to Mrs Wilt to warn her that unless her daughters changed their behaviour and used less disgusting language she would be forced to ask her to remove them from the school.

She decided to prepare a further letter, to be sent straightaway, and would also hand a copy to whichever Wilt came to collect their delinquent offspring, saying that owing to increased overheads the school was having to raise its fees substantially again.

Surely that ought persuade the parents to take them away, she thought sitting back in her chair with a smile.

She was certain the Wilt family were already having a hard time meeting the quads' school fees. They'd entered the girls for every scholarship the school offered – even the one for single parents, with Mrs Wilt arguing that her husband was so useless she may as well be on her own. They'd won nothing, of course, although there had been something of a near miss when Penelope's drawing of her three sisters in minute anatomical detail in the Life Studies class had hugely impressed one of the school governors. Fortunately the man had had to stand down in some disgrace when he was later arrested and charged with lewd behaviour after exposing himself in the local park.

What a ghastly handful those girls were! Goodness knows what the father must be like, to have sired not one devilish daughter but four of them.

Up at Sandystones Hall Wilt was oblivious to the fulminations of his daughters' headmistress. He was finding that he was having a more interesting – if peculiar – time than he'd expected. He'd risen on the first morning to find that Sir George was in court all day and Lady Clarissa was confined to her room with what Mrs Bale described as a 'general poorliness', which he rather suspected had something to do with drink. And once again the elusive Edward was nowhere to be found. As a result Wilt was able to explore the house and grounds, happy in the knowledge that he would not have to spend the day listening to his host grumbling about his step-son whom he called 'the blithering idiot' – or indeed himself attempting to teach the blithering idiot A-level history. Instead Sir George had lent Wilt an old bicycle and told him that, for all he cared, Wilt could go into town and have dinner in a restaurant.

'I don't want to be disturbed when you come back either,' he'd said, to Wilt's delight. This was slightly diminished when Sir George added that Wilt may well come across the little bastard Edward skulking somewhere on the Estate, and to look out for low-flying missiles if he did.

So in fact Wilt was enjoying what amounted to a holiday, and had decided to start it by exploring the house more fully. It proved to be even more peculiar than the ancestral portraits on the staircase and the enormous beds had led him to expect. In search of something interesting to read that evening – having tired of the causes of the First World War – he went into the library. It was a big room lined with the shelves around all four walls. These were filled with dusty old books which didn't look as though they had been opened for years.

But it was the furniture that held his attention. It was all Indian, and not the contemporary sort manufactured in Birmingham or some sheet-metal works in the Midlands, which he'd occasionally seen in suburban houses and pretentious high-street stores. This was authentic nineteenth-century furniture: dark teak sideboards, lots of highly ornamented fretwork screens, and even rattan or bamboo extending chairs, which Mrs Bale helpfully told him later were known as Bombay Fornicators because they could be pulled out so far that one (or two) could lie down on them.

A whole host of miniature carved elephants and other animals cluttered the floor between chairs and screens, so much so that Wilt felt he had wandered into a museum of Imperial relics. This odd menagerie was as visually unsettling as the exterior of the Hall.

He turned away and desperately searched the bookshelves for something light to read, but military history seemed to be this family's obsession, with an emphasis on the 1757 struggle between the British and the French.

Needing to escape, Wilt went to the front door. He crossed the drawbridge and strolled around to the walled kitchen garden and the cottage in which they were going to stay. Once outside it, he decided the cottage looked perfectly acceptable if to his mind rather small. He began to wonder whether he could persuade the Gadsleys that he ought to remain living at the Hall and not in the cottage with Eva and the quads. After all, he would be engaged upon important work – always provided he found the elusive Eddie – and ought not to be pestered and distracted by four raucous girls. In fact, five raucous women since Eva was every bit as noisy and demanding as the fast-maturing quads. No, he couldn't possibly be expected to tutor the boy if he had to endure their horrendous music and violent quarrels all day and all night: he would put this to Lady Clarissa when he saw her and felt sure she would agree.

Having settled that in his own mind, Wilt decided not to bother with the bike but instead went for a walk deep into the woods. It was there that he discovered a caravan, well hidden near the wall which screened the Hall from the road and set behind some shrubs and young fir saplings. He could hear someone moving about inside it and presently an extraordinarily fat and short woman came out with some clothes, which she hung on a makeshift washing line. When she went inside again, Wilt crept back the way he had come. Something about that van and the way it was partly camouflaged had made him feel uncomfortable. He decided not to go near it again. Instead he crossed the lawn to the lake and sat down on a bank to gaze across at the architectural fright show that was the Hall.

After half an hour spent basking in the sun, he went

back into the house and through to the kitchen to talk to Mrs Bale. He found her supervising two surprisingly plump young women who were cleaning the staircase and corridors. The three women together were so large there was actually no possibility of his getting round them to his room so Wilt reached a sudden decision.

'Good morning, Mrs Bale. I wonder if you could tell me if Lady Clarissa is up yet?'

'I'm afraid not, Mr Wilt. Her ladyship has suffered a bereavement . . . although it isn't my place to talk to you about it as I don't believe in gossip. Anyway I don't think we will see her for a good while yet, Mr Wilt. She was very, very upset when she got back late last night, and by the state of the drinks cabinet I'd say that she had to have a drink or two . . . to console herself. Not that I'm one to gossip, you understand.'

'Of course not,' he said hastily, thinking that at this rate he'd be stuck in the corridor for ever. 'Bereaved, you say? How terrible – I do hope it wasn't her uncle.' He continued quickly before Mrs Bale could confirm or deny the matter, 'Well, then, may I ask whether Sir George is back yet, and if so whether he'd mind my having a quick word with him?'

'He is, and provided it's not about his step-son, I'm sure he'd be pleased to see you.' Mrs Bale turned around with some difficulty to pry apart the two cleaners who had become wedged together in the doorway. Wilt went the long way round to the study and knocked on the door.

'Come in,' Sir George called out, and glanced somewhat critically at Wilt as he entered. 'If it's about my step-son . . .' he began, but Wilt shook his head.

'No. I thought you should know that there's some sort of caravan, parked in the woods. It seems to be partly camouflaged by saplings and shrubs.'

'Caravan?' asked Sir George, turning rather crimson. 'Don't know anything about a caravan. Whereabouts is it?'

'Deep in the wood, opposite the kitchen garden and cottage.'

'Dashed if I can spot it . . .' said Sir George, peering out of the window through a pair of binoculars.

'It's some way into the woods,' Wilt told him, pointing in the right direction.

'And, as I said, it looked camouflaged.'

'Well, I'll go down and have those damned trespassers off the premises in no time at all. You stay and see the cleaners don't come in here. I keep telling Mrs Bale not to let them in but she's as bad as they are. Always tidying my things up so I can't find anything I need. Not that I don't like to see them down on their hands and knees, you know . . .' He paused and looked enquiringly at Wilt, who in turn shook his head. He didn't know what on earth Sir George was getting at.

'You know . . . cleaning things?'

Sir George sighed at his reaction and went over to a metal cabinet standing near his desk. He unlocked it and took out a twelve-bore shotgun. 'Always best to be on the safe side when dealing with trespassers,' he explained as he went out of the room.

When he had gone Wilt looked in the cabinet and was horrified by the number of guns he saw inside it. There must have been at least thirty of various shapes and sizes, and all looking absolutely lethal. He felt extremely worried that he'd told Sir George about the trespassers.

From the window Wilt watched his host make his way through the grounds. Once Sir George was out of sight, though, he left the study. Wilt was afraid of guns and certainly didn't want to be left alone in a room with an open metal cabinet filled with weapons. In fact, he felt sure that leaving a gun cabinet unlocked was illegal. He'd go up to his room, he decided, and look at his notes on Austrian/Serbian relations, for the umpteenth time.

But just as he was about to open the door to his bedroom, he noticed another staircase leading off the landing and ending before a closed door. This turned out to open on to a corridor identical to the one he'd just left below, complete with yet another staircase towards the front of the house.

'May as well see where that one goes to,' Wilt said to himself, wondering how on earth he had thought the Hall somewhat small when he first saw it. Presently he found himself in a turret that overlooked the great lawn, the lake, and away to the right the walled kitchen garden. As he gazed out of a window trying to establish exactly where the caravan was, he suddenly saw a youth walking across the lawn. This must be the teenager he'd been hired to get into Cambridge. He looked younger than Wilt had expected. As he turned towards the house Wilt was surprised to see that Edward, if this youth was he, looked so ordinary after all he had been told about him. It was hard to tell from this distance but he looked to be nothing worse than a typical spotty teenager.

Wilt leant on the window ledge and wondered about Sir George's remark that his step-son was a 'Gawd Help Us'. From this angle he didn't look particularly bad nor, it had to be said, very interesting. Still, if Lady Clarissa was prepared to pay him fifteen hundred quid a week to educate the blighter, Wilt was prepared to do his best. Determined to call down to the boy and arrange to meet up in the library, Wilt stepped out of the low window and on to the flat roof outside. For the first time he saw that this was only the front turret and that around the circumference of the roof there were more dotted here and there, with no apparent regard for any architectural or even structural rules. Even more extraordinary were the ancient cannon that pointed out over the grounds from every side of the building, set out of sight from the ground behind a low parapet wall. The taxi driver had been right when he'd said the bloke who'd designed the place must have been either off his head or on opium.

Wilt turned back to the window he'd come out of and made the mistake of looking directly down over the wall. Finding himself far higher up than he'd supposed, and suffering from a phobia about heights, Wilt dropped to his knees and crawled back over the window ledge in a panic. He would go straight down and find the boy, he decided. And he was damn' certain that never again would he climb up on that fearful roof.

He had just reached the ground floor when he encountered Mrs Bale again.

'Lady Clarissa says she will see you in the dining room in an hour's time. She's feeling very much better although still grieving, poor thing. She's very sorry not to have been here to meet you and to show you around, but of course with her poor uncle dying like that . . .'

'Oh, it was her uncle who died? I'm sorry to hear that and I'm sure my wife will be too. Does this mean that they'll all be off to Ipford for the funeral? I can call Eva and tell her not to come, if necessary.'

'Oh, no, apparently the body is coming here.'

'Coming here? How very odd.'

Mrs Bale was about to reply when there was a furious shout from the study.

'Where's that tutor bloke? I left him in here to mind

the gun cabinet. And the idiot's disappeared, leaving it unlocked! What's more, the keys have gone too . . .'

'I think you'd better make yourself scarce. I'll try to cool him down,' Mrs Bale whispered.

Wilt hurried back down the corridor as she called out to Sir George that she was coming.

Lady Clarissa lay in bed nursing a very bad hangover and waiting to feel well enough even to attempt getting up. She had driven back late the previous evening, feeling surprisingly light-hearted. She was looking forward to seeing Wilt again, and besides, now that she came to think about it, Uncle Harold's death was something of a relief. Even the thought of spending every weekend with Sir George from now on didn't bother her unduly. She was sure there would be other opportunities to meet up with the man from the garage, always supposing he recovered from his cold or Swine 'Flu or whatever it was.

The previous evening she had arrived at the iron gates at the back of the Hall, opened them with the electronic gadget Sir George had installed to prevent any car thief stealing his Bentley, or worse still the ancient Rolls-Royce, and then driven the Jaguar into the garage. When she had entered the house she had found the kitchen empty so went down to the front hall to Sir George's study.

'You're back late,' he said, polishing a rifle. The 'pull-through' was lying on the floor.

'I rang your secretary. She should have informed you.'

'Mrs Bale never informs me of anything pleasant. She gave me supper, though, such as it was.'

'And what about Mr Wilt? Did she give him supper too?'

'I daresay. In the kitchen. I don't dine with servants.'

'And how did Edward and Mr Wilt get on?'

'I've no idea. Haven't even seen the boy and I don't believe Wilt has either. You need to give dear Eddie a talking to.'

'Don't call him Eddie. His name is Edward. I expect he was just settling back into being home.'

'God help us,' muttered Sir George.

Lady Clarissa ignored the remark.

'What have you been doing with that gun?' she asked.

'Just polishing it, my dear. Never know when one's going to need a gun at the ready. Even on the way to court this morning some young hooligans attacked my car at the traffic lights. Stuck a wet sponge all over the window and then had the bloody cheek to ask for money. Reminded me of highwaymen or something. Wished I'd had my gun with me then, I can tell you.'

'May one ask why you didn't have them arrested?'

'I just happened to be in a good mood. I'm always in a good mood when you go down to Ipford to see your damned uncle.'

Lady Clarissa sighed.

'I phoned the Bale woman and told her he'd died. I suppose she didn't let you know that either.'

'I've told you, she's my secretary. She does not meddle in your relative's affairs. She knows I'm not interested.'

'Well, he has died, and I expect you'll be pleased not to have the expense of paying for him any more. Although I did have to write a large cheque to the undertaker to get him up here.'

'Get him up here? What on earth are you talking about, you stupid woman?'

'They're bringing him up here to be buried on the Estate, of course. He is family after all.'

Sir George was obviously in an ugly mood. 'He was not a Gadsley, and I'm not going to conduct a ceremony here for someone who isn't even related to my family! I don't care what you say, I'm not having that old fool buried here. You can have him cremated as you said you were going to.'

'But that was before I discussed the matter with Uncle. He wanted to be buried in Kenya where he was born. Well, that was out of the question, of course. I told him it would be far too expensive and no one would visit him out there . . .'0

'. . . and I'll tell you something else. No one's going to visit his grave here either. Just do what any sensible person would and arrange something with the Vicar in the village. I believe they've a graveyard there. Either that or have the old bugger cremated, as you always said you were going to do.'

'I know I did but I've changed my mind.'

'You haven't a mind to change,' her husband snarled. 'Get this into your head: I am not having the cemetery defiled by someone outside the family being buried in it. And that's my final word on the matter.'

With that he had stormed off to bed, leaving Clarissa to drown her sorrows with the help of the well-stocked drinks cabinet.

# Chapter 17

Thoughts of drowning were still on Clarissa's mind once she was finally up and dressed, the next morning although it was a toss up whether she would rather drown her beastly husband after his horrible behaviour last night or – given her terrible headache – herself. Not that the moat was really deep enough. Edward had once tried to demonstrate how long one could hold one's breath underwater, using some poor unfortunate from the village. On that occasion they were fortunate enough to be able to survive a mere three inches of water for really quite a long time.

When Wilt did not appear at the appointed hour she went in search of him and found him coming out of the walled garden. He'd been chatting there with the old man who looked after it and who reminded him of Coverdale on his allotment.

'Ah, there you are,' said Lady Clarissa as he crossed the wooden drawbridge to join her. 'I wondered where you'd got to.'

'I've been looking for Edward – I saw him earlier but he seems to have disappeared again.'

'He'll turn up soon enough.'

'I'm most terribly sorry to hear your sad news, Lady Clarissa. You have my condolences.'

'Thank you, Henry. I appreciate your sympathy, more than you know. Not everyone has been as kind. Now, shall we walk around the moat? I want you to tell me something.'

'That sounds like a good idea. What do you want to know?'

'Mrs Bale tells me you saw a caravan in the woods. Was it a gypsy one?'

'Difficult to say. It was largely hidden by the undergrowth and trees.'

'Was any occupant visible?'

Wilt thought for a moment.

'As a matter of fact, I did see a small fat woman hanging up some washing on a line nearby. I went straight back to the Hall and told Sir George, who said they must be trespassers and went out with a gun. I don't like guns so I left the study and went up to the roof which is when I spotted Edward from a turret.'

'A small fat woman?'

'Yes. There are actually quite a few fat women round here, if you don't mind my mentioning it. With the exception of you, of course, Lady Clarissa. I suppose it's what they call living the good life? Anyway I particularly noticed as it seemed extraordinary that even the trespassers were, well, let's say overweight.'

Lady Clarissa smiled to herself. She had a very shrewd idea who had been in that caravan and doubted very much that the so-called trespasser had been in any danger at all from Sir George's gun. They walked on around the moat in silence. Finally they sat down on the bank and stared at the green water. Wilt tried to think of something to say but Lady Clarissa was obviously preoccupied with her own thoughts and he didn't want to interrupt them. Above them loomed the hideous Hall, casting its shadow over the lawn. Lady Clarissa finally broke the silence.

'I think I'll go up to my room and have another nap. I had such a trying time yesterday. Why don't you join me?'

Wilt was taken aback. Surely she didn't mean that the way it sounded. She must mean, why didn't he do the same thing? He shook his head.

'I don't usually sleep in the afternoon,' he said. 'And in any case, I really feel I ought track Edward down and make a start. Need to earn my keep. And I rather get the feeling that Sir George is a bit cross with me at the moment, for leaving his gun cabinet unattended.'

'Sir George leaves rather a lot unattended himself,' muttered Lady Clarissa darkly as she got to her feet. 'I have just the books you need for reference in my room. So why don't you come up with me and I'll give them to you?'

Wilt wondered why she had them in her room when there was a library at her disposal. But he couldn't say no when she was was the one paying him to tutor her son. He followed her meekly up the long staircase and into her room.

Lady Clarissa waved him over to an impossibly red chaise-longue in the corner and said she'd go and get the books.

Wilt felt himself becoming hot and bothered. The flaming red of the upholstery was getting to him just as Eva's panties had and he knew he had to escape imminently without offending Lady Clarissa. But the next minute she came out of the adjoining room dressed only in her bra and panties. These were of a deep red colour, too, and edged with black lace, leaving nothing to the imagination given that she wasn't exactly waif-like. She posed against the door, one hand draped against the frame and one leg crossed over the other.

'How tall are you, big boy? Five foot nine inches? Let's talk about the nine inches!'

He knew enough to recognise that Lady Clarissa was quoting Mae West. When she saw Wilt gaping at her open-mouthed, she tried again: 'When I'm good, I'm very bad. But when I'm bad, I'm very good.

'Well?' she added, slightly crossly, when Wilt stood gazing at her with a shocked expression on his face. 'Shall we do some research together?'

'Er . . . I suddenly remembered . . . I have to call Eva to let her know the best way of getting here.' And with that, he scarpered off back to his own room and locked the door.

# Chapter 18

In Ipford Eva was preparing to drive down to Sussex to pick up the quads. The Headmistress's letter had arrived that morning with its warning that the school fees were being raised yet again. That had alarmed her so much that she had even thought of phoning Sandystones Hall to ask if she could speak to her husband. She'd finally decided not to because he would only say it was her fault for taking the girls out of the Convent in the first place, and that the fifteen hundred pounds a week he was earning was scarcely going to cover the increase for one girl, let alone all four of them.

Lurking at the back of her mind also was a memory of the way Lady Clarissa had looked at Wilt over lunch. Eva hadn't liked that look at all. It was obvious her ladyship had found him sexually alluring. If that was the case, the sooner Eva and the quads were up at the Hall the better. She'd told Henry there was not to be any hanky-panky when they'd cycled home, and she'd meant it.

Not that he was exactly keen on 'gender' or even the word itself. He said it was an abomination and insisted on referring to political correctness as the 'destruction of the English language'. It was the same with the word 'gay' which he refused to use either except when they'd been to a party he'd particularly enjoyed. In short, he was determined to be old-fashioned and to embarrass her. Eva had tried to fight back but too often had used the word 'sex' instead of 'gender' when she was talking too quickly and forgot. Anyway he wasn't keen on it, whatever you called it. If Lady Clarissa tried to seduce him, or whatever the politically correct word was, she'd have her work cut out. He'd probably run a mile.

There was besides the presence of Sir George, though he had been born under another name or something, according to Wilt, and who according to Lady Clarissa was a very bad-tempered man indeed. He'd soon put a stop to any hanky-panky. And then, of course, Wilt was earning all that extra money on top of his salary at the Technical University and she and the quads were getting a free holiday by the seaside into the bargain. That would save money too. Feeling much

more cheerful, Eva finished packing and took the suitcases out to the car, had a cup of tea and made some
sandwiches for the drive. Then, in a better mood,
she set off down to the school. Come to think of it, she
would need to hurry if she were to get to St Barnaby's
in time.

As she drove she tried to decide what she was going
to say to the Headmistress to persuade her to let the
quads stay on at the school. She was so absorbed in
these thoughts and keeping within the speed limit
that it was only when she reached Hailsham that she
realised she was on entirely the wrong road and almost
out of petrol. She stopped at a petrol station, filled
up the tank and, having paid, asked the man behind
the counter the way to East Whyland.

'You've come a long way out if you want that village.
It's practically in Kent.'

'How far from here?'

'About forty miles, but it's along side roads. You'd
be safer to go back to Heathfield and take the A265
to Burwash. Ask someone there.'

He turned to the next customer, grumbling, 'People
who have no sense of direction ought not be on the
roads in the first place. Or they should at least have
the gumption to get themselves a satellite navigation
system.'

He obviously hadn't met Henry who would sooner find
his way by the alignment of the stars in the night sky
than lash out good money on a box of electronic tricks

when a road atlas would do the job just as well. Not that Eva had ever been any good with maps.

Feeling foolish, she sat in the car studying the road map. East Whyland remained invisible to her. The next problem was that she had to turn round to get back to Heathfield and there was a queue of traffic which made it impossible for her to get across to the opposite lane. After half an hour she managed it thanks to a polite man who left a space for her in front of him. Even then she was stuck in a snarl up for an hour more and it was six o'clock before she reached Heathfield and turned right on to the A265.

By the time she reached Burwash Eva was beginning to wish she'd listened to Wilt when he'd tried to show her how to read a map, but that had been years ago when they were first married and she'd been in love with him. 'I don't need to,' she'd said then, 'I can't drive so how can I get lost?' By the time she'd passed her test Wilt's exasperation with her had grown to such an extent he was more likely to have spent time teaching her how to get lost than how not to.

Well, she was lost now. The last time she'd come down to the school Wilt had been driving and she had been too busy telling the girls to stop squabbling in the back to notice the way they had come. She pulled into the side of the road and was studying the map without much hope when an old woman came out of a house nearby and walked towards her. Eva got out and went around the car. 'I wonder if you could help me,' she said when she'd reached her. 'I'm looking for Saint Barnaby's Girls' School and I've lost my way. It's in East Whyland.'

'East Whyland? Never heard of the place. Mind you, I don't live down here. I'm from Essex. Just visiting my niece, and she's only been here for a month so there's not much point asking her. Sorry, I can't help you.'

When she'd gone Eva consulted the map again and cursed the garage man in Hailsham. The only solution she could think of was that there was probably a hotel in Heathfield and she didn't care if it did cost more than a bed and breakfast, she was throughly fed up and exhausted. She was also desperately hungry. She'd spend the night there after ringing St Barnaby's to tell the Headmistress she'd had a puncture and wouldn't be arriving until the following day. If she found a nice hotel she'd be able to treat herself to a very good dinner with a glass of decent wine. With what Wilt was earning, they could jolly well afford it.

Next morning, armed with painstakingly written directions from the hotel porter, Eva found the school and spent an acrimonious half-hour with the Headmistress who demanded that she remove the quads at once and seriously consider looking for an alternative.

'What have they done now?' Eva demanded angrily.

'What have they done? Well, let me tell you that unless they leave straight away you are likely to end up being multiply sued for the wanton damage your girls are inflicting on staff cars and school property. The only reason I haven't called the police so far is that I didn't want them arrested here – I do have the reputation of the school to consider. All I'm saying is, you'd better consider the legal cost, if members of staff do end up taking you to court. I have so far persuaded them not to but, unless your daughters leave immediately, they may change their minds. One of my best teachers has already resigned thanks to your girls. She had to go to hospital because your daughters deliberately tampered with her car. I hope I've made the situation clear.'

Eva said she had and left the Headmistress's office feeling suitably chastened. She collected the quads from the sick bay where they had been put in isolation. She was already dreading the return journey.

The following day Sir George seemed to be in a slightly more affable mood. 'So where is that son of yours?' he asked his wife at breakfast.

'Why do you want to know? Keeping out of your way, I should think. I'm determined to make sure you won't be seeing much, if anything, of Edward. He'll be spending most of his time being coached by Henry.'

'By whom? If you're referring to Wilt, I'd be grateful if you'd call him by his surname and not his Christian one. After all, he's merely an educated servant. I don't go round calling my secretary Doris or whatever her first name is. She's Mrs Bale to me. Come to think of it, you can address him as Mr Wilt.'

Clarissa glared at him poisonously.

'I'll call him what I like,' she snapped. 'I'm still waiting for an apology from you.'

'An apology? What on earth have I got to apologise for?'

'For being so nasty to me about Uncle. I still don't see why my family can't be buried here. I'm your wife, aren't I?'

'Sadly, my dear, yes, you are. But you won't be if you carry on in this way.'

They sat in silence broken only by Sir George's crunching of the badly burned toast which he had covered with lashings of butter.

'Your manners are disgusting,' Clarissa snapped. 'Thank God Edward's tutor isn't here to listen to you. By the way, where is he?'

'In the kitchen, of course. That's where Mrs Bale eats.'

'In that case, I'll have breakfast in my room and leave you to make a pig of yourself in here. After all, you treat me like a skivvy too.'

She left the table and headed for the door. Behind her Sir George muttered, 'Good riddance to bad rubbish.'

Lady Clarissa turned on him. 'If there's any rubbish in this place, it's what you're currently stuffing down yourself. It looks lethal enough to land you in the morgue. Now that would be good riddance!' And she left, slamming the door behind her.

Sir George went across to the sideboard and helped himself to another portion of fatty bacon from the chafing dish. The only clouds on his horizon were due solely to Clarissa's relations. He was damned if that disgusting old man was going to lay his bones in Gadsley family ground. And as for that moronic son of hers . . . If someone had pilfered the keys to the gun cabinet it was bound to be Edward. Stupid idiot. Wilt was going to find it almost impossible to get that lout into Cambridge. Well, Sir George wasn't going to have the boy cluttering up the Hall much longer, that was certain. He was determined to make dear little Eddie's life so miserable he'd keep out of his step-father's way altogether or, best of all, get a job and leave home. But what work could he possibly be fitted for? Sir George considered the problem and came to the conclusion his step-son might just qualify as an emptier of rubbish bins. He was sniggering over this thought when Mrs Bale came into the room and reminded him that he had to hear a case in twenty minutes.

'What's the charge?' he asked.

'It's the one where the taxi driver was beaten up by drunks who wouldn't pay the fare after he'd taken them back to their village.'

'Oh, that one. Soon sentence him for causing an affray.'

'Fine the taxi driver? Why him? Why don't you fine the drunken hooligans? After all, they started the whole thing?'

'You don't appreciate the pathetic weakness of the twenty-first-century legal system. There aren't enough prisons, and we aren't allowed to use police cells instead because the cost incurred is too great. Oh, yes, much better and more economical to teach the taxi driver not to allow drunks in his car in the future. He won't complain when he sees I'm sentencing him: he'll know he's lucky not to be thrown straight into jail. You should see the other magistrates on the bench . . . as wet as sponges soaked in bathwater! Anyway, please get me my coat.'

Mrs Bale left the room with a sigh, wondering why she'd ever become his secretary. Her late husband had frequently quoted the saying 'The Law is an ass.' If Sir George was anything to go by, it was worse even than that: it was as barking mad as a hyena. She fetched his raincoat and waited for him to come down to the garage. As usual, she pressed the buttons and opened the electronic gates for him.

Lady Clarissa and Wilt were down at the cottage. He had spent three hours that morning trying to teach Edward the rudiments of twentieth-century European history, but had found the boy to be every bit as dull and dim-witted as he'd feared. The only contribution he'd made to the morning's lesson was to draw some idiotic link between the First World War and the Polish man who cleaned the Hall's windows, and when he'd failed to return from a loo break Wilt had decided to call it a day.

He'd tried to broach the subject with Lady Clarissa but she had refused to listen and instead had dragged him off to the cottage in the grounds. He feared the worst, especially when she tried to take his arm which led to a rather ungainly tussle between them as he pretended not to realise what she was doing. But after that one attempt she kept her hands to herself and Wilt wondered if she had given up on him, following the disappointment in her bedroom. He certainly hoped so. It was bad enough fending off Eva, let alone another sex-mad harpy. They walked on in silence for a while.

'I want you to be quite sure your wife will like it here,' his employer announced, producing the key to the cottage from her pocket. 'I don't want her to feel lonely.'

Wilt decided not to mention the quads. The chance of Eva's being lonely while they were around was about the same as his chance of winning the Lottery and retiring to Spain a millionaire. That was to say, zero: the last time he'd bought a Lottery ticket was four years ago and Eva had thrown a fit then, accusing him of reckless gambling.

'I'm sure she won't. I'm away all day during term-time,' he told Lady Clarissa.

'Of course you are. But the Hall can be a lonely place . . . a hell of a lonely place. Take it from me.'

Clarissa sniffed and Wilt pretended to study the ground as he waited for her to rally.

'Perhaps after we've inspected the cottage you could show me where the caravan you saw was parked. You said the woman was short and very fat. I have a shrewd idea who she was.'

They went into the cottage which was built of the same mellow brick as the garden walls. It was surrounded by a pocket handkerchief of lawn and a small flower garden, planted with roses and hollyhocks and edged with lavender.

'This used to be the head gardener's home,' Lady Clarissa explained, 'but now I keep it for visitors who don't find my husband's company to their liking. Frankly, I find him unbearable myself most of the time. He's eating himself into an early grave and I can't say I'll be sorry when he succeeds. You may think that sounds harsh but he treats Edward in the most beastly way.' She glanced at her watch. 'Well, he'll be meting out injustice in court by now so we may as well go and look for that camper thing.'

'Where does the head gardener live now then?'

'Oh, down in the village somewhere. He found it lonely up here when his wife died, and too far from his favourite pub. We get contractors to come in and mow the lawn. It's far too big for the old fellow. How do you feel about the cottage?'

'I think it's a delightful alternative to living in India.'

'I didn't know you had been to India?'

'I haven't, though I feel as if I have been. I was thinking of the Hall.'

Clarissa laughed.

'I try not even to look at the front of the place. I always drive in through the back where we park the cars. Sir George says the hideous look of the place keeps burglars away. The moat and drawbridge help too.'

'So do the guns.'

'The cannon or the ones in the cabinet?'

'I was thinking of the cabinet. I've never seen so many guns in one place. Although I suppose massed cannon aren't exactly welcoming either.'

'George is always showing off his guns, he probably wanted to impress you with them. Although he does have quite a few enemies.'

'Enemies? What sort of enemies?'

'Innocent people he's sentenced to prison terms. He's rather fond of doing that. He's very wary of poachers and trespassers, too. In fact, there are a lot of people who would like to see him dead. Seriously, I wouldn't go wandering about the woods at night while you're here. Someone could mistake you for George.'

'I'll bear that in mind.'

They left the cottage and walked on through the woods, noticing the tyre print of a heavy vehicle preserved on a dusty unsurfaced track to the right. Lady Clarissa put a finger to her lips and whispered, 'Stay where you are. I'm going down there by myself. There's a clearing not far away, I'm pretty sure. I bet that's where he's put the hussy.'

She took off her shoes and handed them to Wilt who watched her move off silently down the track. After a while he sat down under a tree, wondering what on earth he'd let himself in for. Even struggling to overcome Edward's stupidity was preferable to getting embroiled in the Gadsleys' affairs. And he supposed 'affairs' was the right word.

It was twenty minutes before Lady Clarissa returned, put on her shoes and led the way back to the Hall before speaking.

'Just as I thought: Philly's down there. What I didn't know is that there's a gate in the park wall, allowing access to the grazing fields beyond. She got into the wood that way. Well, she's bound to want to get out again sometime so I'm going to go and buy a strong lock in the village, to make sure she won't be able to. You can come with me, if you feel like it.'

'I think I'd better not. I've got some checking up to do on the twentieth-century arms race,' said Wilt, not having a clue who this Philly was, or wanting to. In fact, the only thing he wanted was to keep right out of whatever was going on. And, after their last encounter, he certainly wasn't going to be trapped in any enclosed spaces with Lady Clarissa.

'Do you mind if I head back now? I want to give Eva a ring . . . let her know how much I'm looking forward to seeing her.' Wilt knew that if he said any such thing to his wife she'd think he was suffering from a brain storm. Either that or drunk.

'Make yourself at home.' Lady Clarissa collected her handbag and went out to her car.

Wilt watched her drive off before heading back to the house. Halfway there he heard a loud bang and for a horrible moment thought Sir George's enemies were closing in before he concluded it was just the Jaguar backfiring as it made its way up the lane. As he went inside Mrs Bale was coming out of Sir George's study.

'Just about to call my wife to see if she's back from the school in Sussex,' Wilt explained. 'She went down there to pick up our daughters.'

'If you want my advice, I'd get her up here quickly. Her ladyship is in an odd mood. She's . . . well, if she were an animal, I'd say she was "on heat". If you know what that means. I can't say I blame her. The boss has got someone on the side himself.'

'Really? It wouldn't be someone short and fat, would it?' asked Wilt, who'd rather begun to like Mrs Bale for the light she invariably shone on all of the household mysteries.

'"No names, no pack drill", as my late husband used to say.'

She smiled coyly at Wilt and went into the kitchen.

He decided to ring Eva later and followed Mrs Bale instead.

She started preparing lunch, saying, 'If you're looking for Edward, he's in the study. He always makes a beeline for it if Sir George is out.'

'What on earth is he doing there? He can't be going through the old man's papers, surely. What could there be in there to interest him?'

'The guns, of course,' said Mrs Bale, raising her eyebrows. 'He's mad on the horrid things.'

'But surely Sir George has another lock for the cabinet? It can't be right for it just to be left open. It's illegal, isn't it? Guns . . .'

'And who is the law round these parts? His Majesty, that's who, and if you think he lets the local police into his study to check the security of his weapons, you're mistaken. Anyway, they always phone him up first, if they want a warrant or something like that.'

'In that case, I don't think I'll go near the study just yet. I don't care for guns at the best of times.' Wilt paused and then decided to take the plunge. 'What do you really think of Edward?'

'Thick as two short planks. No, more like four very thick ones. I'll put it another way. If I'd known I was going to have a son like that, I'd have had an abortion. And I'm against that, which ought to tell you some-thing. Fortunately I had just the one daughter. She's a single mother, but that's better than being married to an idiotic self-satisfied shit, if you'll pardon my language. I got the impression from Her Majesty that you've got daughters too?'

'You can say that again,' Wilt agreed, and was about to tell her that he would rather have a dozen daughters who were single mothers than the four she-devils it was his misfortune to have fathered, when over her shoulder he saw the back gates opening and the Jaguar driving through. 'Lady Clarissa has evidently finished her shopping. I think I'll make myself scarce for a bit.'

He scurried along to the library and pretended to be looking for a book to read. Through the partly open door he would be able to hear anything that was said in the hall when Lady Clarissa found out where her son was. He didn't have to wait long. After a hasty exchange with Mrs Bale in the kitchen, she came hurrying down the corridor and evidently entered the study.

'Oh, really, Edward! How many times have I told you never to come in here and play with those dreadful weapons? If George found you, he'd be furious. Why do you continually have to do these things?' Lady Clarissa was virtually shrieking.

'Because I like guns and he won't let me have my own.'

'Well, you can put that beastly thing back in the cabinet at once. And stop waving it round like that! It may be loaded.'

'I'm not waving it round, I'm aiming it out of the

window, and of course it's loaded. No point having a gun if it's not got a bullet up the spout.'

'Well, remove the bullet and get out of here.'

As the pair of them passed the library door, Wilt wondered what the hell he was going to do. He now realised that the noise he'd taken for the car back-firing as he'd walked back to the house was almost certainly the sound of Edward taking a shot at him, and he was willing to bet the boy had ignored his mother's instruction to unload the gun. Wilt certainly didn't relish the prospect of spending the summer trying to tutor a backward lad who clearly had far more interest in aiming loaded guns through windows. History was definitely out – or at any rate it looked as though he'd have to concentrate purely on battles, just to hold the boy's attention.

And what about Eva and the quads? He wasn't worried for their safety – they could more than take care of themselves – but the combination of his girls and the gun-crazy Edward was too dreadful to think about. He'd have to phone Eva and warn her not to drive up. On the other hand, he couldn't phone from the Hall or he'd be sure to be overheard. Not unless Mrs Bale could get him into Sir George's private bath-room, and he wasn't sure that was a risk worth taking. No, he had to get down to the village and use a phone there. He couldn't go through the gates at the back of the blasted house because they were overlooked by anyone in the Hall. Oh well, he'd just have to find his way back down that terrible track through the woods that he'd found so alarming in the taxi. There was nothing else for it.

Wilt set off across the drawbridge, turned to his left, and ten minutes later was negotiating the sharp and dangerous corners that had practically scared the pants off him when he had arrived. Twice he heard the sound of distant gunfire, and spent several long minutes in a ditch after a pheasant scuttled across his path, scaring the life out of him. After losing his way down several wrong turnings, it took him three-quarters of an hour to reach the main road on which he was able to trudge to the nearest village.

The first phone booth he tried seemed to have become something that simply sent emails and the second was vandalised. By mid-afternoon Wilt was beginning to wonder whether he was the last man on the planet not to have a mobile but he finally found a booth that worked, even if it only accepted credit cards and not the 10p he had hopefully got out of his pocket in readiness. He spent at least fifteen minutes trying to get through to Eva's mobile but there was no answer.

Finally Wilt gave up and looked for a pub. It was a hot day and he was desperately in need of a drink . . . several drinks . . . and something to eat. He ordered a pint of beer, finished it and asked for another and some ham sandwiches. The barmaid went off and presently came back with some thick white sandwiches on a plate.

'You're not one of our regulars,' she said when she'd brought the second pint over. 'Are you passing through?'

'Not exactly. I'm staying up at the Hall. It's a weird place.'

'You can say that again! My old man used to deliver brandy up there but he wouldn't go near the place now. You'd best take care . . . I daren't say any more.'

'Why not?' asked Wilt, but two men had entered the pub by then and the barmaid went to serve them and, having poured their beer, stayed on chatting. Wilt finished his sandwiches and went through the door marked TOILET where he relieved his bladder of the beer, estimating that it had taken all of twenty minutes to make its way through his body. When he came out there were half a dozen drinkers in the bar, keeping the barmaid busy. Wilt took out a £5 note and signalled that he wanted to pay.

'You had sandwiches too,' she said as she worked the till. 'That means seven pounds ninety in total.'

Wilt gave her three more pounds and told her to keep the change. She looked at him with some disdain before handing back the 10p, saying that from the look of him he needed it more than she did.

'So why wouldn't you go to Sandystones Hall?' he asked, pocketing the coin.

'They give me the creeps, that lot. They're all . . . Well, I don't like to say really. What with you working for them an' all.'

'Loony?' suggested Wilt, glancing round the bar cautiously as if he didn't want to be overheard.

'You could put it like that,' said the woman. 'Why do you ask?'

Wilt lapsed into Cockney without quite knowing why. 'It's just something I heard. Anyway, I don't think I'll apply for a permanent job there.'

'I don't blame you. I'd get out as soon as I could, if I were you. That's my advice. And it's free an' all.' She glared at Wilt who had the grace to blush.

The barmaid went down the counter to serve a customer who had just come in and undoubtedly looked a more promising prospect. Wilt took a last swig of his beer. When he had finished it he went back to the phone booth and tried to call Eva again. She still didn't answer. He looked at his watch and saw it was earlier than he'd thought but decided enough was enough. He would have to give up. It had been something of a wasted day. But that was a minor problem compared with his real concern, which was the potentially lethal combination of Eva, the quads and a gun-toting Edward. What on earth was he going to do about it? Eva had got them into this mess, of course, just to keep the girls at that damned expensive school and satisfy her own inherent snobbery. Why couldn't he sit back and let her sort it out?

By this time Wilt was back on the winding, overgrown drive to the Hall. Suddenly he stopped in his tracks. A moment later he was crouching down behind the trunk of an enormous oak tree. Round a bend in the road ahead he had caught sight of Edward. The vicious lout was carrying a gun but, fortunately, looking away from Wilt, into the wood on the other side of the drive. A moment later he heard a shot and something thudding to the ground. He peered cautiously round the tree trunk and saw Edward trudging towards whatever poor creature he'd evidently brought down. Wilt fervently hoped it wasn't the Philly woman, although of course Lady Clarissa might feel differently.

He waited no longer but walked diagonally away from Edward in the direction of the Hall, trusting to the pine needles to muffle his retreating footsteps. He came out of the woods after twenty minutes on to what was evidently the back lane. As he stood and watched, the large metal gates slowly began to open outward. Wilt got down on all fours and crawled across to the one on the far side, hiding himself behind it.

# Chapter 19

As Sir George's Bentley passed him and the gates were shutting, Wilt whipped across the yard behind it and into the garage where he lurked for a while. Now all he had to do was reach the back door and he'd be safely inside the Hall. The old devil would almost certainly be in a filthy rage on finding one of his guns was missing, though, and he must have heard the shots from it as he drove in. Wilt dusted down his trousers as best he could, climbed the exterior steps to the kitchen and went into the corridor leading into the main part of the house. All he wanted to do was get up to his room and make himself respectable, but this meant first passing the study door. Oh, well, there was nothing else for it. He walked on, only to find

Sir George standing in the doorway with glass in hand, looking positively genial.

'Come along in and have a glass of whisky. You look as if you need one. Been dodging dear Eddie's gunfire, have you?'

Wilt nodded and dropped into the nearest chair.

'You could put it like that,' he said. The magistrate poured neat Scotch into a glass and handed it to him. Then he took a seat opposite Wilt. 'Did the young bastard take a pot-shot at you?'

'No, I was lucky enough to see him before he caught sight of me. He did hit something, though . . . something heavy by the sound of it,' said Wilt, amazed that Sir George was so relaxed about his step-son running around the Estate, firing at anything that moved.

'Probably one of the deer or a wild boar escaped from the farm where they breed them locally. We occasionally get one or two in the woods. Well, it's a start. Next time, with any luck, he'll have a crack at something human.' Sir George smiled at the thought and winked at Wilt, who was midway through a large gulp of whisky and nearly choked.

'If you'll take my advice,' continued Sir George, fetching the decanter, 'you'll stay in the house while dear little Eddie's out and about. Not that he will be much longer. He's bound to kill someone soon.' And in spite of Wilt's protests that he didn't need any more, Sir George filled his glass practically to the brim before refilling his own. 'You see, I've laid an irresistible temp-tation in his way by leaving the gun cabinet unlocked. Cheers!'

He paused for a moment and then began to explain. 'You gave me the idea when you ran off, leaving the cabinet open. You see, if the brute shoots and kills some poor bugger, I'll be only too happy to have him arrested and sent for trial. Hopefully at the Old Bailey.'

He picked up the decanter again. Wilt shook his head, unable to believe what he was hearing.

'Just as you please. Well, as I was about to say, I have never approved of the modern sentencing system. When my father was a JP, a murderer was hanged by the neck until he was dead. All right, the death penalty was abolished, and frankly I approved of that because the occasional poor devil was found to be innocent when it was too late to matter. Then in place of capital punishment there came life imprisonment, which was far better for three reasons. The first was that there was no longer any possibility of an innocent person going to the gallows. The second was that a life sentence used to mean imprisonment until death – with penal servitude thrown in. Harsh work like breaking rocks and excavating quarries. I can tell you, that did no one any harm at all. Third, and best of all, hanging was too damned quick! Blokes who spent the rest of their natural in prison instead had a long time . . . some a very long time . . . to regret their crimes.

'It was only when the namby-pambies came along that things went wrong. Does "life" mean life today? Not at all. For the most part, it's twelve or fifteen years, and with what they call "good behaviour" the scum can be out in eight years or even less, which is the main reason why there are so many murderers around today.'

He reached for the decanter again. In the momentary silence Wilt tried to think of something to say in answer to this tirade, but Sir George hadn't finished yet.

'As for this bloody government . . . they spend billions on things like submarines and waging a war that has nothing to do with us but haven't the money to build enough prisons. The whole country's gone to the dogs. Yes, may as well give up and go and live in a bloody kennel . . .'

Sir George lurched over to his desk and started looking at some papers. Wilt had no wish to trigger another outburst. He could hear Lady Clarissa and Mrs Bale talking in the kitchen. He tiptoed out of the study and up the stairs, ignoring the dubious safety of his bedroom and choosing instead the bathroom opposite it. He had no intention of further discussing with her ladyship Edward's chances of getting into Cambridge. They were obviously nil. He could no more pass A-levels than fly. In fact, it was a wonder he could even write his name. Wilt locked the door behind him and turned off the light in case Lady Clarissa came looking for him.

He hadn't at all liked Mrs Bale's remark about his hostess being 'on heat'. In fact, he disliked the whole situation. As soon as Edward's gun had been safely put back in the cabinet, Wilt intended to find out what the wretched young fellow really wanted to do. On the other hand, he was glad he'd brought those videos about Verdun and the Battle of the Somme with him. They might just hold the lad's attention in the short term – wholesale slaughter seeming likely to appeal. Best of all, Lady Clarissa would get the impression that the ass really was being tutored.

Wilt waited half an hour and then went very quietly down the back stairs to the kitchen. Having checked that Mrs Bale was alone, he asked in a whisper where Lady Clarissa was and learnt that she was getting sozzled on dry martinis in her bedroom.

'Here's your supper,' said the housekeeper, putting a plate of cold chicken and salad in front of him. 'I'll take hers up when she shouts. She's in a sulk because the boyfriend in the garage is still down with 'flu – or more probably that's just an excuse. Everyone knows he's fed up to the back teeth with too much sex and no booze every weekend because of having to drive her . . . Not that I'm one to gossip. And although she's secretly glad her old uncle has died, I think she feels a bit guilty, too. She'll almost certainly sleep it off before she's even eaten.'

'She's obviously an alcoholic,' commented Wilt.

Mrs Bale smiled.

'And a nymphomaniac. That's why she's got her eye on you! I told you she was on heat . . . I mean, the old man can't do anything for her – he thinks she's too thin – besides which he drinks heavily himself. He eats the most awful food too . . . He'd never eat anything like this unless the chicken had been stuffed with something or other and there were game chips fried in lard to go with it.'

'Sounds grim. Anyway she'd better not try anything with me.' Wilt thought it best not to tell Mrs Bale of the encounter he'd already had with Lady Clarissa. 'Eva . . . that's my wife . . . would kill her. She's already warned me off what she calls any "hanky-panky". What puzzles me is why you stay here?'

'Well, like I said, since my old man died, I have hardly any income. The only good thing I can say about them is that they're rich enough to pay me well. So I just put up with their rudeness. And I do have a soft spot for her ladyship, despite everything. Maybe it's on account of her first husband dying like he did . . . or rather like mine did. She doesn't have a very pleasant time of it, that I do know.'

'I'm desperate to get through to Eva and put her off coming to this loony bin, but I don't want either of them to hear me.'

'Why don't you use the phone in his private bathroom then? I can unlock it for you and keep watch too, if you want?'

Despite his misgivings, Wilt agreed to the plan.

After finishing his supper he found himself inside Sir George's private bathroom, which was equipped with phone and computer, as promised, and also with a large padlocked filing cabinet. To Wilt's disgust, the walls were lined with drawings of obscenely fat women getting up to God knows what. He found it difficult to envisage speaking to Eva, surrounded by such ghastly pictures. He needn't have worried: once again there was no answer from her mobile.

He left the bathroom and waved his thanks to Mrs Bale. He walked to the entrance hall and opened the front door, standing on the drawbridge to stare down thoughtfully at the green scum on the surface of the moat. Where the hell had his wife got to? It was already early-evening – surely she had picked up the quads by now.

He decided to wait on the front step until Edward came back. Wilt wanted to ask him a very pertinent question. He didn't have long to wait before he saw the boy crossing the lawn, swinging the gun carelessly in one hand, the other thrust into his trouser pocket. Wilt started to recede cautiously into the house.

'It's all right. This thing's not got a magazine and I'm out of ammunition. Shot a wild boar or something. Didn't kill it. Couldn't see its head. Brought it down, though. Must have got it in a leg, I think.'

Wilt came back out on to the drawbridge.

'Why don't you put that filthy gun back in the

cabinet? If your father finds you with it, there'll be hell to pay. Besides, I want to ask you a question.'

'Are you scared of guns or something? Anyway it's not filthy. I always wipe it clean before I bring it back.'

Edward went inside the house, presumably to the study, and then returned, the gun still swinging by his side.

'What do you want to know?'

'Quite simply this. Do you want to go to university because if you do . . .'

'Of course I don't. That's all Mother's idea. School was awful enough except for sport. I was quite a good boxer until they stopped me doing that because they said I was picking on the juniors. No, university's my idea of hell. I know she's always bleating on about it but I'll never get in.'

Wilt sighed with relief.

'At least you're honest about it,' he said. 'So what do you really want to do for a career?'

'Go into the army. After all, I'm a good shot and I reckon the Commandos would have me. I've been practising abseiling, and swimming up-stream in rivers like the Teme outside Ludlow, and I've done a lot of long-distance running, too. I don't want to go into some smart regiment, I want to see real action. And kill people.'

Wilt gave up. If Edward wanted to be a soldier in some regiment he wasn't going to be easily stopped, although it sounded as though his motives bore some scrutiny. But given that Lady Clarissa was going to pay for him to be tutored at vast expense he'd at least make a show of it. Wilt informed the boy that if he had an A-level or two, it could help secure him a place with the Commando unit. In truth, he wasn't exactly sure what qualifications were needed for that. All that concerned him was getting Edward interested enough to sit down to some lessons. They both needed to get through the next few weeks, so that Eva could have her holiday with the quads and Wilt could make a few thousand quid to tide them over until he could think of how else to continue to pay the school fees.

'Right,' he said, 'let's see what would interest you before I prepare a schedule for each day.'

'What . . . now?'

'Yes, now,' said Wilt firmly, 'before you disappear again. But, first, please lower that gun. Even if it is out of ammunition.'

Edward sat himself down by a small writing table but kept the gun by his side, his finger on the trigger. He continued to press it now and again, and each time he heard the 'click' Wilt squirmed.

'How much do you know about the Falklands War? The Gulf War?'

'I watch TV, you know.'

'The Second World War?'

'I know lots about that. It was Germany versus England and loads of Jews were killed – maybe two million,' Edward declared, proud that he could come up with such a statistic

'Actually, over six million Jews died in the war, and as it progressed almost all the major countries in the world became allies of Britain against Germany,' Wilt corrected him, inwardly feeling close to despair. How on earth was he going to drum any depth of knowledge into this homicidal brat . . . or even begin to convince Lady Clarissa he'd earned his money? He tried another tack.

'Edward, why don't you tell me what you think you know a lot about instead?'

'I know all about Bravo Two-Zero.'

'Bravo Twenty?' Wilt frowned. He hadn't heard of this conflict before.

'Bravo Twenty?' Edward asked, mystified. 'I don't know anything about Twenty whatever it is . . . I only know about Bravo Zero Two. Or was it Zero Bravo Two? Anyway, just goes to show how dated you are. There's a generation gap between me and you. Why don't you catch up and then we can try talking again? In the meantime, I'm going to go and do some more target practice. It's even better at night-time when you can't see. 'Bye, old man.'

And Edward whistled as he strolled out, with his gun propped against one shoulder.

Wilt shook his head glumly. Somehow his pupil had got the better of him and been bloody cheeky too. Oh, well, he was a completely lost cause in any case. All Wilt had to do now was spend some time with the boy, be seen to earn his keep. There was absolutely no prospect of any repeat visit to this household. And as for Bravo Twenty, he wasn't even going to waste his time finding out what that was. Edward had probably dreamt it up after reading some war magazine.

Eva was having a difficult time, too, thought she hadn't lost her way on this occasion. Nor had she run out of petrol. Instead, to avoid being killed by a huge lorry that had been well over the speed limit when it came round a sharp bend on the wrong side of the road, she had driven her car out of its path and up an embankment, through a hedge and over a ditch into a wheat field where it couldn't be seen by passing cars. The quads had screamed with fright and carried on as though the world had ended, but none of them had been hurt.

Trying to ignore their swearing and shrieking, Eva had attempted to re-start the car only to find that it had died on her. She reached into her bag for her mobile phone and when she finally found it, under the rear seat, discovered it wouldn't work. The quads had evidently spent the entire journey texting – goodness knows who since they appeared not to have any friends whatsover – and as a consequence the battery was now completely dead.

Ignoring their protests that if only they were allowed

mobile phones themselves they would have a better knowledge of how long batteries lasted, Eva forced them out of the car and made them follow her back to the road where she climbed through the gap in the hedge and stood waiting for a motorist to stop and help. Unfortunately it was not a busy road. After half an hour the first car passed without apparently noticing them – a feat Eva found difficult to believe given that by now the girls were amusing themselves by sunbathing topless on the verge, despite all her entreaties to them to cover themselves up. The second car to come along was driven by an elderly man who was concentrating on the sharp bend ahead, although he did look some-what shocked by the sight of so much bare flesh on display and, in the event, barely made it round the corner unscathed. By the time the girls had put their clothes back on, grumbling that they would-never-get-a-decent-tan-with-a-prude-for-a-mother and that they never-wanted-to-go-to-some-Godforsaken-Hall-in-the-middle-of-nowhere in the first place, two open-topped sports cars, obviously racing one another, had sped past. Finally, after another hour, a Mini arrived and the driver actually stopped? But having seen the quads he declared that they couldn't possibly all fit into the back seat of such a small car, shook his head and drove on.

'We'll just have to walk to a telephone box,' Eva told the quads who were tired of standing by now and were sprawling on the verge, although thankfully

fully clothed this time. They got up reluctantly and set off, dragging their feet and walking so slowly that Eva finally resorted to blackmail and promised to buy a pay-as-you-go phone for all four of them if they would only get a move on.

Half a mile further on they at last came to a man who was using a sickle to cut back stinging nettles on the other verge. Eva crossed over and enquired how far it was to the next village.

'I'd say about six miles,' he replied. 'Could be a bit further. You lot on a walking tour or something?'

'No, our car is in a wheat field because a huge truck came round a sharp bend on the wrong side of the road and . . .'

'I saw that raving maniac. He's going to kill someone one of these days. He ought to lose his licence. The bugger must have been doing well over seventy at least.'

'He nearly killed us,' said Eva bitterly. 'Is there some-where nearby where I can phone a garage? Like a farmhouse or just a phone box?'

The man shook his head.

'Not hereabouts. I mean, who'd want to live this far out, like – it's the back of beyond. There used to be a phone box, mind you, but that's long gone. There's a farm two miles off behind you, but Mrs Wornsley had a baby three days ago and she's still in Fenscombe Hospital. Her husband's gone over to see how she is.'

Eva looked round at the flat fields seemingly filled with

wheat for as far as the eye could see. The entire land-scape was flat. Only the trees along the roadside broke the monotony. Over to the right she could see the spire of a church and what looked like some roofs, but that was a long way off. She turned back to the man cutting nettles.

'How do you get here?' she asked.

'Well, I work here and live in a cottage next to the Wornsleys. I'm his pig man, see. He drives me into market once a week when he's going, to get my provisions. And I've got a bike too.'

At this point he paused and looked along the road. A tractor with a trailer behind was coming round the bend. The man crossed over and flagged it down without any fuss at all. 'Ah, Sam! You're just the bloke I wanted to see. This lady was forced off the road by that bloke who drives like he's racing. You know, the bugger in the bloody great truck? Her car went into Volly's field and she cant' get it out. You're heading down that way. Be a good chap and take her and these four lookalike girls of hers down there. See if you can get it back on the road for them.' He leant closer to the tractor driver and said in a low voice so that Eva couldn't hear, 'I reckon she'd make it worth your while.'

'All right, I don't mind if I do. You gone into the wheat or something, missus? Tell your girls to hop up in the trailer. Only I wouldn't like old Volly to find his wheat mucked up. He's a very bad-tempered old sod, he is.'

Twenty minutes later, with the aid of the tractor driver's thick tow rope, the Wilts' old Ford had been dragged back through the hedge, scratched but not too badly damaged. At first the engine still refused to start, but after Sam had opened the bonnet and poked around a bit it coughed.

'I'd better take you down to Jim Bodle to check this over,' Sam told them. 'He's good with motors. I'm not.' The quads got back into the trailer and he set off towing the Ford behind. Several miles down the road he pulled into a garage forecourt. A man in blue overalls came out of the work area while the quads disappeared into the small shop alongside.

'What's the trouble?' the garage man asked.

'Don't know. Wouldn't start. Not a tick over until I fiddled a bit, but it still isn't running right. Ran into old Volly's wheat field but I can't see as there's anything obviously wrong.'

'What was it doing in a field?'

Eva intervened.

'I swerved to avoid being killed,' she said. 'A great big lorry came round a bend on the wrong side of the road, driven far too fast, so I drove through a hedge and this kind man came along and pulled the car out.' As she spoke, the man called Jim opened the bonnet and peered inside.

'Don't see anything bust in here. Must be underneath.' He poked about a bit, shining his torch beneath the car. When he came out he was grinning. 'Next time

213

you haul a car out of a field, Sam, pull it from the front instead of ploughing it backwards. You've blocked the exhaust with earth and straw good and proper. I'll soon fix that.'

Eva went off to find the quads. Twenty minutes later, after she'd paid for various breakages in the shop and retrieved most of the goods they'd secreted about their persons, they were on their way again with Sam and Jim £20 apiece better off. More than could be said for the shop-keeper who had to close for the rest of the day in order to recover from his ordeal. As they drove off, the quads could be seen giggling in the back of the car. They had learnt yet another way of putting a car temporarily out of action and were now so delayed they were going to be forced to stop somewhere for the night. This holiday was already exceeding their expectations and was certainly a million times better than the boring old Lake District.

# Chapter 20

Lady Clarissa got out of bed feeling slightly better for her long drink-fuelled sleep and went into the bathroom, mentally reviewing the way many of her problems were resolving themselves. In fact, if only she could get George to accept Uncle Harold's being interred on the Estate, she would have very little left to worry about. Now that Henry Wilt was tutoring him, she felt sure Edward would get into a Cambridge college. And from the time she had spent with him since he'd arrived, she was convinced that the tutor was interested in her and that – more importantly – he would make a good lover. He'd undoubtedly be a more interesting one than the garage man, who was a little unimaginative except for when car engines were involved. And from all that Wilt had said, it did seem as though Eva was unduly obsessed with their daughters.

Clarissa couldn't imagine that the Wilts had a sexually fulfilling married life. Nor could she imagine that they had much by way of money. She'd seen Mrs Wilt's eyes light up when she'd told them she would pay fifteen hundred pounds a week with a bonus if Edward got into Porterhouse. Uncle Harold's death had actually worked out quite neatly for her, financially speaking: she'd spent far more staying at the Black Bear for her weekend visits than she was paying Wilt per week. Not that she was really bothered about money. After all, she had married Gadsley for his wealth and her first husband's death had left her fairly well off in her own right. She climbed out of the bath, dried herself and got dressed, feeling in a thoroughly good mood.

The same could not be said of Eva. She was in a thoroughly bad mood. In addition to the crises she had already been through on her way to and from the school, she had had to spend another night in a hotel. Although the quads had promised to be on their very best behaviour and she had made absolutely certain the mini-bar in their room was locked and bolted, she had been woken up by the most terrible screeching in the early hours of the morning. It took her a while to realise where it was coming from, and then even longer to persuade the poor woman who had woken to find four girls crawling across her bedroom floor not to call the police. The girls claimed they had gone downstairs to see if they could borrow some books to read and had then returned to the wrong room in error, but that didn't really explain why Josephine seemed to be wearing the woman's make-up and Penelope one of her necklaces.

Eva had spent the rest of the night trying to sleep on a chair in their bedroom and in the morning had found herself paying for the woman's room bill as well as their own. Half an hour later, when she looked into the rear-view mirror and realised that the girls had stolen all of the hotel towels and two of the pillows, she was almost tempted to drive on, thinking that at least they had got their money's worth, but in the end thought better of it and turned the car round.

The last straw was trying to negotiate her way along the deliberately tortuous driveway to the Hall. Eva had completely forgotten Wilt's instructions to use the rear entrance and had instead taken the road from the main gate. She'd made dozens of wrong turns, continually finding herself at dead ends, and had had to back up so many times that even the quads fell silent.

Crossing the drawbridge at last, she told them to stay in the car while she went over to pull the bell rope. She had expected Lady Clarissa to greet her at the front door but instead a youth carrying a gun asked her what she wanted, in a tone that suggested he thought she had come to sell something.

'I'm Mrs Wilt and we have been invited to stay.'

'Nobody told me,' Edward said. 'I'll go and get Mrs Bale. She'll know.' He disappeared into the Hall and presently, after staring down with some alarm at the water below the drawbridge, Eva heard footsteps approaching. When she looked up, she was glad to see what appeared to be a sensible – if rather large – woman standing before her. Mrs Bale introduced herself and apologised for not having answered the bell herself.

'I just hope Edward wasn't rude to you,' she said, eyeing the four teenage girls in the car.

'Oh, that was Edward? I had an idea he would be a little younger. Well, he wasn't particularly polite actually,' said Eva. 'Seemed to think I had come to sell something.'

'He's like that. Thinks anyone coming to the front door is a salesperson and wants to scare them off. Anyway, come down to the kitchen. I've just made a pot of tea.'

'Thank you. I would love a cup. And perhaps some lemonade or squash for the girls? But is my husband about anywhere if he isn't with Edward? And Lady Clarissa?'

'In bed, I'm afraid,' Mrs Bale said as they went down the passage, the quads gaping at the ancient portraits on the walls as they followed.

'In bed? Why? With whom? Whatever is the matter?'

'Well, I'm not one to gossip . . . but you'll find soon enough. Too much to drink, as usual.'

'Oh, no! How disgraceful! I don't know what to say. I feel terrible. Whatever must Sir George make of it?'

'Oh, he'll no doubt shout and yell a bit but he'll get over it. Now don't distress yourself so much. These things happen. Especially in this house.'

'I can't bear it! I just can't bear it!'

'Please don't get upset, there's really no need. In fact, I'm certain I heard noises a bit earlier. I should think she'll be up any minute and will come straight down to see you.'

'What, Lady Clarissa's in bed as well?' said Eva, with some alarm, wondering what on earth was going on. 'Did they both drink too much? Please don't tell me that they're in bed together . . .' She broke off abruptly, only too aware of the girls listening with great interest.

'What? Of course Lady Clarissa is in bed. Who on earth did you think I was talking about? Oh . . . I see. She's in bed on her own, of course. Well, unless Sir George is with her. Which I very much doubt.'

'I feel so stupid,' Eva protested as they entered the kitchen, the quads nodding their agreement unseen behind her. 'But I am sorry to hear about Lady Clarissa.'

'Well, she's had a recent death in the family. Her uncle. She's been consoling herself with dry martinis and the like.'

'Oh, dear. How dreadful. I am sorry. It must be the mourning period.'

Mrs Bale nodded. 'I'm afraid so. Morning, noon and night. I'm sure I don't know how she keeps her figure. Or her liver, come to that.'

At this point Eva gave up and quietly drank her tea. When she'd finished Mrs Bale said, 'I'd better show you where you and your daughters are going to stay. I think you're lucky not to be in the house. It's quieter down there, and I've fixed the fridge and the stove, although I'm hoping that you will take supper with me in here tonight. Your husband does. He doesn't like the atmosphere in the dining room.'

'I'm glad to hear it,' said Eva. 'I wonder where he is now if he isn't in bed. Which he isn't,' she added quickly. 'I'd expected him to meet me.'

'The last I saw of him, he was walking across the lawn past the pond and taking off his shirt. I expect he's gone for a dip.'

After they'd inspected the cottage, Eva excused herself to Mrs Bale and hurried over to the lake, leaving the girls to amuse themselves in the woods. She soon spotted Wilt, lying on the grass reading, and ran over to him, highly agitated.

'Oh, Henry,' she wailed. 'Something too awful has happened.'

'I know. Her uncle has died.'

'It's far worse than that. It looks as though the girls are definitely going to be expelled from St Barnaby's.'

Wilt glared at her.

'As I repeatedly told you, it was bound to happen sooner or later. They should have stayed at the Convent. Anyway, that lets me off the hook here.'

'And what's that supposed to mean?'

'Quite simply that I no longer have to waste my time trying to explain modern European history to someone who can barely read and whose only ambition seems to be to kill people. Which, as luck would have it, seems to be his step-father's ambition for him too.'

'You're just being selfish! We've only this minute arrived and the girls are looking forward to their holiday. And in any case, what about the fifteen hundred pounds a week she's paying? We'd have to pay it back.'

'Oh, no. I was sensible enough not to accept any payment until I'd had a good look at the useless adolescent. Anyway, why are the girls going to be expelled? That's more to the point.'

Eva's face reddened.

'I don't like to say,' she muttered.

'Ah, but I want to hear. In fact, I insist.'

Eva still hesitated. Even the headmistress had been too embarrassed to say it and had handed her another letter as they left.

'Go on then,' Wilt said impatiently.

'Gross indecency,' she whispered.

'Hardly surprising. Now that's not something they got from my side of the family. From what you've told me about that aunt of yours who worked in a pub close to an American air base, I got the distinct impression that she was a . . .'

'Don't say anything about her!'

'All right. Then you tell me what gross indecencies the quads look like being chucked out for.'

'I don't know exactly.'

Eva hesitated again.

'The Headmistress said it had something to do with a condom.'

'Something to do with a condom? I can only think of one thing to do with a condom and I hope to God it wasn't that. Did she say what?'

'I didn't like to ask her. She seemed very angry.'

A shot resounded from the wood.

'What on earth was that?'

'Just Edward shooting something.'

'You mean, he uses real bullets?'

'Of course he does. I've spent the last twenty-four hours trying to get hold of you to warn you against coming here with the girls at all, but your blasted phone hasn't been working. That boy is both fully armed and dangerous and you should all get out of here pronto. If you want the quads to be killed – and from the sound of things that's not a wholly unattractive idea – just stick around.'

'Don't be ridiculous, Henry. But what on earth's he shooting at? And why has a young boy like that been allowed a gun?'

'He's been allowed a gun because his ghastly step-father is utterly brainless, just like his step-son. And as for what he's shooting: any blasted thing that moves. I ought to know. I was coming back from the village and saw him in action. He didn't even know what he'd fired at. Told Sir George it was a deer or possibly a wild boar.'

'A wild boar? But aren't they terribly dangerous?'

'Not half as dangerous as Edward,' said Wilt, who was getting to his feet when suddenly a series of shots rang out.

'Oh my God, why didn't Lady Clarissa warn us?' Eva squawked in terror and clutched at him. 'The girls have gone to play in the woods. How could you have let this happen!'

She broke off at the sound of loud screaming. The quads were emerging from the trees and running towards them.

'How the hell did I know? If I'd been told the mad bastard went round firing at just about anything, I'd never have come within a mile . . .' Wilt was interrupted by the arrival of the quads.

'Mummy, someone's been shooting at us!' shouted Emmeline, shoving herself between her warring parents.

'Well, get into the cottage,' Eva told them. 'As fast as you can.'

Wilt and she dashed after them.

'Now start packing. We're not staying here a moment longer.'

'We only just unpacked!'

'Well, that will make it easier, won't it?'

Wilt smiled to himself. He was delighted to be leaving.

'I suppose we'll be going home. I'll drive as you must be exhausted.'

'Certainly not. We'll find a nice hotel by the sea and stay there.'

'You realise this means they'll definitely be going back to the Convent? Provided, of course, the staff there don't find out they were going to be expelled for gross indecency – especially involving condoms! Are you sure we can afford a hotel?' asked Wilt, brightening up nevertheless at the thought of getting away from this mad house.

'What do you mean? I didn't say you were going to stop tutoring that wretched boy. I said the girls and I were leaving. You'll still be earning fifteen hundred quid a week.'

'Fine, go and leave me here then!' said Wilt angrily. 'I'm merely the financial provider for the rest of you. Oh, well, if I get shot, I daresay you'll be a rich widow.'

'Well, you are insured by the Council. So, yes, I would be quite comfortably off. And, of course, I could also sue the Gadsleys, I suppose, and get enormous damages out of them . . .'

'Well, thanks a lot! I may as well go and find the silly fucker right now and ask him to finish me off.'

'Language, Henry! Not in front of the girls.'

'But it's all right for you to talk about their father being killed in front of them?'

'That was merely speculation. It was your fault for bringing up the subject in the first place.'

Wilt kept his trap shut. He could have said what he really thought: that Eva was the one who had sucked up to Lady Clarissa and got him this infernal so-called job. In fact, if he or any of the quads did get hurt she'd be the one to blame, but he'd keep that to himself for the time being and hope to hell nothing happened. She was in a foul mood already. The sooner she and the quads were out of here the better.

# Chapter 21

Lady Clarissa was in the process of making her way down to the kitchen when she heard the volley of shots although she hadn't recognised what they portended. In any case, she was used to Edward messing about with guns. All the same she went over to the landing window where she was surprised to see four identical girls dashing into the gardener's cottage, followed by Eva and Wilt. For a moment she was stunned before it dawned on her what Eva had meant when she'd spoken about 'the quads', only occasionally naming one of them. Clarissa had failed to take in the fact that the Wilts had quadruplets. Maybe it wasn't so surprising. Sir George talked so frequently about quads in Cambridge colleges and ducking unpopular undergraduates in the quad pond that Eva's use of the word in a family context had escaped her.

Their presence compounded her problem with her husband. Having no children of his own, Sir George hated almost all young people. He had certainly never made any secret of his dislike for Edward, frequently referring to him as 'that verminous son of yours' and on one particularly infamous occasion expressing the hope that 'the swine would fall off a bloody turret'. She couldn't imagine what his reaction would be to having four identical teenage girls squealing and running around the place. It didn't bear thinking about.

She would simply have to impress on the Wilts that the girls were not to come anywhere near the Hall. But, much to her surprise, by the time she reached the cottage there was nobody there. Nor was there any sign that anyone ever had been: no suitcases, no possessions. Back in the house she consulted Mrs Bale.

'They've left in a hurry,' she was told. 'Mrs Wilt said she wasn't having her daughters shot at by Edward.'

'But he surely can't have been shooting at them?'

'I suppose he might have been firing across the road. He frequently does . . .'

'What? When people are passing? He might kill someone.'

'That's what we're all afraid of,' said Mrs Bale with monumental patience. 'Why do you think I always walk down to the village by the back way, where there are houses? It's because it's much safer.'

'Well, of course, I must talk to Edward about it. The sooner he is off to university the better. I assume Mr Wilt didn't leave too?'

'I don't think so. I went up to his room a few minutes ago and his things are still there, which I assume means he's coming back. The last I saw of him he was driving his family off with their luggage. And he looked proper grim about it and all.'

After some wrong turns, the tedium of which was not helped by the quads moaning away in the back about how they'd quite like a gun themselves and that boys had all the fun, Wilt arrived with Eva and the girls outside a hotel on the far side of the village. It overlooked the sea and a sandy beach.

'I must say, it looks very expensive,' he commented when Eva said it was just exactly the sort of hotel she wanted to stay in.

'I'm sure it is,' she replied. 'I intend to send the bill to that beastly boy's mother.'

'What? To Lady Clarissa? Do you really imagine she'll pay it?'

'If she doesn't she'll regret it, I can tell you.'

Wilt sighed. He was used to Eva's threats which were normally directed at him, but this was way over the top. The irony of it was that his wife had been sucking up to Clarissa for months purely to get her to invite the Wilt family to stay at Sandystones Hall.

example of how unfunny this book



'And what do you expect me to do all day?' he asked as they carried the suitcases up the steps and into the hotel. 'Bond with the quads on the beach?'

Eva turned on him.

'Bond? Certainly not. You're not tying them up, no matter how badly they behave! Anyway, as I've already told you, you're to go back and earn your fifteen hundred quid a week tutoring that murderous lout so he gets into Cambridge.'

'Like hell I am! In the first place he's never going to get into Cambridge or any other university. And secondly, I don't want to be shot by the idiot. Get that into your head.'

'Don't you dare speak to me like that,' Eva snapped.

But Wilt had had enough.

'I'll speak any way I choose. You got us into this bloody mess by sending the hell-cats to a school we could barely afford, and when they get threatened with expulsion you still expect me to spend my summer with a psychopath.'

'You'll have to talk to the Gadsleys and get them to sort out the boy. They can't allow him to go on behaving like this. Besides he ought to be busy having lessons with you.'

'Try telling Edward that. Since I've been there all he's done is wander the woods trying to destroy things. The day after I arrived, I was minding my own business when I saw him attack something hidden in the long grass when he hadn't a clue what it was. And you heard the bastard firing round after round near the quads. Do you honestly expect me to go back into that mad house?'

'Yes, I do. In fact, I insist upon it. We've got to have that salary. I've spent all our money coming down here and now we have to pay for this hotel. You've been there a week already: that's fifteen hundred pounds you're owed. You're going to stay there at least until you've been paid.'

Wilt gave up. He'd never seen Eva in such a state. He felt too tired to explain that if they all left for home now, there wouldn't be any hotel bill to be paid.

'Oh, all right. If you want to be a widow, don't blame me,' he muttered, and went back to the car.

'And where do you think you're going?' Eva shouted.

'Where you want me to go, of course. Back to the mad house,' he called as he drove off. Left behind, his wife marched into the hotel and asked for two rooms – only to be told that all of them were taken.

'There are some guest houses in the village. You could try there,' the receptionist told her with a disdainful expression.

Wilt stopped off at the pub where he'd had beer and sandwiches and ordered a whisky and soda, ignoring the barmaid's glare. What the hell was he going to do? It was all very well leaving Eva and the quads in the safety of what was obviously an expensive hotel, but he didn't much fancy returning to the Hall to be shot at by blasted Edward or to spend the next few weeks dodging his mother's amorous advances. In any case, what was the point in Eva's landing them with some enormous hotel bill when they had a perfectly good home to go back to in Ipford? And God knows what those blasted she-devils would get up to on the beach: he'd bet they would spend a fortune on slot machines and bikinis, and most likely end up earning ASBOs for molesting pensioners at bus-stops.

Over lunch in the pub dining room he continued to try and make up his mind. There had to be some way of getting out of this mess Eva had got him into. If only the damned woman had given birth to one blasted baby. But no, like everything else she'd ever done, she'd gone clean over the top and had four diabolically ingenious daughters all in one go. After the recurring thought that he'd been insane to marry the wretched, sex-obsessed woman, Wilt contemplated the future. He would obviously have to return to Sandystones Hall, if only to collect the clothes and belongings he had left there. Then again, however poisonously he felt towards Eva, he couldn't abandon her and the quads at that damnably swanky hotel without any means of support. God alone knew what rooms cost there. His wife's threat to send the bill to Lady Clarissa was, in all likelihood a bluff, but even if it wasn't, it might all too easily backfire and land the family in unpayable debt. There had to be some way of preventing that. His thoughts went round and round.

Wilt ordered another whisky and soda to give him the Dutch courage to go back and tell the Gadsleys to their faces that the idiot Edward hadn't a celluloid rat's hope in hell of passing an A-level exam, let alone of getting into any university. At least he was sure Sir George would side with him even if Clarissa kicked up one hell of a fuss, as she undoubtedly would. Wilt paid up, enduring yet another sarcastic comment from the barmaid when he rounded up his bill with a fifty-pence tip.

He set off in the car and drove towards the safer back way to the Hall. But much to his surprise he saw that the main gates were open and a big black car was in the process of driving in. Wilt hadn't any intention of following it and drove past, studiously looking away just in case one of the Gadsleys was a passenger. He parked up for a while and then, once he was certain the coast was clear, drove through the rear gate and was presently in the kitchen discussing with Mrs Bale the big car he'd seen turning into the fearsome road through the woods.

'Oh, that will be the coffin,' she told him cheerfully. 'Didn't you know?'

'Coffin? I most certainly didn't. Has some poor devil been shot?'

Mrs Bale laughed.

'He was certainly shot at, but a long time ago. You wouldn't have known.'

'Let me guess . . . He wouldn't by any chance have been a colonel with a wooden leg, would he?'

For a moment the secretary gaped at him and then burst out laughing.

'You're spot on. How did you guess?'

'To be truthful about it, I overheard Lady Clarissa begging Sir George to let Uncle Harold be buried here on the Estate, and once I realised it was a hearse I'd seen I put two and two together.'

'I hadn't realised you'd met the uncle, poor old sod that he was. He just hated that home she made him go into.'

'I hadn't met him but I know quite a lot about him simply because my wife is the greatest damned gossip I have the misfortune to know. And a snob into the bargain. She loved her little tête-à-têtes with Lady Clarissa. Why else do you think I landed up here, trying to teach her moronic son?'

'Oh, yes, I see. I presume you haven't enlightened your wife about their having no real claim to the title?'

'Goodness, no! If Eva knew that she could just as easily buy herself one, I'd never hear the end of it.'

'Has she gone back to Ipford?'

'Like hell she has. She and the quads are spending what must amount to a fortune in a very smart hotel on the other side of the village. At least, they were about to when I was sent back here in the hope I'd get shot.'

Mrs Bale raised her eyebrows.

'You don't sound too pleased with her. I mean, does she always order you about?'

'Since she had the quads, I have to say yes. Not that I invariably obey her commands. Anyway I'll go up to my room and brood for a bit.' He moved towards the door and then turned back. 'Is Clarissa about anywhere? I've decided to tell her the truth about Edward's chances of getting into university.'

'The last time I saw her she was going down to the family graveyard, presumably to wait for the coffin.'

# Chapter 22

Eva had finally found two spare rooms in a guest house. She was already cursing Wilt for having taken the car. Without it she was stuck. While the hotel had at least had a restaurant as well as a courtesy minibus, the guest house had nothing and there was nowhere to eat within walking distance. She didn't even have the telephone number of Sandystones Hall to let Henry know that she'd had to move. Having called directory enquiries she had been given two numbers, both of which she had tried several times only to find they appeared to be permanently engaged. To add to her troubles the landlady had come upstairs twice already to complain about the din the quads were making in their room next-door.

'If you don't stop those girls making such a dreadful noise, I'm afraid I'll have to ask you to leave,' she said. 'I have a permanent resident, an old lady who has had a very serious operation recently from which she's recuperating.'

'Oh, God,' muttered Eva, trying to think what on earth to do. It looked as though she'd have to go back to Sandystones Hall if only to collect the car since she couldn't reach Wilt to tell him to bring it back. What the hell was she going to do with the quads? If she left them behind she'd probably get back to find that they'd all been thrown out. The only thing she could think of was to leave them outside the gate of the Hall and hope they could stay out of trouble there for half an hour.

Having come to this decision, she silenced the quads for the umpteenth time and called for a taxi to take her back up to Sandystones Hall. By the time she got there she had changed her mind about leaving the quads. They had spent the entire journey in a sulk at not being allowed to stay in the guest house on their own and were now threatening to hitchhike all the way home if this holiday was going to be so boring. Eva apologised to the driver for their terrible manners and tried to hide the rip they had made in a seat with her coat. 'Would you please go in through the back gate? I want to collect our car and get straight out of here again, ideally without being seen.'

'You won't get in unless you know the security code,'

he told her. 'They're very strict about that and I don't know it. We'd best go round to the front door.'

Very reluctantly, Eva agreed.

'Just go slowly,' she warned. 'It's terribly dangerous.'

The taxi driver said he knew that all too well and his cab had several dents in it to prove it. When she heard this Eva felt a bit better about the damage to the inside of the taxi: at least it wasn't a new one.

Fifteen minutes later they had reached the Hall and were staring with some surprise at the hearse parked in front of it with the outline of a coffin just visible inside.

'Looks like someone's bought it at long last,' the driver muttered. 'I've said it before . . . they should have done something drastic about that blasted young maniac. Spoilt he is. Mind you, they're a queer bunch altogether.'

He got out of the taxi and went over to one of the pall-bearers to have a word with him.

Eva knew perfectly well who was in the coffin but she let the quads go on thinking that someone on the Estate had been shot and killed. Perhaps that would quieten them down a bit.

For Wilt the arrival of the hearse changed nothing. At least Eva's staying at the hotel would give him a chance to recuperate alone at home from the horrors of the past week. After looking in vain for Lady Clarissa to tell her he'd had enough, he'd decided simply to leave a note and his phone number. Since then he had been busy packing and getting ready to leave this place and all its mad inhabitants for good. He went down to the kitchen to tell Mrs Bale he was definitely leaving, though not where he was going.

'I can't say I blame you. I'd do the same myself if I had the money and there was a better job to be had round here, but I have a very small house with a mortgage so I couldn't sell . . . and besides, at my time of life I've good friends here and I've never lived anywhere else. Still, I'm sorry you're leaving. Is your wife going home with you?'

'I've tried ringing her but there was no answer. She's doubtless too busy having a wonderful time with the quads in that luxurious hotel. I've a good mind to leave it to her to explain why I'm leaving to Lady Clarissa: Eva got me into this idiotic situation. By the way, is the parson already down there? I saw a taxi arrive just now.'

'Oh, no,' said Mrs Bale with a laugh. 'They don't bother with a priest . . . or haven't since I've been here. Sir George dons a parson's collar and paraphernalia and conducts the service himself. Claims he has the right to as head of the family, in the family chapel. I wouldn't know whether it's legal or not.'

'But are they really just going to stick the old man in the ground down there? It doesn't sound right to me,' said Wilt.

'I agree, but apparently that's always been the custom

in the family. Of course, they don't bury strangers in the graveyard, only close relatives.'

'Extraordinary. It certainly makes the place more interesting . . . but not interesting enough to make me want to stay, I'm afraid. And my advice to you is to find yourself a bullet-proof vest if you really are stuck here.'

Wilt said goodbye to Mrs Bale. Feeling only a twinge of guilt at leaving without telling the Gadsleys, he took his suitcase out to the car and presently was driving up the family lane and out through the gate on to the road.

Behind him the late Colonel Harold Rumble's coffin was being lifted out of the hearse and carried round to the family graveyard. At the gate Wilt thought he caught the sound of 'Abide With Me' being sung but decided he must have imagined it.

As he left the Hall by the back road Eva was making her way in at the front, having made the quads swear they would sit quietly on the lawn and wait for her. Once in the house she found her way to the kitchen where a surprised Mrs Bale almost dropped the tea things.

'I'm afraid that if it's Mr Wilt you're after, you've just missed him.'

'Missed him? Did he tell you where he was going?'

'No, I'm afraid he didn't.'

'Well, didn't you ask him?'

'No, I'm afraid I didn't.'

'Why didn't you?'

'What business is it of mine?'

'But didn't he even mention whether he was coming to see me and the girls?'

'No, he didn't. I've told you that already, several times,' the secretary replied brusquely. She found Eva's manner decidedly irritating and by now understood Wilt's simmering resentment. It was one thing being browbeaten by Sir George – at least she was paid well to put up with his rudeness – but she wasn't going to endure any more of this obnoxious woman's intrusive questioning, which almost amounted to an interrogation. And Eva's next question definitely did.

'Did my husband make love to Clarissa? I want an honest answer.'

Mrs Bale decided to get her own back for this impertinence.

'Of course he did. I mean, after all, they were in neighbouring bedrooms and your husband is a very attractive man. You can hardly pretend Sir George is of an age to satisfy – sexually, I mean – a woman as beautiful as her ladyship, so what else did you expect? That she really paid him a large salary to tutor her idiot son? I mean, that's pretty unlikely, isn't it?'

It was a speechless and furious Eva who stormed upstairs and threw open the door of the first bedroom she came to. And sure enough there was Lady Clarissa, staring at her reflection in a huge mirror.

She was dressed in her panties and little else. When she spotted Eva's reflection, she turned to stare at her in person.

'What the hell do you want?' she snapped.

'You've been sleeping with my husband, you whore!' spluttered Eva, unfortunately gaping at Clarissa's breasts as she did so.

'How dare you burst in here making accusations! And what in God's name are you staring at? Haven't you seen a pair of breasts before? You're not bisexual, are you?'

'Certainly not! You really are disgusting.' Eva hesitated for a moment. 'What I want to know is, where is Henry? He's obviously just got out of bed with you so you must know where he is.'

Lady Clarissa didn't bother to correct her. 'I've no idea where your wretched husband is, and if you bothered to look after yourself like I do you might be better able to hold on to him. Just get out, will you, or I'll be late for the funeral.'

Eva went slowly back downstairs. Her worst fears had been confirmed: Henry was an adulterer. She looked around for Mrs Bale but the secretary/housekeeper had made herself scarce. She'd had enough of Mrs Wilt.

Eva went outside to gather up the quads and take them back to the guest house, but despite their promises there was no sign of them. She tried quizzing the cab driver but he said they must have gone off when he had his back turned, talking to the pall-bearers, and

243

anyway he wasn't a bloody child minder and she should take better care in the first place.

At this final straw a distraught Eva sank to the ground and began to wail.

The quads had grown bored of staring across the lawn at the yew hedge and wondering what was happening behind it. They had never seen an actual burial, only the occasional brief film clips on the television of coffins being lowered on straps into oblong holes outside churches or disinterred in autopsy cases where murder was suspected. Here was an opportunity to see the real thing. So while Eva searched for Wilt they made their way cautiously down to the family grave-yard, mindful of Edward's propensity to shoot anything that moved.

They dashed into the kitchen garden and climbed the wall into the field behind it. From there they crept along behind the cottage and a hedge towards the pine wood beyond the lake and then around the boat house. In short, they kept well out of sight and spoke in whispers when they spoke at all. Finally they reached the rear of the tiny unconsecrated chapel which was itself hidden by the yew hedge surrounding the cem-etery. All the same, they took the precaution of taking it in turns to lie on the ground and keep watch at the entrance to the graveyard while the others exam-ined the coffin. Just looking at it soon grew boring. They started to wonder whether the coffin lid was nailed shut: much to their delight it wasn't. When – after much daring and goading on of one another – they opened the lid there was a corpse inside.

'Bloody hell! I can't believe they left it open.'

'That'll be so as people can say a proper goodbye to him. You know, like you see on the telly. God, he's ugly, though. And, look, he's got a wooden leg, hasn't he?'

'I bet you it's that old uncle Mummy told us about in Ipford,' said Josephine with some disappointment. She'd hoped it might really be someone who had been shot and killed on the Estate. Or someone rotting away at least.

'He's a colonel in the army.'

'Was. I don't think he'll be doing any more fighting.'

'With that wooden leg, I don't see how he could,' said Samantha. 'And anyway he's too old.'

At that moment Emmeline ran up from her hiding place by the hedge. 'Quick, shut that lid! There's two people coming down, arguing their heads off.'

A moment later the coffin was shut and the quads were on the ground, keeping well behind the chapel where they couldn't be seen but could hear everything that was being said. The man who had to be Sir George was obviously in an ugly mood.

'He was not a Gadsley – how many times do I have to tell you? I'm not going to conduct a ceremony for someone who isn't related to the family. And I don't care what you say about getting the local Vicar in, I'm not having that old fool buried here and that's that. You should have had him cremated as I told you. In fact, I've half a mind to set light to the blasted box here and now. Except that would mean his rotten ashes would be here on the Estate.'

'Don't be ridiculous! Someone would see the smoke and wonder what was going on. I can't see why you're being so horrible, George. He's my uncle and I'm your wife so he is family. You'll be telling me next that Edward isn't family.'

'Eddie? Christ, no, he bloody well isn't,' spluttered an irate Sir George. 'If he were in my family I'd have had him castrated years ago, to make sure his useless genes didn't carry on down the line. He's not going to be buried here either, when and if we're fortunate enough to be rid of him.

'Now listen, Clarissa, you'll do what any sensible person would and go and arrange something with the Vicar in the village. Either that or have the old bugger cremated. That's what you always said you were going to do when the time came.'

'Oh, you are so vile, George. I know I did, but I changed my mind.'

'You haven't a mind to change,' he snarled. 'Get this into your head. I am not having the cemetery defiled by burying someone outside the family in it. And that's my final word on the matter.'

Peering round the side of the chapel, the quads saw him stride off.

Lady Clarissa leant against the coffin, crying audibly

for five minutes, and then she followed him. When they had both gone the quads came out of their hiding place.

'Lady Clarissa was crying,' Emmeline said. 'And that horrible man didn't care.'

'Well, she's horrible too,' said Josephine. 'I overheard that fat woman telling Mummy she's been having sex with Dad. Every night,' she added, embellishing the story a bit to make it more salacious. 'Why don't we teach them both a lesson?'

'How?'

'Let's pinch the body, and then he'll think she's gone ahead and had it buried here in the cemetery and she'll think he's burned it!'

'All right, but where can we hide it?'

'I suppose we could bury it. Neither of them would find it then and all hell would break loose.'

'But we'd never dig a grave big enough to hold it,' Emmeline objected. 'I mean, that coffin's huge.'

'We could take the dead body out, so it would look like it had been stolen.'

'Who on earth wants to touch a dead body? I know I don't.'

Samantha spoke up next.

'Don't be such a stupid coward. All we'd need would be some plastic gloves or something. That way there would be no need actually to touch the body, and there'd be no fingerprints if anybody did find him.'

'I still don't see what we're going to do about digging the grave.'

'Don't have to dig one,' said Josephine. 'We can always take him into the woods and make a big pile and do what Sir George wanted to do.'

'You mean, burn him? How horrible.'

'It isn't. They cremate dead bodies all over the country every day. A lot of people put it in their wills that they don't want to be buried at all. They want their ashes scattered over their gardens. Or somewhere beautiful.'

'That's true. I read about some man the other day who wants to be taken to the moon and scattered there when he kicks the bucket.'

'Silly sod. He'd just float away, wouldn't he?'

'OK, we'll burn him. But we'll need some matches.'

'Check no one's coming, I'm going to the cottage. There was a packet of plastic gloves in the kitchen and there are bound to be matches as well,' Samantha told the others.

She set off, keeping well under cover, and twenty minutes later had returned with eight disposable gloves and a matchbook.

At the gate to the graveyard Josephine called out, 'Something weird's going on up by the drawbridge. They have two furniture vans and men are unloading tables and chairs. Anyone would think they were going to have a garden party.'

'For a funeral? Don't be silly.'

'Well come and see for yourselves.'

The other three did, lying one at a time where she had lain. Then they all went behind the hedge.

'More likely the guests will be mourners coming for the burial which isn't going to happen.'

'With coloured umbrellas?'

'No, I have to admit, that's odd,' agreed Emmeline. 'Now if they were black it would make more sense.'

'I bet it's the food bit and not the mourners. They'd have to set up first and they might need brollies in case of rain.'

'Oh, well, never mind that,' said Samantha. 'We've got to get the body out very quickly and hide it somewhere. We can come back later and take his uniform off.'

'How gruesome. Why can't we burn him with it on?' asked Penelope.

'Because his medals and belt buckle and cap badge are made of metal and it doesn't burn.'

'What are we going to do with his clothes and the wooden leg?' Emmy asked.

'We can't leave them here or anywhere nearby. Someone is bound to find them.'

'The wooden leg will burn, won't it, stupid? And as for the clothes, I suppose we could take them out to sea in a plastic bag and weigh them down with a rock. Nobody would find them there,' Josephine declared.

'Except for a skin diver,' Samantha replied. 'Or someone fishing with a hook and line.'

'Please, can we just get on with it before someone comes and catches us? We'd never get all his stuff back to the guest house without Mummy seeing us, in any case. We'll just have to bury it all somewhere they won't think of looking. We don't need to decide where now.'

'There's no need to be so bossy! OK, let's see if we can move him.'

They pulled the late Colonel out of the coffin quite easily and disappeared with him into the thick stand of pines behind the chapel

# Chapter 23

Up at the Hall Eva was hoarse from calling for the quads and had begun to think they might have gone off in search of the beach. She'd had to borrow money from Mrs Bale to pay the taxi driver, who'd turned quite nasty when she had told him she'd pay him as soon as her husband came back.

'All I'm telling you is that I'm adding all this waiting time and I'll bloody well get my solicitor to take action if . . .'

There was no need for him to go on. Eva had dashed back to the kitchen where, to her relief, Mrs Bale had re-emerged and asked if Wilt had returned. Mrs Bale had said she scarcely thought so given that his car was not parked in the yard. She was about to say she could

TOM SHARPE

understand why, with a wife like Eva, but changed her mind because the woman was on the verge of tears. A moment later she was crying properly and tears were coursing down her cheeks.

'I don't know where my girls are and Henry's gone off with the car and I've got no money . . . We should never have come.'

'All right, I'll lend you enough to pay the taxi out of the housekeeping tin, but I'll have to tell her ladyship. She may want to deduct the charge from this month's earnings.' Eva gave another great sob and Mrs Bale felt even guiltier for misleading her over Lady Clarissa and Wilt. 'Don't worry, it's going to be all right. Now, it's about time we both had something to eat. I've got a steak and kidney pudding which needs warming, and you'll feel better after a spot of gin and tonic. I know I would.'

After paying the driver, Eva let Mrs Bale lead her to a chair and for once appreciated the extremely strong gin with a minimum of tonic that she was given. In fact, she had three altogether, after which she felt decidedly better. So much so that she forgot all about the girls' disappearance and let herself be helped up to Wilt's bedroom where she promptly fell asleep.

In his study, Sir George was still extremely angry. On the way back to the Hall he had decided his violent quarrel with Clarissa in the cemetery should be resumed more decorously in the house. He didn't

252

want Mrs Bale to hear him shouting so waited for his wife to catch him up and then shut and locked the study door behind them. Clarissa still maintained that, because she had married into the Gadsleys, she was now a member of the family, and Sir George still maintained that she wasn't.

'George, I haven't wanted to bring this up before now but you're being so horrible you've forced me to. Mrs Bale told me that you're not even a Gadsley yourself.'

'Downright nonsense!' Sir George yelled at her, forgetting to lower his voice. 'I'll sack the bloody woman for impertinence! I'm more of a Gadsley than even the Gadsleys were.'

Clarissa wondered what on earth he meant by this, but before she could ask him he went on.

'I know the family history better than anyone. Ask me anything. Go on, ask me.'

'I have no desire to ask you anything, you stupid, horrible man.'

'Well, I'll tell you then. I'll tell you all you want to know about the cemetery you want to bury your bloody uncle in. It was first created by a Gadsley Blisett after the Battle of Hastings and remained private and secret so as to prevent the Normans from desecrating it by burying their own dead in it. And it's not going to be desecrated now!' He glared at his wife. 'It's remained private and to an extent secret ever since. In fact, the headstones were always laid horizontal, level with the ground, so that it wasn't immediately obvious anyone lay in graves below them – a small detail you might have observed for yourself if you hadn't been so intent on annoying me.'

'What about the chapel? Is it consecrated ground?' asked Lady Clarissa, thinking that if only she could calm him down they might at least have a rational conversation.

'Of course it isn't now, but it was when it was built in the sixteenth century. It's merely ornamental today, but recognised by the family as a fitting burial place.'

This reminded him of their original argument and he banged his fist on the table so loudly that Mrs Bale rushed to the study, thinking she was wanted. An embarrassed Sir George unlocked the door and claimed that he needed to make a phone call, an important and confidential one that he needed her to take notes on, and after hustling Clarissa out of the room promptly phoned directory enquiries. Getting through, he left the receiver on the desk and helped himself to a large brandy before picking it up again and starting a one-sided conversation about shares with his non-existent financial adviser. Every now and then he paused for a couple of minutes before going on. Finally he put the phone back in its cradle, dismissed a perplexed Mrs Bale, and poured himself another brandy.

He'd have needed several more had he known what the quads were doing in the pine wood.

\* \* \*

They had dragged the Colonel's body to the edge of the plantation, where a band of mature conifers extending from the massive screen of mixed woodland helped to conceal the Hall from passers-by on the main road. Two hundred yards beyond them, in a wide meadow, cows and what looked suspiciously like a bull grazed.

'We'll cover him up for now and go back a bit into the wood to gather some sticks and things to make a pyre,' Samantha told her sisters who had slumped on to the ground, exhausted after dragging the body over fallen branches. 'There's plenty of dry stuff there. But first we have to remove all the metal from his uniform and anywhere else he might have it.'

'Even coins in his pockets?' asked Emmeline.

'There won't be any. If the family haven't taken it, the undertakers will have. That's probably what they regard as their tip, like you give a taxi driver or a waiter.'

They moved back through the pine wood, gathering twigs and branches and stopping every now and then to listen for voices. While they worked they wondered what to do with the coffin.

'Well, we definitely can't take it anywhere and hide it.'

'Why's that?' asked Josephine. 'It isn't as heavy as it looks. And without his body in it, it will be lighter still.'

'Which will make the blokes carrying it suspicious. It's a pity we can't burn it too.'

'Wood does burn,' said Samantha helpfully. 'That's what we're going to use to get rid of the Colonel when we set him on fire, isn't it?'

'If only the thing had a lock and key. If it did, we could lock it and throw the key away.'

'What are you on about? I thought the whole point was to let Lady Clarissa find it empty and think that Sir what's-his-name, her husband, had done something?'

But Josephine came up with another idea.

'Why don't we put something heavy inside? Not too heavy, of course. The Colonel wasn't a heavy man. And then, when they open it up for a last look, they'll be even more shocked.'

'Now that is good idea. Let's separate and look for a big log,' said Samantha, the leader of the group.

By the time they had found a broken branch that fitted the coffin perfectly they were worried that they really had been gone too long and that either Eva or Wilt would have a search party out. They quickly cleaned themselves up in the lake, deliberately getting their hair wet, and returned to the kitchen where a slightly sleepy Eva sat nursing a black coffee and trying to wake up properly. 'Where on earth have you been?' she demanded.

'We went down to the beach,' Josephine lied.

'And swam in your clothes, by your appearance. They're wet through.'

There was a moment's silence and then Samantha spoke.

'There was a small boy of about five who got out of his depth and obviously couldn't swim so we had to go in and get him out.'

'Where were his parents?'

'His father wasn't down on the beach and his mother . . . I suppose it was his mother . . . was hysterical. So then we had to stay a bit longer and help calm her down. Anyway, we're really sorry.'

Eva sighed. She'd never seen the quads looking less sorry but she wasn't sure she had the strength right at this moment to find out what they had really been up to.

Mrs Bale took the girls off to her room to get their hair dry and left Eva wondering what on earth she had done to deserve all this.

'That's much better,' she said when they all came back. Behind her Mrs Bale smiled to herself. She had not smelt any seawater on the blouse she was wearing when Emmeline had brushed against her. She'd felt the wet patch with her hand but there had been only fresh water and not a trace of salt on her finger when she'd licked it. She was certain the girls had been nowhere near the sea.

Wilt sat on the beach below the hotel, wondering where on earth his wife was. The receptionist at the desk swore she had no one by the name of Wilt staying, and in any case they were fully booked with no new arrivals all week. He ought never to have left his family here, but at the time Eva had so annoyed him that he hadn't considered the consequences.

He was wondering what to do next when, to his surprise, the barmaid from the village pub sat down beside him.

'Good Lord. What on earth are you doing here?' he asked.

'Well, I do have some time off, you know. In fact, I've been for an interview at that posh hotel. I'm fed up with working in the pub and never meeting anyone properly. Or at least only meeting men like you who are too mean even to leave a decent tip.'

'Yes, well, I was just about to go actually. I don't think I should stay here any longer,' he said hastily, getting to his feet.

'Why is that? You're all right. Don't leave on account of me.'

'Oh, no, I'm not. I'm growing worried about my wife and daughters.'

'They aren't ill or anything, are they?'

'Good Lord, no. But I thought they were staying here at the hotel and it turns out they aren't and never were in the first place.'

Seeing the puzzled look on her face, Wilt sat down again and told her the whole story.

'So they left the Hall after they got shot at, yes? And then your wife insisted on staying here, but you weren't happy?'

'Well, it looked bloody expensive. God alone knows how much it was costing.'

'So? You don't have to pay. They're not here.'

'Theoretically, no. But if they were Eva had threatened to send the bill to wretched Lady Clarissa.'

'By the sound of it, this Lady Clarissa could easily have afforded to pay?'

'Ah, but if she refused to. What then?'

'You mean, you're going to be left with an enormous bill? Or, rather, you would have been left with an enormous bill had your wife and daughters been staying there. Here. Which they aren't,' said the barmaid, wishing she'd gone straight home after her interview.

'Worse even than that, Eva said she was going to sue the Gadsleys if they didn't pay up. And if she did sue, they'd hire the most experienced and expensive lawyers. And if we lost, as seems only too likely, the cost would bankrupt us. In fact, it's not just likely: it's damned well certain. And what really pisses me off is that Eva sucked up to this bloody woman like mad because she thought she was a so-called aristocrat and my wife is a raving snob. And she isn't even a Lady!'

'No, she doesn't sound like one.'

'No, she really isn't a Lady.'

'Yes, as I said, she doesn't sound like one,' said the barmaid, feeling increasingly puzzled.

Wilt began to wish he'd never started. They sat there in silence for a while and then the barmaid said, 'I've been thinking about the teenager with the gun. Do you think he's got a licence for it?'

'Probably not. On the other hand, his step-father is bound to. He has a cabinet full of the beastly things . . . not that I've seen him use them much. He did charge off once when I'd just told him I'd seen a caravan in the grounds and a woman hanging up washing on a line. He took a gun with him because he's got some sort of obsession about trespassers. Mind you, he didn't fire the thing.'

'Does he keep that cabinet locked?'

'He didn't on that occasion. I didn't stick around. I don't like weapons.'

'What I'm getting at is the fact that he left the cabinet open, and that when you went out of the room anyone could have nicked one of the guns – it sounds like there were a lot of them.'

'I never counted the confounded things but I'd say about a dozen, maybe more,' Wilt replied. 'Why do you want to know?'

'Never you mind. I'll get to the point in a minute.'

'If you say so. All I can see is Eva landing me in the shit again and there's sod all I can do about it.'

'Oh, but there is. You're in a far stronger position than you realise. Number one – what was a teenager doing with a firearm for which he had no licence? Number two – why did Sir George Gadsley leave you alone in his study with the gun cabinet unlocked and open? Number three – why were Eva and your daughters driven out of Sandystones Hall. Ask yourself that and you'll come up with the answer to your worries.'

'They left, as I keep telling you, because someone – presumably that young maniac – fired a series of shots at or near the quads when they were down by the lake and scared them out of the place.'

'Exactly. Put the situation like that and the finest lawyer in Britain isn't going to prove you guilty of anything. Add the unlocked gun cabinet and Sir George is bound to find himself in trouble with the law and lose his gun licence or be fined. Oh, yes. You'll have them Gadsleys by the short and curlies.'

Wilt sighed and said he certainly hoped so, although privately he wondered how he had ended up in this increasingly mad and muddled conversation.

'One thing you're forgetting,' he went on, unable to resist, 'is that Sir George is a magistrate and must have influence in legal circles.'

'That makes his position even worse! First he breaks the law himself by leaving his weapons unattended. And second, he knows that his son . . . all right, step-son . . . illegally has a gun because you told him the boy shot a deer or something.'

'He said it might have been a wild boar which had got out of a farm where they breed the brutes.'

'Well, there you are. So you've nothing to worry about.'

261

Wilt wasn't at all sure that the barmaid's logic made any sense whatsoever but felt grateful for her support. He rather regretted not having tipped her more, once he came to think of it, but suspected that offering her money now might not be viewed in the best light. Thanking her, he got up and offered her a lift back to the pub but she said she was going to stay on for a while.

As he drove back to the Hall he felt a little more cheerful. He'd enlist Mrs Bale's help and ring round all the local hotels: he was certain Eva and the quads wouldn't have gone all the way back home without him. They couldn't be that difficult to track down. Certainly once seen, never forgotten. And once seen and heard, never recovered from. He parked in the back yard and went up the steps to the kitchen.

'Oh, you're back. Your wife's been here looking for you,' Mrs Bale told him. 'She wanted the car.'

'I don't believe it! Why on earth didn't the stupid woman ring me? I've been sitting outside the hotel like an idiot waiting for her. Where is she now?'

'Well, she and Lady Clarissa had a flaming row about Clarissa having slept with you . . .'

'What? We never did any such thing!'

'I know you didn't,' Mrs Bale said, looking rather shame-faced. 'Anyway, before Mrs Wilt realised that she was wrong, she'd said so many dreadful things that Lady Clarissa had to go and lie down to recover.'

'Oh, Eva, what have you done now?' muttered Wilt, seeing the legal bill mounting by the minute.

'To make amends, she volunteered to go down to the Vicarage to make arrangements for the Colonel's funeral.'

'I thought he was being buried here on the Estate, and that all the trestle tables and umbrellas were for a funeral tea afterwards?'

'Well, no. Sir George refuses to allow him to be buried in the family's private plot. We've had to turn the mourners away at the main gate and the caterers are packing up now, Not that they were real mourners mind you. Just a load of nosey parkers from the village come to gawk at the house.

Wilt gaped at her.

'And my wife has gone to make alternative funeral arrangements? How extraordinary!'

'I would have thought you'd have realised by now that everything about this establishment is extra-ordinary.'

'Yes, it's a complete mad house, populated by lunatics.'

'Well, I did warn you. Even though I thought you were her latest fancy man.'

'Thanks for the compliment,' said Wilt.

'Having met your missus, I'd realise how wrong I was. She's not someone I'd want to cross.'

'Eva gives me absolute hell sometimes, it's true, though I'm used to that. But if she's in the village, then where are the girls?'

'Goodness only knows. They said they were going down to the beach again . . . but if you ask me they never went there in the first place. You've got your hands full with those four.'

'Don't I know it,' said Wilt bitterly. 'I'd better go and look for them. They'll be up to something disreputable, you can bet on it.'

# Chapter 24

In the graveyard the quads had placed the suitably sized piece of timber in the coffin, wrapped in a blanket they'd taken from the cottage earlier. After putting the coffin lid back on they returned through the pines, though this time taking a totally different route to avoid leaving an obvious trail to the corpse. They put their plastic gloves on and piled more dry wood around the body.

Samantha was about to strike a match to begin the cremation when the sound of Wilt's voice calling reached them through the trees.

'Oh, Christ,' Josephine said. 'All we need is for him to bloody well find us.'

They stayed quiet until their father's voice started to recede.

'Look, it's too exposed here. Someone's sure to see us. And we'd better go and head off Dad before he finds us here.'

'It's absolutely fine,' said Samantha angrily. She was eager to begin and bored stiff by all the delays.

'No, Josephine's right,' agreed Emmeline. 'Let's cover him up again and find another place . . . somewhere they would never think of looking. I suggest we spread out and search for the thickest patch of young pines, where grown-ups would find it very difficult to get through. In fact, we may even have to crawl ourselves.'

'What are we going to be looking for?' asked Samantha crossly. 'I still think we should get on with it here.'

'Somewhere not too far away but really dense, with lots of pine needles so we can cover the body with them and anyone looking for it will think it's a fallen log.'

'But logs don't fall on newly planted pines.'

'Of course they don't. But haven't you seen the sawn-off stumps of much older and bigger ones they've used for firewood in the Hall? Those pines shed needles in hundreds and thousands and could easily cover something up.'

'Provided whoever is looking doesn't step on it. They'd be puzzled to find a soft log.'

'He's hardly soft now, is he? He's got rigor mortis.'

'Yes, but you wait. In this hot weather he'll start to

rot any minute, and then he'll turn all soft and squidgy, not to mention smelling to high heaven.'

'That won't matter if we cover him really well with plenty of pine needles. You two' – Emmeline pointed at Josephine and Penelope – 'go over that way, and we'll go this side where the trees are much thicker.' A minute later all four quads had disappeared into the young trees.

Half an hour later, Emmeline had found a hollow which was filled with fallen leaves and pine needles. She showed it to Samantha who was delighted. Best of all it was screened by a thick undergrowth of young saplings.

'It's exactly right. We'll get the other two and bring the Colonel down. We can shove him in there for now.'

'Hadn't we better clear all these leaves out and have it ready for him before we fetch him? And what about the bonfire we build? People are going to wonder what on earth it's for.'

'What people? Nobody comes up here. They'll think it's for Guy Fawkes Night or something like that. Anyway, the quicker we can get the body into that hole the better. You go and find Penelope and Josephine and we'll meet up at the wood pile. It won't take me long to get this lot out.'

Back at the wood pile the four of them started to drag the Colonel's body back to the hollow, Penelope grumbling loudly that this wasn't as much fun as she'd thought it was going to be. Suddenly there was the sound of a shot and a bullet embedded itself in a nearby tree trunk, narrowly missing the girls. Three of the quads instinctively dived for cover and flattened themselves amongst the pine cones and bracken on the floor of the woods. Samantha, however, hid behind the nearest tree and so was able to see Edward walking towards them. To her amazement he reloaded and carried on firing his rifle, this time aiming for the dead body which lay where they'd dropped it, propped against a tree.

'Killed you, you bastard!' yelled Edward as he drew closer to the body. 'Teach you to trespass, you dirty Hun!'

'North by north-west!' whispered Samantha, which was their code for going anywhere but north or north-west. She needn't have worried since the gormless Edward didn't know his north from his west from his east. He moved steadily forward, oblivious to the three girls creeping sideways out of the line of fire.

Samantha had picked up a few stones and was throwing them to distract him when a particularly large one accidentally hit him on the head. Edward looked startled and began to topple forwards: trying to save himself he tripped on an exposed tree root and the gun went off, shooting him between the eyes. There was a sudden silence.

'Oh, shit,' said Samantha. The others stood up and joined her.

'Bloody hell!'

'Bloody hell is right. Now we're for it.'

'Oh, never mind all that! Quick, change of plan. Help me lift Edward up and let's put him closer to the Colonel's body,' said Penelope, which they did. She then took the gun from where it had fallen and fired a few more shots into the Colonel's body, then pushed the gun back under Edward's body so it was clear he had fallen on it after it had gone off.

'Now it looks as though he was the one who pinched the body and was using it for firing practice or something when he tripped up and killed himself. Which, of course, is exactly what he did.'

'Genius,' said Samantha, 'except now we don't get to burn anything, which is a pity.'

'Don't whine. Come on, let's get on with it before someone arrives to see what all the noise was about.'

Half an hour later the quads had removed any sign of the track they had made while dragging the naked corpse through the pines and had headed back to the Hall, having buried the Colonel's medals and clothes in the hollow.

Not long before that, at the insistence of Sir George, the coffin had been removed from the family plot by the pall-bearers and returned to the hearse. As it wound its way back up to the gate and on to the main road, Eva could be seen getting in a taxi and following on.

'Don't forget to insist that he's cremated,' Sir George

told her as she left. 'I don't want to hear any more nonsense about his being buried here.'

Eva nodded, knowing full well that she had promised Lady Clarissa that her uncle would be buried and not burned.

Feeling distinctly self-conscious, she followed the hearse all the way to the Vicarage where she got out and knocked on the door. A few moments later it was opened by a woman who looked at her enquiringly.

'Is there anything I can do for you?' she asked.

Eva said she'd come to speak to the Vicar but, by this time, his wife had spotted the coffin.

'Well, I'll tell my husband it's urgent although he is rather busy writing his sermon for Sunday,' she replied, and went back into the house. Presently, an elderly man wearing spectacles and a dog collar came out.

'I take it you want me to conduct a funeral. Is the deceased a local person?'

Eva shook her head. 'I am certain he isn't.'

'I can tell you're not from your accent,' he commented.

Eva replied that she lived in Ipford herself, but had been asked to accompany the coffin to the Vicarage.

'I know he was a colonel in the war and had a wooden leg,' she added inconsequentially.

The Vicar looked at her over the top of his glasses.

'I ask because the graveyard is almost full and we can only bury people who live hereabouts. Where exactly are you living?'

'Actually I'm not living here. I was going to be staying here for the summer, up at the Hall . . .'

'Sandystones Hall?' asked the Vicar, looking shocked.

Some years before he had played golf with Sir George and been disgusted by his filthy language when he had hit a ball into a bunker. He had also strongly disapproved of Sir George's habit of taking regular swigs of whisky from the silver flask he kept in his back pocket. Above all the Vicar objected to the Gadsleys' refusal to attend any religious services on Sundays or any other day of the week, and was more than aware that everyone in the village disliked them intensely too.

He had just decided that anyone who stayed for the summer at Sandystones Hall must share all their undesirable attributes when Eva broke into his deliberations.

'The four men who brought the coffin down have gone away,' she said. 'If you won't take it into the church, I don't know what I'll do. I can't possibly take it away by myself.'

'I'm afraid I can't be of any assistance. It's not as though I could even get such a huge thing into my small car, and in any case it's in the garage being serviced.' He paused for a moment then went into the house and phoned the service station.

'I wonder if you would mind sending a lorry up to the Vicarage to take a coffin up to the Hall.'

'Somebody died up there?' said the man who had

answered the phone hopefully. 'Like that horrible bugger Sir-my arse-George?'

'I'd be glad if you didn't use that filthy language,' snapped the Vicar. 'I'm calling from the Vicarage . . .'

'Cor blimey! I do apologise, sir,' said the mechanic, who knew the Vicar's views on swearing and bad language. He put the phone down and turned to the only other man in the service station. 'You're to take the pick-up and transport a coffin up to the Hall. Evidently some sod's kicked the bucket up there. Let's hope it's that bastard Gadsley.'

The trainee started the pick-up and drove to the Vicarage. The coffin lay just inside the gate with a fraught-looking Eva standing guard over it. But even with her help, the garage man found it too heavy to lift. Finally he ventured to the front door of the Vicarage to ask if there was anyone to help him get it into the pick-up. By this time the Vicar had finished his sermon and agreed to assist the young man. They each took one end of the thing and Eva tried to lift the middle, but it was still too heavy.

'There must be a very heavy deceased person in it,' observed the Vicar.

'Well, it took four men to get it here,' Eva pointed out helpfully.

'I suppose we'd better open it and take whoever it is out and then put the body back when we've got the coffin up on the truck.'

Eva thought how much Clarissa would hate her

uncle being hauled about the place, but then again Sir George was going to go mad when the coffin was returned. It was hardly her fault. She stood by as the two men lifted the lid, took hold of the blanketed shape and pulled it out.

'The deceased's lighter than I expected,' said the Vicar. 'And a lot stiffer.'

By the time it was in the back of the pick-up, the blanket had slipped off.

'Bugger me!' said the young mechanic, and for once wasn't rebuked for using filthy language. The Vicar was in too great a state of shock himself to hear or care what anyone else said.

His thoughts were fully concentrated on that broken branch and the motives of the person who had tried to make a sacrilegious idiot of him by conducting a church service for a piece of dead wood. By the time his pulse had returned to its normal rate and he could think sanely again, he was sure he knew who had set this disgraceful trap for him. The Vicar realised exactly who his enemy was: that monster Sir George Gadsley. They had always been at odds with one another, and this was the other man's damnable way of trying to make the Vicar the laughing stock of the village.

Ignoring Eva's cries of horror and determined to turn the tables on Sir George, he went to his study and phoned the police. 'I have reason to believe there has been a very serious crime committed,' he told the Sergeant who answered. 'I want you to come up at once and see the evidence.'

'Coming straightaway, Vicar.'

The clergyman put down the phone with a smile. He had begun to think it really was possible a crime had been committed at the Hall. He had often heard gunfire in the grounds there, and the villagers refused to go anywhere near the place unless they were collecting someone by taxi or delivering large quantities of alcohol or other expensive goods that made it worth the risk.

By the time the Sergeant and a Constable had arrived they were greeted not only by the Vicar but also one of the local men who had delivered the coffin in the hearse. He said that he was often up at the Hall as he had a contract to cut the grass on half the lawn each week provided, as he put it, the 'bloody boy with the gun' was guaranteed to be inside the Hall and forbidden to come out before he left.

'I've been there when he's shot a deer,' he'd already told the Vicar, 'and I wouldn't be surprised if he'd killed other stuff too. He used just to throw stones at people, but it looks like he's moved on.' The Vicar repeated this to the Sergeant who nodded as he took it all down. He had had past experience of the lad's misdemeanours but it looked like this time it was too serious for anyone to intervene, magistrate or no magistrate.

'And now you'll want to see the so-called corpse,'

the Vicar announced. 'And I can certainly corroborate the fact that there's frequent gunfire up there. A bullet passed overhead when I was walking past along the road a month or so ago. But come and look what we found in the coffin.'

They went round to the yard where the Vicar kept his car.

'Just open it up,' he said. He'd closed the lid to add to the policeman's surprise when he opened it again. A wooden corpse was the last thing he'd be expecting to see.

'Blimey, that's not a dead body! Why on earth did they bring a piece of wood down here?'

'They were ordered to bring the coffin and had no idea what was inside it.'

'They came with a woman who said she was from Ipford, but that's miles away,' put in the garage man.

Again the Vicar intervened. 'She claimed she was from Ipford. She also told me she was supposed to have been spending the summer up at the Hall, which was why she was accompanying Mr Whoever was meant to be in the coffin. Gadsley asked her to arrange the burial.'

'So where is she now?'

'As soon as she saw the piece of wood in there she took off smartish,' said the garage man. 'Come to that, I wish I'd done the same. If I'd know it was going to take as long as this, I'd have buggered off too.'

'Of course, she may well be back up at Sandystones

Hall by now. I think you ought to check. You can use the phone here,' said the Vicar, giving the garage man a disapproving look.

'Do you know her name? I mean, I can't just ask for the lady who was meant to be staying for the summer and has brought a coffin down here.'

'Oh, I think you can. They're bound to give you her name and address even if she has gone back to Ipford,' said the Vicar, eager to create an embarrassing scandal for Sir George. He was helped by the Constable who announced that he'd found what looked like a bullet hole in the log.

'It certainly appears to be one,' said the Sergeant, to the Vicar's delight. 'We'll just have to wait and see when forensics have done an or . . . auto . . . made a thorough examination of the log.'

By this time the Vicar was in a state of high excitement. The fact that the Sergeant had almost said 'autopsy' had been a moment so perfect he would treasure it for as long as he lived. He decided it was time to call in a senior detective to take charge. That way the scandal would really escalate, with Sir George's name appearing on the front page of every dreadful popular paper. The best thing of all would be for the detective to find a genuine murder victim, though the Vicar was too godly to actively hope for that.

Instead he discreetly suggested bringing in higher police authorities.

The local Sergeant was only too ready to agree.

He was feeling distinctly peculiar, looking at that branch and trying to make sense of its sinister presence in the ornate coffin. The Vicar's wife came out into the yard then and asked if they would like some tea or coffee. The Sergeant shook his head and thanked her. He really wanted something much stronger, like brandy, but it didn't seem appropriate to say so in the present company. Instead he accepted the Vicar's offer of the use of his telephone and called the Chief Superintendent at Ligneham, who took some persuading that the Sergeant wasn't mad, pulling his leg, or more likely drunk or at any rate suffering from some morbid hallucination.

'No sane person puts a piece of timber into an expensive coffin and expects a respectable parson to bury the damned thing,' he barked.

'Well, someone has done so. And, to cap it all, there appears to be a bullet wound in it.'

'A bullet wound? In a tree trunk? You're having me on. You can't get . . . Well, I suppose if it's a very small tree.'

'It isn't. I mean, wasn't. It is the branch of a moderately sized tree that's been pollarded.'

'Pollarded? And that would be your professional opinion, would it? Are you a policeman, Sergeant, or a bloody gardener?'

Half an hour later two police cars with plainclothes officers in them had arrived and were parked conspicuously outside the Vicarage, much to the annoyance of the Vicar who was wondering what rumours about him were now being spread through the village. On the other hand, the Superintendent no longer doubted the Sergeant's sanity. The lump of wood in the back of the truck proved he had indeed been telling the truth. Now the Vicar was telling him how he had been fired at, and only narrowly missed, close to the Hall by a youth with a gun the previous Wednesday.

'With an utter disregard for public safety, Sir George seems to encourage the boy to use lethal weapons on innocent people walking past the Hall,' the Vicar continued damningly. 'He is either a very bad shot or may, I suppose, be deliberately aiming above people's heads. I suspect it's because that family are so determined to prevent anyone intruding on their property. In fact, they've always been like that. One of these days a passerby is going to be killed, you mark my words.'

'And how old would you say this boy is?'

'He can't be much more than seventeen. Maybe younger, for all I know,' the Vicar exaggerated.

'Sounds like he's the same lad who was in trouble before, but now he's using a rifle and a powerful one at that. It would account for the depth of the bullet hole in the log,' said the Superintendent.

'There's no doubt about that, but if we're to prove it we'll need to match the bullet to the rifle, which could take a while,' said the Sergeant. 'Hope he doesn't do any more damage in the meantime.'

The Vicar looked puzzled.

'Why not remove the bullet now and take it with you when you go to the Hall? It shouldn't be too difficult,' he said. 'I have an excellent electric saw and chisels galore. We could hack it out in no time at all.' But the Superintendent shook his head.

'No, we'll need to leave this as it is. It's evidence, you know, so we can't touch it.'

'Well, if you can't touch it, how on earth are you going to be able to identify the gun?'

'Calm down, sir. Calm down. From what you've told me about pot-shots over the wall and the like, I reckon we've already got enough to nail these friends of yours.'

The Vicar almost levitated from his chair in disgust.

'They're no friends of mine, I assure you. That infernal man has hated me for years.'

'It was just an expression, Vicar. But I thought your lot were everyone's friends – aren't you meant to love your fellow men?' asked the Superintendent.

'Yes, yes. And of course I do – on one level,' protested the Vicar, growing increasingly irate. 'But you know, officer, he has always refused to let me carry out Christian burials in his private graveyard.'

'Has he actually buried anyone there?' The Superintendent looked particularly interested in hearing more about that.

'Not as far as I know. But, don't you see? That must be why he sent down this coffin with a log in it – to try to make a fool out of me because I wrote a letter to the local paper saying that private graveyards are wrong.'

The Sergeant and Superintendent exchanged glances. 'And is that it, sir?'

'Well, no. Since that piece appeared he's cut me – not that it bothered me. But then he began to spread really scandalous rumours about me . . .'

'If they are as nasty as you're suggesting, why haven't you sued him? It seems the obvious thing to have done.'

'Because the villagers generally dislike Sir George so much he wasn't believed. And in any case, I don't want an accusation like that spread all over the news-papers.'

'What sort of accusation? Perhaps we could pros-ecute Sir George.'

'Oh, the usual. That I'm a pervert who interferes with small boys,' the Vicar told him.

The Superintendent thought this over for some moments.

'And are you, sir?'

'How dare you! Of course I'm not. You can ask my wife, if you don't believe me. I don't even like small boys . . . nasty, vicious little things. Or big boys, come to that.'

The Superintendent thought about reminding the Vicar about the inclusiveness of Christian love again, but thought better of it. There was a short silence and then he announced, 'I think it's about time I met Sir George Gadsley. In the meantime, Sergeant, can you get that branch back to Ligneham and have it locked up in the evidence room? Now then, Vicar, is there anything else we should know?'

'Well, I ought in all conscience to warn you that Sir George can be a difficult customer. Drinks like a fish as does his wife – and, of course, she's very keen on men. Frankly, if it weren't uncharitable I'd call her something worse.'

'What would you call her then?'

'There's really only one word for it,' said the Vicar with relish. 'Nymphomaniac.'

'Now now, Vicar, we'll be cautioning you next, for spreading malicious rumours.'

The clergyman turned red but couldn't resist saying, 'I think not, Superintendent, since all I've said is absolutely true. You can ask that boy outside. He works at the garage.'

Bidding him good day while thinking once again that this man of the cloth wasn't all he was cracked up to be, the Superintendent went off to question the trainee mechanic about the woman who had accompanied the coffin. The young man had never met her before.

'Proper scared she looked when she took off, saying something about needing to get back to her daughters. Mind you, I'm not sure she was entirely all there in the first place. When she saw the branch, she kept saying it was a leg.'

'Was it her accent? Perhaps she meant log?'

'No, she definitely said a leg . . . when anyone could see it was just a lump of wood. And pollarded at that.'

# Chapter 25

Back at the Hall, Wilt felt as though he had been tramping the woods for hours. Although he'd shouted and sworn and then resorted to broadcasting black-mail and promises, the quads had failed to materialise. He found one of the girls' cardigan and a pair of socks at the edge of the lake and briefly wondered whether something terrible had happened to them. It seemed unlikely that all four would have drowned at once, but neither would he have put it past them. On the other hand, it was more likely that they would fake their own deaths and were at that very moment hidden somewhere nearby, giggling at him. He experimented with whirling round suddenly, hoping to catch them out, but just received some very curious looks from the caterers who were busy packing up their stuff.

He was seriously unnerved when he heard the sounds of gunfire in the distance, followed by some squealing, but when all fell silent again he concluded that Edward must have bagged yet another wild beast.

Wilt must have been on his fifth or sixth circuit of the grounds when he came across the half-concealed caravan. Although it seemed unlikely the quads would be hiding there, he thought he should probably look inside. As he drew nearer he saw the branches around it shaking and the caravan itself rocking from side to side.

'I bet that's the quads,' he said to himself. Then, quietly creeping up to the window, decided he would give them the rude shock they deserved. But in fact it was Wilt who had the shock, and it was a rude one all right, when the sight of Sir George's rear end, bouncing up and down on what appeared to be the trespasser, came into view.

Fortunately they were both too preoccupied to notice him peering in at the window. He beat a hasty retreat, deciding he had better head back to the Hall.

Mrs Bale met him at the top of the kitchen steps.

'Thank goodness you've returned,' she said. 'Your wife's in a terrible state.'

'She's always in a terrible state. What's happened

now? If it's those damned girls, you can tell her from me I've spent hours looking for them. It's no good: they're officially missing.'

'The girls? No, it's the uncle. He's the one who's gone.'

'I know he's gone, poor bugger, and I'm very sorry for him. But I don't know what that has to do with me or with Eva, for that matter.'

'No, he's gone. As in, his body has gone. Disappeared. Vanished. Vamoosed. Mrs Wilt has had a terrible shock and she's worried sick about telling her ladyship the truth.'

With this, Mrs Bale rushed back to the kitchen from where, as he followed, Wilt could hear the sound of Eva's hysterical sobbing. His first instinct had been right. This was a bloody mad house.

It was some while before he was able to calm Eva and in the meantime the girls had slunk back into the house, saying they'd only been to the beach again and didn't know why there was such a fuss. Looking at their four guilty faces, not to mention the pine needles all over their clothes, Wilt didn't believe them for one second but, given the state Eva was in, decided not to say anything. He was about to ask them whether they'd heard all the gunfire when there was a bellow from the study. Sir George was obviously back and in a temper. Mrs Bale got up hurriedly and dashed out, thinking she had better be with Lady Clarissa. Wilt shut the door and sat down again next to his wife. He didn't want to know what the latest row was about.

The quads were certain they already knew and stealthily made their way into the corridor to eavesdrop. They soon discovered they were wrong: no one seemed to have found the bodies yet. Instead Sir George was furiously berating a Police Superintendent and shouting that he must be mad to accuse him of putting a log in a coffin.

'What the fuck would I do that for? You're lying through your goddamn' teeth. Now get out of my house!'

There was a pause which allowed the quads to slip into the library and hide behind the open door where they could hear what was said or shouted in the study.

'If you really want to know, the Vicar found it when the coffin was opened,' the Superintendent told him.

'And you believe that old fool? He's off his head. A piece of wood in a coffin? That is absurd.'

'Absurd it may be, but we have witnesses.'

'So what makes you think this wood or whatever it was came from here?'

'Because the pall-bearers who brought it down said it did. There was a woman with them, too, who apparently said she was staying at the Hall for the summer.'

'Christ, the Wilt bitch!'

'I've another question for you, Sir George. Do you always keep that gun cabinet locked?'

'Of course I do. What's it got to do with you?'

'Then why was it unlocked when I was shown in here and you hadn't arrived from wherever you'd been? Leaving a gun cabinet unlocked is against the law. I trust you have a firearms licence?'

Sir George replied that of course he did and produced one from a drawer in his desk. He was beginning to grow slightly alarmed by the way this plainclothes policeman remained so calm, in spite of having been shouted at and ordered to get out of the bloody Hall. The Superintendent's next question made him even more wary.

'How old is your step-son?'

'I've no idea. Can't stand the boy.'

'Does he do much shooting? I mean, does he have a gun?'

Sir George hesitated and then said he had not noticed. 'Why do you ask?'

'Because there's a bullet hole in the log in the coffin, and I just thought there may be some connection between a boy with a gun and that hole,' said the Superintendent. 'Is it possible you might not have "noticed" one of your guns missing too, do you think? It's a very serious matter, permitting unlicensed young people to use powerful firearms.'

Sir George was beginning to sweat. This wasn't going at all the way he'd expected it to. 'I don't know what you're talking about. There was no funeral here so why would we have a coffin? There hasn't been one for over a thousand years . . . except for family descendants, of course, but the last of those was an age ago. The Vicar must have explained all that to you.'

'He did, but we've also been in touch with all the undertakers in the vicinity and had it confirmed that an Ipford hearse was seen making its way to the Hall. The locals noticed it because of their not getting the business themselves, of course.'

'They must have been mistaken. No one's died. Now bugger off!' said Sir George.

'We've a hearse and a coffin but no body, and that doesn't look good to me. It's why we want to search the Estate.'

Sir George knew he ought to restrain himself. He couldn't.

'Search the Estate? You bloody well won't! I'm damned if I'm having policemen poking their noses in all over the place,' he shouted.

'There'll only be a few of us and the dogs. Sniffer dogs. If the real corpse is in the grounds, the dogs will find him,' the Superintendent told him with a smile. 'They've never been known to fail.'

'To hell with your sniffer dogs! This is my private property and you're not bloody well searching any part of it.'

The Superintendent shrugged.

'If that's your attitude then I'll have to get a warrant,' he said. 'I'll be back in the morning.' And stalked out of the front door and got into his car.

# Chapter 26

The quads sneaked back through the kitchen and out into the grounds where they watched the police car go off up the driveway, clipping its wing mirror as it failed to negotiate the first of the terrible turns. Emmeline laughed loudly, earning herself a filthy look from the police driver, and then went to sit next to her sisters on the grass.

'Sniffer dogs! What are we going to do now?' asked Josephine. 'I hope they won't sniff up to us after that pulling and pushing we've done. The smell of the bodies must be all over us.'

'It's not as though we haven't washed since,' Emmeline reminded her. 'But I should think the dogs are bound to find the bodies.'

'Yes,' said Penelope. 'And when they do, what about the medals and clothes and stuff? It'll be very difficult to come up with a reason why they've been buried by Edward if the dog finds them as well.'

'They won't be found, stupid. Bet they'll be there forever.'

Samantha thought for a moment and then spoke.

'Not necessarily. You remember that TV programme with dozens of hounds who followed pieces of cloth that had been rubbed against a fox, so they could smell it and chase it?'

'But fox hunting is against the law. They aren't allowed to do it now,' Penelope protested.

'They aren't allowed to kill a fox, I know that. But they can hunt one.'

'Oh, for goodness' sake, shut up. What's it got to do with us anyway? We aren't going to go fox hunting. Look, it doesn't matter if they find the bodies or the uniform or whatever, does it? It's whether they believe Edward did everything and don't suspect it was really us.'

There was a brief silence. Then Emmeline spoke.

'Maybe if they don't find them for a bit there's less chance of any forensic evidence.'

'Forensic evidence?'

'Yes, you know, stuff that shows we were there and it wasn't all him.'

'I think we should plant lots of false leads to muddle

them and then they can't prove anything,' said Josephine.

'Like what?'

'Well, if the police are bringing in sniffer dogs, ones that can find dead bodies and things that are lost, we need to confuse them. So if we collect all the Colonel's clothes and medals and shoes and scatter them all over the woods, it'll throw the dogs of the scent.'

'Now I'm the one who's confused,' said Penelope. 'Shouldn't we be worrying about our alibi, not the sniffer dogs?'

'Oh, Lord! You're right: there's that too. But I bet we can make Dad say we were somewhere with him.'

'Huh! Why would he? He'd rather we were in jail than bothering him. I heard him tell Mum he thought we were little psychopaths who were going to end up in prison anyway.'

'Because we'll tell him that if he doesn't say we were with him all the time, we'll let Mum know he really was sleeping with Lady Clarissa. We can say we saw him.'

'But we didn't. And he wasn't, was he?'

'No, but he knows Mum will never believe that.'

Pleased with their plan, the quads went back into the Hall where they discovered that it had been decided everyone would stay the night rather than go back to the guest house. They were going to be in the cottage with Eva, and Wilt would stay in his room at the

Hall. Much to their surprise Sir George and Lady
Clarissa had already gone to bed, but when the quads
suggested it must be because they wanted to get sexy,
Mrs Bale told them there was more chance of seeing
some pigs fly past.

It was only later that evening, when Eva said she
was still frightened of being shot at by Edward, that
Mrs Bale realised no one had seen him all day. By
now it was too dark to conduct much more than a
cursory search of the grounds so, concluding that the
boy was skulking out of sight somewhere, she left out
some sandwiches for him and went off to bed.

Down at the cottage, the quads stayed awake for
hours, trying to think up better alibis in case they
needed them, but their whispering didn't disturb Eva
who had taken a sleeping tablet and was snoring
loudly. Wilt, however, slept only in fits and starts. In
his wakeful intervals he spent much of his time unable
to forget Sir George's first enraged bellow and the
subsequent calm questioning of the Superintendent.
He couldn't help thinking that the quads must be
involved in the business of the coffin with the lump
of wood in it . . . although surely even they would
stop short of actually moving a body? And what was
Lady Clarissa going to say in the morning when she
heard that her uncle was missing and some kind of
log had appeared in his place? And when he finally
managed to get his mind off the puzzle of the empty
coffin and the quads' putative involvement, it was

only to start thinking about the missing boy. Eva would undoubtedly insist that he continue wasting his time supposedly coaching the lad when Wilt knew perfectly well that Edward's education was a lost cause.

His mind went round and round, thinking about the useless boy and the guilty looks on the quads' faces and the missing body and the terrifying roars he had heard coming from the study . . .

It was obvious the dreadful Sir George was an extremely dangerous man. His collection of rifles was proof of that, and he had the most uncontrollable temper. Goodness only knew what he would do if he learnt Wilt had seen him and the trespasser through the caravan window. Probably shoot him.

At about five in the morning Wilt finally gave up any pretence of sleeping and decided to go for a walk. He'd go up the back road and stick close to the wall on the far side of the woods screening the hideous Hall. With dense forest on one side and a high wall on the other he should be safe from Edward and his damned gun if he'd been out there on night target practice, not that Wilt had heard any gunfire since the previous afternoon. All the same, remembering that Sir George had warned him that his step-son shot at anything that moved, Wilt kept his eyes skinned for the brute. At least he couldn't open fire from the wall without being easily spotted.

Half an hour later, Wilt had reached the high hedge behind which he had last seen the caravan, but although he went to the gate through which it must originally have come he could see no sign of it now. The padlock Lady Clarissa had attached looked to have been smashed although he thought it might just as easily have been shot off. To his right lay the entrance to the family graveyard. Wilt crossed the short open space to it and felt safer. On the slope above it he would be hidden by the dense pine plantation. He followed the path that led through the trees to the top, unknowingly passing by on the other side of the tree where the Colonel's corpse was propped up and Edward's body lay a short distance away, face down in the bracken.

Finally he found himself standing beside what seemed to be a small hollow: looking down the hill he could just see a corner of the chapel's roof. In short, the view was as calm and tranquil as he could have wished. Feeling peaceful at last, he turned to carry on up to the top of the slope where he stopped to rest in a little clearing among the pines.

As he sat and thought about all that had gone on, his mind kept returning to the puzzling disappearance of the Colonel's body. Its whereabouts could easily become something of an obsession since it had scarcely left his mind since he'd first overheard the gossip about it. The more he thought about it, the more Wilt felt sure that it lay somewhere in these woods although at the same time he was conscious he had no real reason for this conviction of his. It was based on nothing more than intuition and the knowledge that, whenever something went wrong, those blasted girls of his were somewhere at the root of it.

Wilt glumly pondered his future. It was years until he'd be rid of the quads. Knowing his luck, they'd want to go to Fenland University when they finished whatever school could be made to now take them, so that they could live at home and save money. It didn't bear thinking about.

He leant back against a trunk, his spirits sinking as he watched the sun gradually appear above the tops of the pines below.

# Chapter 27

In the study, Sir George and Lady Clarissa were having a particularly vicious argument. Lady Clarissa had started it over breakfast, much to the embarrassment of Mrs Bale who had come to report that the boy still hadn't turned up.

'Edward's probably run away because you're so hateful to him!' Clarissa shouted at her husband. 'You've never liked him, I don't care what you say. In any case, it's your fault he likes shooting. You encouraged him from the start.'

'I did nothing of the sort. That's a downright lie, and you know it.'

Lady Clarissa was driven to fury.

'I will not be called a liar by anyone . . . and you're

the last person to talk about lying! I heard what you said to that policeman last night even if you won't tell me why he was here. When he comes back, I'm going to let him know that you always leave that gun cabinet unlocked deliberately. That's why Edward can always get his hands on a gun. Oh, yes, I've seen the look of hatred on your face when he's out with one. I wish to heaven I'd never married you.'

Sir Georges face had turned almost purple. 'Aren't you forgetting you married me for my money? You knew I was extremely wealthy and, like an idiot, I thought you were charming and gave you a very generous allowance as well as a wedding ring. All you've done since then is spend it on that bloody moth-eaten old Colonel and the yobs you've been shagging. Or, more likely, paid with my money to sleep with you. If I had known what a whore you are, I wouldn't have come near you with a bargepole. You're nothing but a slut!'

'You bastard!' Clarissa screamed. 'My uncle has just died and what sympathy do I get? You won't even let him be buried in the family plot so I'll have to go into the village whenever I want to visit the grave. And now you've driven my son away with your hateful remarks and insults. Well, I'm going to see that you pay for it, if it's the last thing I do. And don't think I can't ruin you. I've kept a record of all the financial rackets you've been involved in, let alone all your nasty little perversions. It's not just me who hates you either:

you should know by now how loathed you are by all the staff, not to mention the locals.'

They were still shouting at one another when the police van drove up to the drawbridge and the sniffer dogs were led out. Behind them two Constables were holding pieces of clothing while a third carried a rifle. The Superintendent's car followed. He got out and crossed the drawbridge where he almost tripped over the quads who had raced to be the first to the door, flinging it open before he'd even rung the bell.

'Damn those bloody police!' shouted Sir George, having seen them arrive through the window, while in the background Lady Clarissa could be heard sobbing and moaning about her darling boy.

She left the study when the Superintendent arrived escorted by Mrs Bale, the quads and Eva, who had come to see what on earth was going on.

'Good morning Sir George.'

The old man nodded.

'As a magistrate you must realise what this situation entails,' the Superintendent said with the same air of calm assurance he'd shown the previous evening. 'I have a warrant here to search the grounds and the Hall itself, and I've had some officers investigating in Ipford where they've ascertained that there was indeed a body dispatched to the Hall, that of an old man whom I further believe was related to you.'

'He wasn't any bloody relative of mine,' growled Sir George.

'That's as may be, sir, but we've also obtained some of the old gent's clothing. We'll find out soon enough if his body is here on the Estate.'

'Don't be bloody ridiculous. Of course he's not here on the Estate, you idiot. And by the way, do you have any idea who I am? I only need put a call in to your superiors and you'll be back plodding the beat, you wait and see.'

'Are you threatening me?' the Superintendent asked, having had more than enough of Sir George's ranting and raving already. 'I'm putting you on a caution for Corruption. Let's wait and see what other charges we'll be making by the end of today, shall we?'

The quads were agog at this drama which was already turning out to be better than they could possibly have hoped. They couldn't decide whether to stay in the study and listen to Sir George and the policeman or whether the best of the action was outside, where they could hear the dogs barking loudly and Mrs Bale asking if anyone wanted a cup of tea. In the end they decided to split up into pairs. Josephine and Penelope went into the garden where they watched as the dogs were made to sniff some pieces of clothing and then started to strain at their leashes, yelping as they sought to be let free to run off after the scent.

Back in the study, the Superintendent continued to caution Sir George.

'Now then, we also need to talk to that boy of yours. We have the lad's birth certificate and your step-son is way under-age to be using a powerful rifle. Forensics have been working overnight and the bullet we exhumed from the log was found to be a .303 from the Second World War . . .'

'So what?' interrupted Sir George. 'My father brought it back as a memento.'

'So you admit that the bullet was fired by your gun? And that your step-son in all probability fired it?'

'Yes, of course I do. He was probably shooting at something in the woods, the silly oaf. He's the one you want to arrest, not me. I didn't tell him he could take the gun.'

'But you left the gun cabinet unlocked all the time, didn't you?' said Lady Clarissa, who had come back into the room just as Sir George was protesting his innocence. 'You encouraged him to fire at people and property, and I'm willing to testify to that in court.'

'Shut up, you stupid woman. Look, he's obviously stolen the gun,' said Sir George, flinging open the doors to the cabinet to show that there was a weapon missing. 'He'll have gone off and fired it at things in the woods, which is when that blasted branch must have got winged, and then run away to join the army, I should think.'

'It seems to me that you allowed your step-son il-legally to use a dangerous weapon. That's the first offence. The second is that we've witnesses to say he fired from what you call your private property across the road, which is a public thoroughfare. And let's

not forget your threat to get me into trouble as well
– an even more serious crime – which brings the
running total to three, so far.'

The Superintendent spoke to the Sergeant behind
him.

'Let's get the tracker dogs on to it,' he ordered, then
turned back to Sir George who was looking distinctly
pale now. 'We are going to ascertain where the body
of the Colonel has actually been buried, whether on
the Estate or nearby. It's difficult for us not to suspect
foul play, if not actual murder. At the very least, we'll
probably have you for burying someone on unsanc-
tified land.'

Lady Clarissa was looking extremely confused,
having no reason to believe that her uncle's body was
anywhere other than at the Vicarage.

'I did nothing of the sort! I sent his damned coffin
down to the village. We only bury members of the
family in our cemetery.'

'George, what's going on? Where is Uncle?'

'Looks like you've some explaining to do, Sir
George. I'll leave you to it – for now. We'll be back
to search the house once we've gone through the
grounds.'

The Superintendent left the room followed closely
by the two remaining quads. Out in the yard, the
sniffer dogs, both Collie crosses, had finished snuf-
fling at some of the Colonel's possessions and old
clothes. As they were let off their leads the dogs out

to have been able to find the dead man twenty miles away, let alone on the Estate. But to their handlers' confusion they started running round in circles, with one dog going first to the four girls standing watching and the other heading straight for the woods. The policemen looked very taken aback. After a few moments the one left behind dragged his dog off the girls and started running after his colleague. The quads looked rather shaken by this but after a few moments set off in pursuit.

Back in the study, Lady Clarissa confronted her husband. 'What on earth is all this about a log full of bullets found in a coffin? And why does the Superintendent think you've done something to Uncle?'

But Sir George had slumped back in his chair, powerless to answer her. He didn't understand a thing that was going on but he knew he was up to the eyeballs in terrible trouble, with incriminating circumstances stacked well and truly against him.

Still slumped against the tree, Wilt had been thinking back over his conversation with Mrs Bale the previous evening. She'd told him how furious Sir George was at the thought of the police returning with a warrant to search the Hall and Estate.

'Whoever put that wooden thing in the coffin knew he'd create one hell of a row. Lady Clarissa will go mad when she hears about it.'

'I suppose the disappearance of her uncle's body will really upset her.'

'Not on your life! She'll be more upset by the thought of losing all of ghastly Gadsley's fortune if he does divorce her. They were having a terrible fight about it before the police arrived. He'd threatened to cut off her allowance and sue her for adultery, and he could do that easily enough. After all, she didn't go down to Ipford every weekend just to see her uncle . . . I happen to know she didn't even like the old man much.'

Mrs Bale stopped gossiping while she made the tea. It was Wilt who broke the silence.

'I must say, I find Sir George a singularly horrible man. There's a degree of suppressed violence in his character I have never encountered before. I can't imagine what he'd be like as a magistrate. I certainly wouldn't want to be sentenced by him.'

'Now you see why he's detested in the village. The man is a monster,' Mrs Bale agreed, handing him his cup of tea. 'Though to be honest, the pair of them are as bad as each other.'

'When do you think he'll tell Clarissa that her uncle's body is missing?'

'Never, if he has any sense. Let's hope it turns up before things get much worse.'

Wilt had privately thought that things couldn't be much worse than having four terrible daughters running riot at school and destined to be his responsibility for the rest of his life – and sadly not one he could simply divorce himself from.

As he sat there in the woods he thought, for the umpteenth time, that he should never have married wretched Eva and then he wouldn't have had four hell-cats to show for it. Looking back on that awful occasion, he reminded himself that he hadn't actually proposed to her at all; she'd proposed to him when he was drunk and hadn't known what the hell he was doing. He knew now.

The first tracker dog shattered his reflective mood as it appeared round a bend in the path, barking excitedly, with three plainclothes policemen trailing behind it. Before Wilt realised what it was doing, it had dashed into a thick clump of young pines.

'Go in and see what the dog has found. I'll stay here and see if this bloke knows anything,' said one PC, taking a notebook out of his pocket. 'May I take your name and address, sir?'

'Wilt . . . Henry Wilt. I'm staying at the Hall with Sir George. He'll confirm my identity.'

'How do you spell your name?'

As Wilt began to tell him there was a shout from deep in the pine wood.

'He's found a naked body with a wooden leg . . . and we are coming out fast!'

'Why?'

'Because it stinks to high heaven, that's why.'

Two minutes later the dog handlers, clutching

handkerchiefs to their white faces, came hurriedly out of the trees.

'Bloody hell! There's two of them in there.'

'Two what?'

'Two corpses! One lying face down on the ground and the other propped up against a tree. I thought we were only looking for one?'

'Well, yes, we are. Were. But at least we've done what the chief told us to do. And he ought to be especially pleased 'cos we found two. Where's the dog?'

'Probably vomiting its guts out. Another five minutes in there and I know I'd have been doing the same. Now where is that bloke who was here when we arrived . . .'

But Wilt had taken the opportunity of all the shouting and confusion to dash down to the cemetery and had hidden himself behind the altar in the chapel. He had already had too many encounters with coppers who tried to pin crimes on him he'd never committed. He'd left before hearing they had found two bodies and before the quads turned up in hot pursuit of the lead dog, closely accompanied by the second animal which seemed unable to stop sniffing at them.

After three-quarters of an hour, Wilt was so uncomfortable he crawled out of hiding and headed away from the cemetery. He kept close to the wall beside the road until he reached the back gate and could hurry into the parking area. For the first time that morning he felt safe from both bullets and police. He ran across the yard and up to the kitchen where Mrs Bale was having a cup of tea as usual.

'You look as though you could do with some too,' she said. 'And where on earth have you been? In a jungle of fir trees from the state of you.'

'You're right about the jungle, and I'd certainly appreciate a cup of tea. I've been watching the police find the stark bollock naked body of the Colonel, which stank to high heaven – or more accurately high hell.'

Mrs Bale shuddered.

'I'm not surprised. What I don't understand is why he had been stripped naked? It doesn't make any more sense than hiding him in the wood in the first place. And why put a log in his coffin?'

Wilt shrugged and said he had no idea. 'Someone round here must be crazy. What does Sir George say?'

Mrs Bale hesistated before answering.

'Well, when he heard about the empty coffin, he reckoned it was either you or Edward who took the body.'

'That's ridiculous!'

'I'm not saying you did, just that that's what Sir George thinks. Is it definitely the Colonel, though? Did he have a wooden leg?'

'Who else would it be? And he certainly had only one leg, according to the Constable I heard shouting.'

'That means it really is the Colonel. Lady Clarissa will be beside herself, though it could have been worse: at least the body has been found, I suppose. I tell you, I'm sick to death of seeing her drooping about the place.'

'You mean, she's in mourning for him?'

'Mrs Bale laughed.

'Not on your nellie! It's mainly because she's got no excuse to go down to Ipford every weekend and sleep with the garage man.'

'Yes, well . . .' said Wilt, who still felt very uncomfortable talking about Lady Clarissa's sex life. 'I suppose I'd better go and tell them about the body.'

'He left the kitchen and went down the corridor to the study, only to find the Superintendent already there with Sir George and Lady Clarissa, who was bawling her eyes out.

The Superintendent looked at Wilt suspiciously.

'And where did you get to?' he demanded. 'Come to that, what were you doing so near the corpses? According to my men, when they arrived you were sitting no more than forty yards away.'

Wilt thought he had a strange turn of phrase, pluralising everything, probably attempting to impress Sir George. He glanced nervously over at Lady Clarissa, wondering why she was quite so upset given that her uncle's body had at least been recovered.

'So what? I wasn't to know there was a grave nearby. I told the officers I was simply going for an early-morning walk, well away from the idiot I'm supposed to be tutoring. You might not have noticed but the boy spends his time shooting anything he sees moving. That's why I can only take a walk at first light. And that's also why my wife went away with the quads.'

'With the whats?'

'Our four daughters, born at the same time. Quads is short for quadruplets,' Wilt tried to explain over the noise of Lady Clarissa's wails which had become even louder.

The Superintendent decided to change his line of questioning.

'And what about the smell? The men on the scene said it was disgusting . . . utterly revolting. How did you get to be relaxing about the place, without a care in the world, that's what we want to know? Only forty yards away and yet you didn't smell anything? The sniffer dog did as soon as it got there.'

'I am not a sniffer dog. I simply sat down to have a rest and look at the view. Anyway there was a strong breeze blowing from the east which probably carried the stink off in the opposite direction. If the corpse was smelling so foully it could be noticed from where I was, your men wouldn't have gone in in the first place. They came out fast enough.'

'True,' said the Superintendent desperately. This bastard had a logical answer for every question.

'But tell me,' said the Superintendent, screwing his

eyes into slits, trying to look shrewd and professional, 'what do you have to say about the second, non-smelly body?'

# Chapter 28

As he stood listening to the Superintendent subject Wilt to a barrage of questions, Sir George began to put two and two together. God, how he cursed the day he had married a good-looking woman with the morals of an alley cat on heat and a son who could no more get into university than run a mile in ten seconds. And now this! He just knew that the young imbecile had been the one who'd emptied that coffin and taken the body – probably for target practice, knowing him. And then the bloody fool had obviously gone on to shoot himself accidentally! Clarissa, who was by now in an inconsolable state, would make her husband pay dearly, though, of that he was sure.

That Edward had brought this upon himself Sir

George was completely convinced, but he was already struggling to think of a way of avoiding the scandal that was bound to ensue and would in all probability focus on himself. God knows, that bloody Vicar was going to have something to gloat over now. If he could somehow pin Edward's death on Wilt, that should give him a chance to get himself off the hook . . . And, now that he thought about it, if Wilt were found guilty, Clarissa would only have herself to blame, given that she'd brought the man to the Hall in the first place.

Sir George reckoned he'd have the Superintendent on his side, too, as he seemed to view Wilt with the utmost suspicion and his interrogation was already taking on a particularly nasty tone.

'What other body?' asked Wilt, bewildered.

'My darling Edward . . . Edward, my son and heir. My beloved Edward!' bawled Clarissa, racked with grief. 'It's all your fault,' she cried, turning on her husband. 'You never liked him. You let him have your guns and encouraged him to shoot himself.'

'I did nothing of the sort. I can't help it if Eddie was stupid. Anyway, it must be Wilt here who's to blame.'

'Now hang on,' protested Wilt. 'What are you on about? I'm not involved in anything. Is Edward dead as well?'

Sir George ignored him and carried on shouting at his wife. 'You were the one who brought him here to teach your idiot son, and I know for a fact he's been teaching him the history of warfare. Eddie must have got worked up then stolen your uncle's body to use for target practice. For all we know, Wilt might even have helped him set up the corpse in the woods.'

Wilt turned pale and sank down on to a chair.

Sir George seemed quite pleased with his argument and carried on: 'And how did the Colonel come to die so conveniently, I ask you? Just when Wilt was coming. And don't think I didn't know you could hardly wait to shag him . . .'

'You complete bastard,' Clarissa sobbed. 'Uncle died and you couldn't have cared less. You wouldn't even let him be buried in the family graveyard. And now you're insulting the memory of my dead son. And it's you who got Edward killed, not me. Yes, you! All because you want to make sure there's none of us left who aren't Gadsleys by blood.'

'Oh, no, not me, my dear. You and your lover Wilt have probably been in league together.'

Wilt could not believe what he was hearing. 'Contact Detective Inspector Flint in Ipford. He can vouch for my innocence,' he insisted.

'We've already done that,' the Superintendent told him, just as the man himself walked in to join the fray.

'Flint!' shouted Wilt. 'Am I glad to see you! Tell them I couldn't kill a flea.'

The Inspector remained poker-faced. 'But maybe

this time you have. It was just that I could never pin anything on you before. Looks very much to me as though we've finally caught you red-handed.'

Wilt realised he was in deep trouble and very much on his own. This situation was rapidly becoming a nightmare. He knew who he blamed for everything: Eva. This was all her doing, and when he got out of this mess he intended to put his foot down. The quads were definitely going back to the Convent.

'But why would I want to get Edward killed?'

'Because you yourself thought him a fool and he has been taking pot shots at your quads,' Sir George answered.

'Well, yes, but . . .'

The Superintendent felt he was losing control of the situation.

'Lady Clarissa, I must ask whether you have been having . . . well . . . relations with Mr Wilt here, as your husband claims?'

'Don't you try to pin this on me, you bastard!' yelled Lady Clarissa, turning on Sir George.

'Now let's all calm down,' Flint said in a calm but firm tone, trying to exert some authority over the situation.

'Wilt, are you saying you were nowhere near the scene of the crime?'

'No, I haven't said that. I was near the place where the bodies were found as I walk there pretty often.'

'So you admit you are involved?'

'No, I don't! As I just said, I was near the scene of the crime, but that does not mean I was involved in the crime itself or that it was a crime to be there.'

'If you were not involved, although you were there, why were you there?' Flint was experiencing the usual sense of incipient mental collapse which always descended when he was confronting Wilt.

'Look – I had no interest in getting Edward killed. Why would I when I only took a job here in the first place because I needed the money I was paid to teach him? No more Edward means there will be no further need of my tutoring services.'

'Ah! But that leaves the way open for you to start dispensing your services in other ways,' cried Sir George, trying desperately to steer the blame back on to Wilt.

'I wasn't going to pay him for that!' cried Lady Clarissa, before she could stop herself.

'So what were you going to pay him for?' asked Flint.

'I wasn't going to pay him for anything. Sir George was going to pay him.'

Wilt, Flint and the Superintendent all turned and stared at Sir George.

'What? I haven't arranged anything, I tell you. It was Lady Clarissa who arranged for Wilt to come here. She was the one.'

Wilt, Flint and the Superintendent all turned and stared at Lady Clarissa.

'Are you suggesting that I could have arranged for

Wilt to kill my own little Edward? He was only meant to tutor him – to get him into Cambridge!'

Flint thought that an unlikely story judging from what he had heard about the boy. However, he was by now totally confused as to who had arranged with whom to do what, and where exactly Wilt fitted into what was clearly a carefully laid plan . . . before it had gone wrong along the way. Or had it? Flint was completely flummoxed because he couldn't make sense of any of it.

'Look – we're not getting anywhere. Let's break for a bit and carry out some interviews with the rest of the household, not to mention Mrs Wilt and those four girls,' he suggested. He, the Superintendent and the Constable went off to the kitchen to try and find someone to make them a cup of tea, only to find it empty. They had to settle for helping themselves to tap water instead.

Mrs Bale entered the study by the other door, carrying a mug of tea for Wilt, whom she had rightly guessed was in dire need of it, and a glass of whisky for Sir George. Lady Clarissa was left to help herself to some cognac.

Wilt drank his tea down quickly then left the study to find Eva and the quads and tell them to get ready to leave, with or without him. They were all sitting together on the edge of the moat, the first sniffer dog having now been joined by the second and both of them pawing occasionally at the quads, despite Eva's best efforts to repel them.

'Mummy, is Daddy going to be arrested?' asked Emmeline.

'It's not fair if he is. That stupid boy shot himself,' Samantha added.

Wilt stared at her.

It was at this juncture that it suddenly dawned on him that his terrible quads were definitely involved in this freebie holiday-turned-tragedy. God, he might have known it. He daren't let Flint and the other policemen anywhere near them: he had to keep the girls out of this at all costs. He told them not to speak to anyone but to go and sit in the car and wait for him there, then handed over two £10 notes when they refused. The quads ran off, secretly glad to get away from all the sniffing and pawing. Wilt ignored Eva's questions and ordered her to follow him. After looking at his face, she obeyed him for once and let him steer her back into the house.

Left alone in the study, Sir George and Lady Clarissa glared at each other over their drinks.

Sir George knew that he could not get out of this plight without his wife's support, but at the same time couldn't see how he might call on it. Eddie was dead, and he himself had been reckless about his gun cabinet precisely because he had secretly hoped the boy would kill himself or someone else and thus be off their hands.

Lady Clarissa sobbed into her drink, feeling guilty that she had treated Uncle Harold with less respect than she should have, and certain that her harbouring lustful thoughts about seducing Wilt must have brought about the death of her beloved son.

For the first occasion in a very long time, Sir George went over to Lady Clarissa and put his arms around her as if to comfort her. Drastic situations called for drastic measures so he said, 'Darling, I'm really sorry about Eddie . . . I mean, Edward. I didn't want him killed – I just wanted him to have some fun with my guns because that was the only thing he seemed to enjoy. If it's any consolation, you can bury him here. Even though, strictly speaking, he's not one of the Gadsley family . . .' He broke off as Lady Clarissa started to wail even louder, '. . . he must of course be buried nearby. And, what's more, I'll pay for you to fly out to Kenya with your uncle's ashes so that his last wishes are respected. And, while you're there, why don't you take a long holiday at the same time?'

Lady Clarissa was no fool. She turned her tear-stained face towards him and demanded, 'And what do I have to do in return for this display of generosity?'

'Oh, nothing at all. Except to tell those policemen that Edward must have known where the keys to the gun cabinet were kept. And I swear to you on my mother's grave that I never wished him to get himself killed. It was a tragic accident, poor boy.'

It was a most convincing act by Sir George. It was only much later, when Clarissa was on the plane, in first class of course, that she remembered Sir George's mother was one of the few Gadsleys who was not buried in the family graveyard. In fact, Sir George had never known where his mother's body had ended up after she was swept away by a freak wave on a family holiday on the Costa Brava. Or so his father had claimed.

Inspector Flint and the Superintendent returned to the study filled with new resolve: to get to the bottom of this death or two deaths or two murders or one murder and one death or God knows what.

They found a completely different atmosphere inside the room from the one that had pervaded it barely half an hour before. Sir George had clearly made things up with his wife and there was an air of reconciliation between the two of them as they exchanged contrite smiles with one another.

'Superintendent . . . Inspector,' began Lady Clarissa grandly, 'I'm very sorry that you've had your time wasted investigating what was obviously a terrible accident. My poor silly boy,' and here she paused to sniff loudly, 'was probably trying to help me by taking charge of Uncle's body after my husband misguidedly refused to recognise him as family. I expect he thought he could bury him here himself, tripped as he tried to do so and was fatally wounded.'

'But why did he take the clothes off the body?' asked Flint.

'Only Edward will ever know that,' said Sir George

as he slid his arm supportively around his wife's shoulders. 'But I expect he wanted to give his poor mother the medals to remember her uncle by.'

He stopped as Wilt came in, tugging Eva behind him. Having forgotten the rude behaviour of Lady Clarissa earlier on, she said how sorry she was about Edward's tragic end, and added that it would probably be best for all of them if the Wilts left the Hall immediately. They could 'settle up' later, once the police inquiry was over.

'What do you mean by "settling up"?' queried Flint.

'The money that Lady Gadsley owes Henry for teaching Edward,' replied Eva. 'In the circumstances we'll forget about the other costs we've incurred along the way.'

'So the payment to Wilt was for tutoring your son and not for . . .' Flint stuttered.

'That's what I said but you didn't believe me,' retorted Wilt. 'And now that you have the Colonel's body, you can easily find out if he was done to death or in fact died from something self-inflicted. There is a certain taste for alcohol in the family. You know where to find me in the event of any suspicious circumstances.'

'Tell me, Flint, did you really believe I would have stayed anywhere near someone firing live ammunition? You know me too well to believe that. Just as you already knew it was highly unlikely I could ever have killed anyone. I am really disappointed in you for considering it a possibility.'

From having three suspects, Flint and the Superintendent found themselves left with none. But the Superintendent had one last ace to play. 'Perhaps Edward's death was a case of death by accidental means or misadventure, but I'm still going to charge you, Sir George, with contravening the law by leaving a gun cabinet unlocked, a dereliction of duty which has inadvertently led to the demise of a young lad.'

At that Lady Clarissa took up her handkerchief and wailed convincingly that Sir George always kept it locked but Edward must have found the keys and helped himself to the gun. The Superintendent's shoulders slumped. He was going to have to leave this place without charging anyone, not even the dreadful Sir George, and his dream of slapping the smug pseudo-aristocrat in irons and earning a slap on the back from the Chief Constable dissolved.

The Wilts departed, leaving Flint feeling once again, defeated and deflated. He'd been so sure that this time Wilt would not get away, but he had. Yet there were still so many questions left unanswered . . .

Why was the log put into the coffin?

Why strip the Colonel naked just to remove his medals?

Why was Wilt always there when there were bodies about?

And why was Flint the unlucky sod whose path had crossed Wilt's in the first place?

# Chapter 29

Edward was buried in the family graveyard with Sir George officiating at the ceremony. At the same time the Colonel was cremated, but not before an autopsy had found no trace of any poison or suspicious substance. His remains were put into an urn and delivered to Lady Clarissa. His medals had finally been found by a sniffer dog borrowed from the local police force by Sir George, in return for his resignation from the bench, and were stuck inside the urn so that the Colonel would be symbolically reunited with his old regiment.

Clarissa flew to Kenya the next day with the urn travelling in her excess baggage. She spent a three-month holiday in several five-star hotels. The man from the garage drove her to the airport and then, strangely, went missing for the next twelve weeks. When Lady Clarissa returned to Sandystones Hall she had a wonderful glow to her cheeks, but, as Mrs Bale was overheard to remark to the postman, no suntan.

While she was away Sir George borrowed the sniffer dog once again and tracked down his beloved Philly's caravan. He welcomed the cook back into the kitchen and then into his bed. He died suddenly two months later but it was said that he had a wide grin on his face when the doctor was called to pronounce him dead. Whether it was one suckling pig too many or some other strenuous activity that his heavily clogged-up arteries could not support, no one would ever know for sure. When his will was read, as expected everything went to his wife – with the exception of the computer, fax and telephone in the secret lavatory which he left to Mrs Bale together with the torch.

The quads were reluctantly readmitted to their private school: Lady Clarissa had forked over the bonus plus the weekly fee she owed Wilt as she said it wasn't actually down to him that Edward had failed to pass his university entrance exam. The Headmistress was very alarmed to see the girls arrive back armed with both mobile phones and iPods, but Wilt's parting threat to them that he'd have all of their electronic equipment confiscated unless they stayed out of trouble for at least one term seemed to be working.

Back in Ipford, Wilt and Peter Braintree shared a pint at the Hangman's Arms as they caught up with each other before the new term started. Peter had been looking forward to sharing his latest news with Wilt, and the latter more than fulfilled Peter's expectations by being absolutely stupefied to hear that Fenland University was going to be closed down and a technical college re-opened in its place. Wilt sat back in his chair with his mouth half-open.

'Good God, I never thought I'd live to hear that,' he said. 'I really didn't. It's incredible . . . and absolutely marvellous. The damned place should never have been opened in the first place, and wouldn't have been if it hadn't been for that lunatic Mayfield and his crony Vark.'

'You are forgetting that vile multi-billionaire crook Pinson who wanted to be in the House of Lords and donated a billion to the two main political parties to ensure he got in. That's how Fenland was allowed to build such ghastly buildings and get away with it.

'Talking of money, what will happen to us? I've just sent the quads back to boarding school and it costs a damn' fortune.'

Peter thought for a bit.

'I suppose we'll have to wait and see what the authorities want us to do. Or what they intend to do, more to the point. They may want to bring in fresh lecturers. Or, then again, fresh subjects with old lecturers, like us.'

'Do you think they'll bring back Liberal Studies? I enjoyed being head of that, and I'm sick to death of bloody computers,' said Wilt.

'Goodness only knows, though the Government is frightfully worried about the huge unemployment figures and lack of skilled workers so I'd be surprised if we weren't still swamped with youngsters signing up for one heavily promoted scheme or other. You'd only need the Government to bring back something along the lines of the 1944 Act, which included a compulsory hour of Liberal Studies a week, and then you'd be back in your old position pronto. But you're already Head of Computer Studies, so come what may I don't expect you'll be for the scrap heap.'

'Well, we're still speaking English – just – so you'll be all right as well. Perhaps we'll all get better salaries in compensation for being downgraded from a so-called university.'

'Oh, quite. In devalued pounds. Big deal,' sighed Braintree. 'I'll get another round in.'

And at that, Wilt felt quite hopeful.

He'd deal with Eva and the quads when the next full-blown situation arose as he had no doubt it would. But he hoped to God it was a long way off.

# Acknowledgements

I would like to thank my superb editor, Susan Sandon, for her immeasurable help and sound advice, and all her team at Random House for their continuous support and great enthusiasm. But most of all, my special thanks to my agent, Sonia Land, ever positive and always there for me whenever I hit a writer's low ebb, and without whom this book might never have been finished. Her team, Leila Dewji and Gaia Banks at Sheil Land Associates, have been equally supportive and an author cannot ask for more.